'Afraid you will lose again?'

'Not at all,' Charlie drawled. 'My interest is waning. I'm afraid I need more of a challenge.'

Merry eyed him suspiciously. 'Fifty guineas a point and a hundred for a win is reasonably challenging.'

'I'm not trying to fleece you, Merry, but I think both of us can lose a few hundred guineas in a night and not turn a hair.'

Her eyes widened a fraction. 'Do you want to make it thousands?'

He grinned and leaned on his cue. 'That is more of the same, isn't it?' Oh, God, he was going to hell for this. 'In this next game, how about for each point we lose we remove an article of clothing?'

AUTHOR NOTE

This is my second story about the Mountford twins. You will recall Robert in THE GAMEKEEPER'S LADY. This is his older brother Charlie's story. Charlie is the heir to the dukedom, and you couldn't meet a man more different from his brother—although their twin bond is strong. The women who catch the eye of these brothers are not at all alike. In this story Merry surprised and intrigued me, I must say. It was only when we had completed our journey together that I fully understood her.

I had fun writing the same scene in both books from the perspective of each brother, though it is the only place their stories intersect. The fact that this summer I visited the place where this scene occurs made it all the more interesting.

The story is set against the backdrop of Yorkshire, with its moors and sheep and woollen mills. I enjoyed my visit and I hope you do too.

If you want to know more about my books and my research, you can visit me at http://www.annlethbridge.com. I love to hear from readers.

MORE THAN
A MISTRESS

Ann Lethbridge

MILLS &
BOON

First published in Great Britain 2011
Harlequin Mills & Boon Limited,
Eton House, 18-24 Paradise Road, Richmond, Surrey TW9 1SR

© Michèle Ann Young 2011

ISBN: 978 0 263 21815 2

Harlequin Mills & Boon policy is to use papers that are natural, renewable and recyclable products and made from wood grown in sustainable forests. The logging and manufacturing process conform to the legal environmental regulations of the country of origin.

Printed and bound in Great Britain
by CPI Antony Rowe, Chippenham, Wiltshire

Ann Lethbridge has been reading Regency novels for as long as she can remember. She always imagined herself as Lizzie Bennet, or one of Georgette Heyer's heroines, and would often recreate the stories in her head with different outcomes or scenes. When she sat down to write her own novel, it was no wonder that she returned to her first love: the Regency.

Ann grew up roaming England with her military father. Her family lived in many towns and villages across the country, from the Outer Hebrides to Hampshire. She spent memorable family holidays in the West Country and in Dover, where her father was born. She now lives in Canada, with her husband, two beautiful daughters, and a Maltese terrier named Teaser, who spends his days on a chair beside the computer, making sure she doesn't slack off.

Ann visits Britain every year, to undertake research and also to visit family members who are very understanding about her need to poke around old buildings and visit every antiquity within a hundred miles. If you would like to know more about Ann and her research, or to contact her, visit her website at www.annlethbridge.com She loves to hear from readers.

Previous novels by this author:

THE RAKE'S INHERITED COURTESAN
WICKED RAKE, DEFIANT MISTRESS
CAPTURED FOR THE CAPTAIN'S PLEASURE
THE GOVERNESS AND THE EARL
   (part of *Mills & Boon New Voices…* anthology)
THE GAMEKEEPER'S LADY
   (linked to *More Than a Mistress*)

and in Mills & Boon® Historical *Undone* eBooks:

THE RAKE'S INTIMATE ENCOUNTER
THE LAIRD AND THE WANTON WIDOW
ONE NIGHT AS A COURTESAN

This story is dedicated to the memory of my good friend and supporter, Jacques. He always gave me lots of encouragement and helped out with the French in several stories. He is missed.

Chapter One

January 1820

*O*nly *a man dedicated to duty travelled to Yorkshire in January.*
Hunkered against the cold, high on his curricle, Charles Henry
Beltane Mountford, Marquis of Tonbridge, couldn't miss the irony
in his father's proud words. What choice was there for Charlie, other
than duty, if Robert was to be accepted back into the family? If he
was found. No. Not if. When he was found.

Face stinging and ears buffeted by the wind, he lifted his gaze
from the road to the leaden sky and bleak stretch of moors ahead.
Three years and not one word from his wayward twin. While on
some deep level, he knew his brother hadn't come to physical harm,
every time he recalled Robert's face as he left, Charlie's gut twisted
with guilt.

He should not have said what he did, imposed his own sense of
duty on his brother. They might look alike, but there the similarities
ended. Their lives had followed different paths and each had their
own roles to play.

Finally, after three years of arguing and pleading, he had sold
his soul to bring his brother home. He would visit Lady Allison
and begin the courtship his father demanded. The weight of duty

settled more heavily on his shoulders. The chill in his chest spread outwards.

Damnation, what in Hades was the matter with him? Lady Allison was a modestly behaved, perfectly acceptable, young woman of good family. She'd make a fine duchess. Marriage was a small sacrifice to bring Robert home and banish the sadness from his mother's face. Sadness he'd helped cause.

He urged his tired team over the brow of the hill, eager to reach the inn at Skepton before dark.

What the hell? A phaeton. Sideways on. Blocking the road. Its wheels hung over the left-hand ditch, its horses rearing and out of control. Coolly, Charlie pulled his ribbons hard right. The team plunged. The curricle tilted on one wheel, dropped and swung parallel to the obstruction. It halted inches from catastrophe, inches from a slight young man in a caped driving coat bent over the traces of the panicked animals of the other equipage, unaware of the danger.

Damn. What a mess. Charlie leaped down. Nowhere to tie his horses. He clenched the bridle in his fist. 'Need help?' he yelled against the wind.

The young man spun around. 'By gum, you scared me.'

Not a man. A woman. Charlie stared, felt his jaw drop and could do nothing to stop it. Her eyes were bright blue, all the more startling beneath jet brows. Her cheeks were pink from the wind and black ropes of hair flew around her oval face in disgraceful disorder.

A voice in his head said *perfect*.

Her arched brows drew together, creasing the white high forehead. 'Don't just stand there, you gormless lump. If you've a knife, help me cut the bloody traces.' She hopped over the poles and began sawing at the leathers on the other side with what looked like little more than a penknife.

Charlie snapped his mouth shut, pulled the dagger from the top of his boot and slashed the traces on his side. 'Here, use this.' He passed her his knife, handle first.

She grabbed it, cut the last strap and proceeded to untangle the horse's legs with very little care for life and limb.

Charlie grabbed the bridle of her horses while hanging on to his own.

The young woman straightened. She was tall, he realised, her bright sapphire eyes level with his mouth. 'Thank you.' She dragged strands of hair back from her face and grinned. 'The damned axle snapped. I must have been going too fast.'

Another Letty Lade, with her coachman-style language. 'You were lucky I managed to stop.' He glanced around. 'Where is your groom?' No gently bred female travelled alone.

'Pshaw.' She waved a dismissive hand. 'I only went to Skepton. I don't need a groom for such a short journey.'

Reckless, as well as a menace on the road. 'It seems on this occasion you do.' He huffed out a breath. He couldn't leave her stranded on the side of the road with night falling. 'A broken axle, you say?' It might be a strap, in which case he might be able to fix it. 'Hold the horses for a moment, please.'

With a confidence in her abilities he didn't usually feel around females, he left her holding the horses and went to the back of her carriage. He crouched down beside the wheel and parted the long yellowed grass on the verge.

Blast. No fixing that. The axle had snapped clean in two near the offside wheel. She must have hit the verge at speed to do so much damage.

He returned to her. 'No hope of a makeshift repair, I'm afraid. I'll drive you home.'

'That's reet kind of you,' she said, her Yorkshire accent stronger than ever. Then she smiled.

It was as if he'd looked straight at the sun. The smile on her lips warmed him from the inside out. *Lovely.*

A distraction he did not need.

He glared at her. 'Where do you live?' His tone sounded begrudging. And so it should. The careless wench could have killed them both, or damaged some very fine horses. She'd been lucky. And she should not be driving around the countryside without a groom.

Her smile disappeared. She cocked her head on one side. 'No need to trouble. I'll ride.' She jerked her chin towards her team.

'One is lame. And the other is so nervous, it is sweating and likely to bolt. It is my duty to see you safely home.'

And his pleasure, apparently, from the stirring in his blood.

Damn it.

He looked up at the sky, took in the fading light. He'd be finding his way to Skepton in the dark if they didn't get started. 'I insist.'

'Do you, by gum?' She laughed, probably at the displeasure on his face. 'I'll not deny you your way, if you'll tie these beasts on behind.'

Kind of her to oblige him.

Leaving her with his horses, grateful they were tired enough not to protest a stranger's hand, he led her team to the back of the curricle and jury-rigged a leading string.

Returning to the girl, he shouted over the rising wind, 'I'm going to push your vehicle further off the road.'

He strode to her wrecked equipage, put his shoulder to the footboard and pushed. The phaeton, already teetering on the brink of the shallow ditch, slid down the bank, its poles tilted to the sky. No one would run into it in the dark.

'Strong lad,' she yelled.

Good God, he almost felt like preening. He suppressed an urge to grin, climbed up on to his box and steadied his team. The perfectly matched bays shifted restlessly. Probably feeling the chill, as well as the panic of the other horses.

'Can you climb up by yourself?' he asked, controlling the beasts through the reins.

She hopped up nimbly. He caught a brief glimpse of sensible leather ankle boots and a silk stocking-clad calf amid the fur lining her driving coat before she settled herself on the seat.

A very neatly turned calf, slender and sweetly curved.

Bloody hell. 'Which way?'

'You'll have to turn around. I was on my way home from Skepton.'

Skepton was at least five miles on. A mill town. Not a place a respectable female went without a groom. Just what sort of woman was she? Not gently bred obviously, despite the fine clothes. Apparently, he was soon to find out. He manoeuvred his carriage around in the road, the prospect of a warm fire any time soon receding.

He cast her a sidelong glance. She was as lovely in profile as she was full face. She had a small straight nose and full kissable lips. If Robert was in his place, he'd be enjoying himself by now, making love to her.

But he, Charlie, was a dull dog according to his last mistress. A prosy bore. Robert's parting shot rang in his ears. *Try to have a bit of fun, for once.*

That was all right for Robert. He wasn't the ducal heir with hundreds of people relying on his every decision. Hades, the last time he'd done as he pleased it had ended in disaster. For everyone, including Robert. Never again.

He'd do well to keep this woman firmly at a distance.

Mindful of the lame horse following behind, Charlie walked his team. He raised his voice to be heard over the wind's howl. 'As travelling companions, I believe introductions are in order. Tonbridge, at your service.'

'Honor Meredith Draycott,' she said. 'Call me Merry. Thank you for stopping.'

As if he'd had a choice.

'Tonbridge,' she said. 'That's a place.'

He felt slightly affronted, as if she'd accused him of lying. 'It is also my name.'

She considered this in silence for a second, perhaps two. 'You are an of.'

He blinked. 'Of?'

'Something *of* Tonbridge. Duke or earl or some such.'

He grinned. Couldn't help it. 'Marquis of,' he said.

'Oh, my.'

The first thing she'd said that hadn't surprised him, he realised. Which in and of itself was surprising.

'What are you doing in these parts?' she asked.

'I'm going to Durn.'

'Mountford's estate. Oh, you are that marquis. You still have a long way to go.'

'I do. I plan to put up in Skepton for the night.'

They reached the top of hill and the road flattened out. The clouds seemed closer to earth up here, the wind stronger, more raw, more determined to find a way beneath his coat.

She inhaled deeply. 'It's going to snow.'

Charlie glanced up at the sky. The clouds looked no more threatening than they had when he set out earlier in the day. 'How can you tell?'

'I've lived on these moors all my life. I can smell it.'

He tried not to smile. He must not have succeeded because she huffed. 'You'll see,' she said. 'I can smell when it's going to rain, too, or feel it on my skin. You have to feel the weather or you can get into trouble out here on the moors.'

He chuckled under his breath. 'Like running off the road?'

'That was not my fault,' she said haughtily. She glanced back over her shoulder at her horses. 'I think his limp is getting worse.'

Charlie didn't much fancy leaving the horse out here, but he might be forced to do so if the animal became too lame to walk. He slowed his team down a fraction. 'How much further?'

'Two miles. Turn right at the crossroads.'

At this rate it was going to be midnight before he reached the next town. Blasted woman wandering around the countryside alone.

'You can leave me at the corner,' she said.

Had she read his mind? More likely she'd seen the disgruntlement on his face. Clearly, he needed to be more careful about letting his thoughts show. 'I will see you to your door, Miss Draycott.'

'Pigheaded man,' she muttered.

Definitely not a lady. Most likely bourgeoisie, with lots of money and no refinement.

As they turned at the crossroads, white flakes drifted down and settled on the horses' backs where they melted and on Charlie's coat where they did not.

'See,' she said.

He shot her a glance and realised that she didn't look all that happy about being proved right. 'Should we expect a significant amount?'

She shrugged. 'Up here on the high moors? Like as not. The wind will drift it, too.'

Hardly comforting. The few flakes turned into a flurry, and pretty soon he was having trouble making out the road at all. Only the roughness at the verge gave him any clue he was still on track since there were no trees or hedges. Even that faint guide wouldn't last long. There was already a half-inch of pure white blanketing everything in sight. In the growing dusk, he was beginning not to trust his vision.

She gave a shiver and hunched deeper in her coat.

The cold was biting at his toes and fingers, too. If it came to a choice between the lame horse and the two people in the carriage, he was going to have to choose the people, even if he valued the horses more.

'There,' she said, pointing.

A brief break in the wind allowed him to see the outline of a square lump of a house. A monstrous ugly house. Not what he'd been expecting. Though he should have, given the expensive clothes, the fashionable phaeton and the mode of speech.

'Good,' he said. He glanced back. The lame horse didn't seem any worse though it made him wince to see how the animal favoured his right front leg. 'I assume you have someone who can care for that animal?'

'Yes.' She turned in her seat, her knees bumping slightly against his and sending every nerve in his body jangling.

Her eyes widened as if she, too, felt the shock.

It was the cold. It couldn't be anything else.

'You will stay the night, of course,' she said.

He opened his mouth to refuse.

'Don't be an ass,' she said. 'You won't find your way back to the main road.'

He raised his gaze. All sign of the house was gone. The snow was blowing in his face and it seemed a whole lot darker than it had a minute or two before.

'It looks as if we will not find your house after all.'

'Let the horses have their heads. They will keep to the road. Since I'm expected, someone is sure to be waiting at the gate with a lantern.'

They should not have let her drive out alone, and he intended to tell them so, but he did as she suggested. It felt odd, handing control of their lives to a couple of dumb beasts, but their ears pricked forwards as if they knew where they were going when he let the reins hang slack. After only a minute or two, he saw a light swinging ahead of them, a faint twinkle rocking back and forth. Within moments a wizened man in a coachman's caped coat was leading them between the shadowy forms of a pillared gate. They rounded a turn in the drive and more lights glowed through the swirling snow. They pulled up at a magnificent portico.

Two more men rushed out of the dark with lanterns.

'We'll see to the horses,' the coachman bellowed over the wind. 'Get yourselves inside afore ye perish, Miss Draycott.'

One of the grooms helped her down.

Charlie jumped down on his side.

'This way,' Miss Draycott called, hurrying up the steps.

Charlie followed. The blast of heat as the front door opened let him know just how cold he'd become.

* * *

Merry stripped off her coat and handed it to Gribble, whose smile expressed his relief.

'We were beginning to worry,' he said.

'Gribble, this is the Marquis of Tonbridge.' She gestured towards the stern dark man who was looking around him with narrowed eyes. She suppressed a chuckle. Grandfather's idea of the style of a wealthy industrialist was a sight to behold. 'My rescuer will need a room for the night.'

Tonbridge's gaze shot to her face, dropped to her bosom as he took in the low-necked green muslin gown. It barely covered her nipples. She'd worn it quite deliberately today. Clearly her guest did not approve, for his firm lips tightened, before his gaze rose to her face again.

She cast him a flirtatious sideways glance. 'You don't have a choice, my lord.'

'The green chamber is ready, Miss Draycott,' Gribble said. 'I'll have Brian bring up your valise, my lord. He will serve as your valet while you are here. May I take your coat?'

Still frowning, Tonbridge shrugged out of his fashionably caped driving coat and handed it over, along with his hat and gloves. The lack of a coat didn't make him look any less imposing. His black morning coat clung to his shoulders as if it had been moulded to his body, an altogether pleasing sight. Or it would be if she cared about that sort of thing. Without his hat, his jaw looked squarer, more rugged, but the smooth wide forehead and piercing dark eyes surprisingly spoke of intelligence. She doubted their veracity, because although his thick brown hair looked neat rather than fashionable, his cravat was tied with obvious flare. It must take his valet hours to turn out such perfection.

Merry knew his sort. An idle nobleman with nothing to do but adorn his frame. And there was plenty of frame to adorn. A good six feet of it, she judged. Tall for a woman, she still had to look up to meet his gaze. But she'd known that already. He'd loomed over her out there on the moors. And made her heart beat far too fast.

And the odd thing was, it was beating a little too fast now, too. And grasshoppers in hobnail boots were marching around in her stomach.

Surely she wasn't afraid of him?

Or was it simply a reaction to the events of the past few hours? The disappointment at the mill owners' intransigence, followed by the accident. It had not been a good day. She straightened her shoulders. She wasn't beaten yet.

She needed to talk to Caroline. 'Where is Mrs Falkner, Gribble?'

'In the drawing room,' the butler replied. 'Awaiting dinner.'

Blast. She'd have to change, which meant no time to talk over what had happened with Caroline until later. She turned to Lord Tonbridge. 'Gribble will see you to your room. When you are ready, please join us in the drawing room.'

She ran lightly up the stairs. Dandies took hours at their toilette. She stopped and turned. Tonbridge was watching her with an unreadable expression.

'Dinner is in one hour. Please do not be late.'

His slackened jaw made her want to laugh. He must think her completely rag-mannered. And so she was.

She continued up the stairs to her chamber. If she was quick, she could speak to Caroline before their guest arrived downstairs.

A frown gathered beneath the chestnut curls on Caro's brow. Her hazel eyes filled with sadness. 'There is no help from that quarter, then,' she said, at the end of Merry's swiftly delivered report.

No matter how drably Caro dressed—tonight she'd chosen a dark blue merino wool with a high neck and no ornament—or how serious the expression on her heart-shaped face, the petite woman was always devastatingly lovely.

'None at all, I believe,' replied Merry, who always felt like a giant next to her friend. 'Do not worry, the women can stay here for as long as is needed.'

She paced the length of the drawing room and came back to face Caro. 'I'm so sorry I could not convince them.'

Caro gently touched her friend's gloved hand. 'It is not your fault. We will find another way.'

'I wish I knew how.'

'We will think of something. What is our visitor like?'

A generous change of topic given Caro's disappointment. Merry filled her lungs with air. 'Tonbridge? Handsome, I suppose. Rather disapproving of me, I'm afraid.'

'That's because he doesn't know you.'

If he knew her, he'd be more disapproving than ever. She sat beside her friend. 'I hope he doesn't take too long. I'm starving.' She looked at the clock. In one minute the hour would be up.

Tonbridge stepped through the door. He had shaved and changed from his driving clothes into a form-fitting blue evening coat, starched white cravat and ivory waistcoat. His tight buff pantaloons fitted like a second skin over muscle and bone. One would never guess from his languidly fashionable form he had recently heaved a wrecked carriage off the road single-handed.

He'd looked magnificent, like Atlas supporting the world.

'Come in, Lord Tonbridge,' Merry said. 'Let me introduce you to my dear friend and companion, Mrs Caroline Falkner.'

'I am pleased to meet you, Mrs Falkner.' Tonbridge made his bows, gracious, elegant and formal. Coolly distant. The highborn nobleman meeting the unwashed masses. No wonder Caroline looked thoroughly uncomfortable.

'I hope my unexpected arrival is not a dreadful inconvenience,' he said, moving to stand beside the fire.

Polite blankness hid Caroline's thoughts. She sounded calm enough when she spoke. 'I am so grateful you were on hand to help Miss Draycott.' She rose to her feet. 'I hope the servants took good care of you?' She went to the console on the far side of the room.

'Excellent care,' he said.

'And your quarters are to your liking?' Merry asked.

'Indeed.'

A consummate liar. Merry hid her smile. Like the rest of the house, the green guest chamber was a nightmare of ostentation.

'Let me pour you a libation to warm you after your ordeal,' Caroline said. 'Sherry for you, Merry?' She turned to look at Tonbridge. 'A brandy, my lord?'

Tonbridge was looking at Caroline with a frown of puzzlement. And no wonder. Caro's ladylike airs and modest appearance would seem at odds with this house of gross opulence.

Oppressive scarlet velvet curtains, gilt scattered with abandon, garish fabrics on the floors and wildly patterned silk on the walls— she could almost see Tonbridge wince as he looked around.

Grandfather had wanted no one to underestimate his wealth.

'Takes a lot of brass to fill a room like this,' she said.

His gaze came back to her face. 'Beauty needs no adornment.' Mischief gleamed in his eyes. Not the reaction she'd expected. The man had a sense of humour lurking beneath that haughty lift of his deeply cleft chin.

Dash it. She did not want to like him. It would only lead to embarrassment. He was simply being polite. A gentleman. No doubt when he joined his friends, he would have a mocking tale to tell.

Oh, how she'd like to peel off the polite veneer and reveal his true nature. Prove she was right and stop her foolish heart's flutters every time he sent that cool dark glance her way.

'A pox on your sherry,' Merry said with a quick laugh. ''Tis brandy for me. I vow I am still chilled to the bone. Perhaps *you* would prefer a dish of tea, my lord?'

As she'd expected, Tonbridge turned with a frown. Clearly she'd shocked him with her teasing. Blasted nobility. They thought everyone who didn't conform to their idea of polite society to be beneath them. While they gambled away their fortunes, men like her grandfather accumulated great wealth by hard work. He could look down his nose all he liked, she wasn't ashamed of her background.

A small smile curved his lips, a brief softening of his harsh features and her heart gave a lurch, the kind that hurt and felt good at the same time. Not a feeling to have around such a powerful man. If he sensed it, he would see it as weakness.

'Brandy would be equally welcome to me, Miss Draycott,' he said.

Did nothing put him out, or did he just never show it? Too well bred. Too reserved. 'Call me Merry,' she said, as she had on the moors, an inner wildness overcoming good sense. 'Everyone does. I hate formality, don't you?'

He looked more than a little startled at that, which gave her a moment of satisfaction.

He responded cheerfully enough. 'As you wish, Merry.' He didn't offer his own first name. She guessed he'd already placed their relative stations in life and knew he was far above their touch.

Caroline poured the brandy. Merry took both glasses and handed one to Tonbridge. 'To my knight in shining armour,' she toasted boldly and tossed off the fiery liquid. It burned its way to her stomach.

She really didn't need any more heat. The proximity of this man made her skin glow. She cocked a challenging brow.

He raised his glass, a smile curving his finely drawn mouth. 'To a lovely maiden in distress.'

More devastating charm. He must practise in front of the mirror, the way the girls practised simpering before the glass at school.

He took a cautious sip and then nodded. 'Excellent.' He swallowed a mouthful.

'My grandfather kept a very fine cellar,' she said, not without a little pride. Grandfather might have lacked town bronze, as the *ton* called it, but he knew quality. Unfortunately, he had no sense of style. Hence the costly but dreadful décor.

Gribble opened the door. 'Dinner is served, miss.'

Tonbridge held out both arms. 'Ladies?'

Gribble's grey brows shot up, wrinkling his forehead.

Speechless, Merry looked at Caroline, who lifted her shoulders in a slight shrug. As usual her hazel eyes gave nothing away. Merry had found Caroline serving at an inn in York and had instantly seen her predicament. A well-bred lady brought low. She'd offered her the position of companion on the spot. But Caroline never talked about her past. And she rarely offered an opinion.

Not that Merry relied on anyone else's judgement. Grandfather would never allow it. She made her own decisions.

She placed her hand on his right forearm and Caroline did the same on his left. As they walked, she glanced at his face and saw nothing but bland politeness. And that made her nervous. Because politeness hid lies and knives in the back.

She had a strategy for dealing with practised deceit, developed after years of misery. Frontal attack.

Chapter Two

'Is this your first visit to Yorkshire, my lord?' Caroline asked when the food was served and the butler had withdrawn.

Tonbridge paused in his carving of the roast duck and smiled politely. 'Not at all. I came here often in my youth with my family. It has been some years since my last visit, I must say.'

'Lucky for me you chose today,' Merry said, fluttering her eyelashes in a fair emulation of the girls she'd despised at school.

Caroline cast her a startled look.

Tonbridge continued carving. 'It seems we were both lucky. I doubt I would have made it to Skepton in the snow and I would never have found hospitality on so grand a scale elsewhere in the wilds of the moors.'

Grand meaning horribly bourgeois, no doubt.

'May I help you to some of this fine bird, Mrs Falkner?' he asked.

'Thank you,' Caroline said.

'Not for me,' Merry said, then waved her fork and the carrot on its tines airily at the picture behind her. 'That is my grandfather, Josiah Draycott. He rose from shepherd boy to owning one of the largest wool mills in Yorkshire.'

'Impressive,' Tonbridge said. He put the best slices of the bird on Caroline's plate and took the remainder for himself.

Merry wasn't sure if he referred to the portrait in which her grandfather, with his full-bottomed wig and eagle-eyed stare, looked as if he could eat small boys for breakfast, or his accomplishments. Strangely enough she had the impression it was the latter when she'd expected the former.

She cut her roast beef into bite-sized pieces. 'He left it all to me.'

He stilled, his duck-laden fork hovering before parted lips. Lovely full lips. The kind of lips that would cushion a girl's mouth. No awkward clashing of teeth for him, she felt sure.

His eyes widened. 'You are a mill owner?' he asked.

Hah! She'd managed to surprise him. At least he'd managed not to sneer. 'Owner of Draycott's Mills.'

His gaze met hers. 'I recognised the name, of course. I just didn't expect...'

'A woman in charge?'

'We sell Durn's wool to Draycott's,' he said, neatly sidestepping her question. He put the duck in his mouth and chewed. How could anyone look so scrumptious, just chewing?

She dragged her gaze from his mouth. 'And very fine wool it is.'

'The best,' he agreed.

'But not producing as much in recent years.'

He blinked and she felt a little glow of satisfaction. She wasn't just a mill owner, a reaper of profits. While she rarely visited the mill because the blunt Yorkshire men felt uncomfortable around their female employer, she received weekly reports, statements and accountings. She knew her business. Grandfather had insisted.

'We've seen revenues fall off,' Tonbridge admitted. 'One reason for my visit.'

One reason? What would be the others?

He turned to Caroline. 'Are you also involved in Draycott's, Mrs Falkner?'

For a man of such an exalted position, he had exquisite manners.

Merry found herself warming at the way he included Caroline in the conversation. But he'd not get carrot juice out of that turnip.

Caroline shook her head. 'Oh, no.'

'I don't know what I would do without Caroline's companionship,' Merry said on her friend's behalf.

Caroline smiled at her with gratitude.

Tonbridge's dark eyes looked from one to the other. A question entered his gaze, a dark thought that caused a slight tightening at the corners of his mouth. More disapproval? 'You are lucky to have such a good friend,' he said quietly. The words seemed to hold more meaning than she could work out.

What on earth was he thinking? She found she couldn't hazard a guess and that was annoying. Accompanying her grandfather on his business dealings had taught her how to read men very well. This one, however, was a bit of a mystery. A challenge.

'What do you do when you are not visiting the outposts of the Mountford empire?' she asked.

He laughed. 'You are nothing if you are not direct, Merry.' He held up a hand when she began to apologise. 'I like it. It is refreshing.'

Refreshing meant naïve. Ignorant of the social niceties. She flashed him a sultry smile. 'I'm glad you find it stimulating, my lord.'

Glints of amber danced in his eyes. 'You have no idea.'

Oh, but she did, because her blood was stirring and her pulse fluttering in places she shouldn't be aware of in polite company. She felt more alive than she had for months, perhaps years. For the first time since her fall into disgrace, she felt her body tingle with interest and excitement.

Lust.

Thank goodness she knew it for what it was and could resist it.

Caroline cast her warning glance, an admonition that the flirtation was getting out of hand.

What did it matter if she flirted a little? It wasn't as if she could be ruined. And this man with his icy reserve deserved a little shaking up. Pretending not to notice Caroline's unspoken message, she raised a brow. 'Well, Lord Tonbridge? You didn't answer my question. Perhaps you are a gambler or a rake?'

'Both,' he said, his expression suddenly darker. 'Have you a wish to test my skills?'

Caroline coughed and picked up her water. 'My throat is dry,' she muttered after a sip.

Merry only knew one way to deal with a man of his sort. Call his bluff. 'La, sir, where would we start? With a wager? Or a seduction?'

Dark eyes observed her intently, then flicked to Caroline, who was bright pink and looking mortified. 'I bow to your wishes,' he said, his deep voice a silky caress on her ears.

Her stomach did a long slow lazy roll that left her breathless. And speechless. Blast him, he didn't scare easily. Most of the noblemen she'd met in the past would be running a mile by now at the thought of an entanglement with Merry Draycott.

Gribble entered quietly with his minion at his heels to clear the table for the remove, affording her the opportunity to marshal her defences.

'Do you plan a long stay at Durn, my lord?' Caroline asked, covering an awkward silence as the servants went about their business.

'I'm not sure,' he said, looking at Merry. 'It depends on several factors.'

Merry really didn't like the thrill that rippled through her at the thought that she might be a factor. Did she? He might be the handsomest man she'd ever seen, but he had an arrogance about him, a sense of entitlement, put there by wealth and position. There was also a coldness. It wafted from him like a chill wind. He'd judged her instantly and sensed his superiority. Perhaps he thought she should be honoured to fall at his feet. The thought jangled her pride. A need to take the wind out of his sails was pushing her into outrageous behaviour she could not seem to stop.

Finished with their tasks, the servants withdrew.

'Can I offer you some of this very fine aspic, Mrs Falkner?' he asked.

Caroline inclined her head. 'Yes, please, my lord.'

He raised his gaze to her face. 'Merry?'

She should not have given him permission to use her first name. It put her at a distinct disadvantage. 'A small amount. Thank you.'

He served Caroline first. He had large strong hands. The fingers were elegant, yet not at all limp or fluttery. Grandfather always knew a man's nature from the way he shook hands. Most of the time, men bowed over hers, so she never got the opportunity to judge their grip. She'd found other ways to assess their worth.

The way a man handled his knife and fork and the business of eating told her a great deal. This one used his implements with casual ease and ate with firm elegance and a pleasing economy of movement. The Marquis of Tonbridge exceeded all her standards.

He'd been good with the horses, too, she recalled, firm, yet gentle. Not once had he pulled on their delicate mouths while keeping firm control.

Was she letting her biases lead her astray in regard to this man? Was he merely following her lead out of politeness? If she truly believed so, she should simply bid him goodnight after dinner and retire. It would not be difficult to declare a headache or weariness from the day's events.

But she didn't believe he was just being polite for a minute. He wanted to put her in her place. She could see it in his eyes.

'You haven't answered my question,' he said, raising a brow.

Clearly, he needed a lesson in humility. 'Why don't we start with a wager?'

He raised a brow. 'Cards? Or do you prefer dice?'

'Billiards,' she said. 'If you play?'

He nodded. 'Billiards it is.'

The conversation passed on to more mundane topics and it was not long before Caroline was making her excuses, leaving Merry to deal with the fruits of her challenge.

The billiard room was, without a doubt, the most comfortable room Charlie had entered so far. Linen-fold panelled walls of oak provided a warm background for comfortably heavy wooden furniture dating back to the last century. An equally impressive green baize-covered slate table stood in the centre of a red-and-green-patterned rug.

Not a scrap of velvet or gilt in sight. A relief to his weary eyes. The only glitter beneath the overhead light was Miss Draycott herself. Merry. What an apt name for such an unusual female.

She eyed the balls, running her palm up and down her cue. Her fingers were long and fine and the action brought other images to mind. Sensual images.

The simmering arousal he'd been fighting all evening made itself known with a disgruntled jolt.

He'd never before felt such instant attraction for such a—how did one describe this woman? Statuesque, certainly. Gloriously so. She didn't have to crane her neck to see his face. He'd thought he liked his women small and delicate. Until now.

He certainly wouldn't worry about hurting her when romping around in a bed. His body stirred in approval. He tamped down his desire. The last thing he needed was a distraction like Merry Draycott.

For an unprotected woman, she was far too bold for her own good. Many men would have no qualms about taking advantage. He had to admit he found the prospect tempting.

Her behaviour had him thoroughly off kilter, too. On occasion, her manner of speech left much to be desired. At other times she seemed almost genteel. She confused him. And, unfortunately, intrigued him.

For an instant at dinner, he'd suspected the two women of being more than platonic friends, that they might worship at the altar of Sappho, but as the meal progressed he had not sensed anything warmer than friendship.

Not that he was averse to the special friendships some women preferred. It just put those particular women out of reach, and, in her case, he'd felt disappointed.

The truth was, he wanted her. He couldn't remember the last time he'd felt so urgent about having a woman. He fought to control the impulse to seduce her. As her guest, good manners required he accommodate his hostess's wishes. A part of him wished those desires included more than a high-stakes game of billiards. The undercurrents swirling around them suggested they might. And no matter what he thought, his baser male nature wanted to oblige.

A man about to become betrothed did not enter into an entanglement with another woman. Hell, he'd just got rid of his long-term mistress for that very reason.

Meeting this particular woman on the road was, without a doubt, a confounded nuisance.

She played a damned fine game of billiards, too. She'd won the first game, mostly because he had been focusing too much on her sweet little bottom when she'd leaned over the table. A quite deliberate ploy on her part, no doubt. Not unlike a Captain Sharp plying his mark with gin.

He watched her saunter around the table with a jaunty swing of her hips and clenched his jaw. She was deliberately tormenting him with a gown that skimmed her breasts and revealed every curve when she walked. While her gown wasn't any more provocative than many respectable married ladies of the *ton* wore to a drum or a rout, on her, it seemed positively decadent.

The woman was a menace. Teasing a man came with consequences she might not like. Perhaps she needed a lesson in acceptable behaviour. A warning.

He covered his mouth and yawned widely. 'Excuse me. It's been a long day. I think I am ready to retire.'

She frowned. 'Afraid you will lose again?'

'Not at all,' he drawled. 'My interest is waning. I'm afraid I need more of a challenge.'

She eyed him suspiciously. 'Fifty guineas a point and a hundred for a win is reasonably challenging.'

'I'm not trying to fleece you, Merry, but I think both of us can lose a few hundred guineas in a night and not turn a hair.'

Her eyes widened a fraction. 'Do you want to make it thousands?'

He grinned and leaned on his cue. 'That is more of the same, isn't it?' Oh God, he was going to hell for this. 'In this next game, how about for each point we lose, we remove an article of clothing?'

It was the kind of thing he would have proposed during his misspent youth, before his stint in the army. Before he became duller than ditchwater, more sedate than a spinster walking a pug. The sharp voice of his handsomely paid-off mistress rang in his head.

Merry was staring at him wide-eyed, shocked to her toes.

A rueful smile tugged at his lips as he waited for her to retreat in disarray and leave him to take his brandy to his empty bed.

'An article of clothing per point?' she said, a little breathlessly, her cheeks flushing pink, but her shoulders straightening.

A breath caught in his throat. By thunder, she wasn't going to back down. The naughty minx. Someone ought to put her over their knee. He drew on every ounce of control, the kind a man needed going into battle.

Clearly there was only one way to teach this young woman not to play with fire. Singe her eyebrows.

'Anything on your person,' he said as if the whole topic bored him.

'Including jewellery? Because it seems to me I have far less clothing than you do.'

'Certainly.'

She boldly ran her gaze down his body as if considering whether seeing him disrobed would be worth the risk. He pretended not to notice the heat of desire flaring in the depths of her summer-blue eyes and let her look her fill.

She parted her lips and his body hardened to granite. He forced himself not to shift to find ease for his confined flesh.

Some women found him too large, too overpowering physically, when the fashion was for lisping mincing dandies. In her case the thought of doing a bit of overpowering made the prospect all the sweeter.

If she dared take his challenge.

She drew in a deep breath. 'All right,' she said. 'Fifty guineas and an article of clothing per point to twelve points. The hundred guineas for the win remains unchanged.'

She expected to win. It was writ large on her face. He took a slow inward breath, controlling the surge of heat at the thought of seeing her naked. 'That sounds fair,' he said coolly.

And then she laughed. A low chuckle in the back of her throat. 'Perhaps I should ask Gribble to have the fire stoked before we start. So no one catches a chill.'

'I don't think that will be necessary. Our blushes will keep us warm.'

Her shoulders tensed. 'Your blushes, you mean.'

What a surprise, this woman—the first who had dared challenge him for years. They usually simpered and flattered. If he was any kind of gentleman he would stop this right now, but he wouldn't. Not if his life depended on it. He was having too much fun. He smiled at her, a sweet, but slightly devilish grin. 'It seems you are first, my dear Merry.'

She missed her first shot. Nerves. Not as blasé as she pretended.

'Bad luck,' he said. 'A one-point penalty.'

She removed the pearls at her throat and placed them on a side table with a little toss of her head. 'You will not be so lucky in future.'

He eyed the board, and played his shot carefully. His ball missed hers and came to rest temptingly close to the pocket.

'You missed. One point for me,' she said.

He bowed and removed his coat and draped it over a chair back, while she walked around the table, looking at the balls from all angles.

He waited, leaning nonchalantly on his cue.

With a small smile of triumph she lay across the table and eyed the balls. An easy shot. Just as he'd planned. He and Robert had actually orchestrated one of these games with a couple of the village tarts at Durn. It was all coming back.

The sweet curve of her bottom as she stretched over the table tempted unbearably. From this angle, the draping fabric left little to the imagination and put her at just the right angle to receive his attentions. Two steps closer and he could slide his hands over the soft flesh and press his groin against the full roundness of her buttocks.

He drew in a swift breath. Brought his body under control. Passion, strong passions, led to nowhere but disaster. And even if she was wriggling that little posterior on purpose, she was doing it as a distraction, a way of putting him off his own shot.

She knocked the white ball with a swift jerk of her elbow. It caromed off the red and hit his ball with a crack, sending it into the corner pocket.

He smiled. 'Good shot.'

She lowered her feet gracefully to the floor. She cast him a glance over her shoulder. 'I know.'

He grinned.

She raised her brows.

He removed the diamond pin from his cravat, adding it to her pearls, then unknotted and slowly unwound his cravat. She looked highly pleased with herself, but he couldn't help wondering if it was because she wanted to see more of him, or because she'd won.

The former, he evilly hoped. He had no qualms about removing his clothes before a woman, despite the scar.

He draped the long strip of cloth over his coat. He glanced down at himself. 'What next, do you think? Ah, yes.' He toed off his shoes and, standing first on one leg, then the other, divested himself of his stockings. He did not miss her sidelong glance at his feet and bare calves, or the quick swipe of her lips with her tongue.

Heat flowed to his groin.

Ignoring his burgeoning arousal, he sauntered around the table, replacing the balls, while he felt the touch of sparkling eyes on his body.

'How many pieces of clothing do you think you are wearing?' she asked.

'Less than the number of points required to finish the game,' he said, instantly guessing the direction of her thoughts.

'Good,' she said, but there was an undercurrent of nervousness behind her bold front. An unease. Unless he wanted her to be better than she appeared? Surely not?

'You didn't tell me you were an expert at this game,' he said, rubbing the end of his cue with chalk.

Her gaze flew from the cue tip to his face. 'I used to play with my grandfather all the time. It passed the long winter evenings and while we played he taught me about the mill.'

'He sounds like a grand old gentleman.'

'He was. A darling.' Her face brightened. It was as if she'd lit a candle inside, she became so dazzling. The brightness wasn't true, he realised. It flickered and wavered as if a sharp gust of wind would blow it out. But why would he care? He had enough baggage to shoulder of his own without delving into hers. She'd made it quite clear from the beginning of the evening that she was interested in a dalliance. The idea became more attractive as the evening wore on. He didn't remember the last time he'd felt quite so enlivened.

Her ball was easily accessible. His guarded the red. She played her next shot with consummate skill, knocking his aside and giving her access to the red ball.

He leaned in for his shot. A flick of the wrist and he struck the red and white in quick succession. They fired off into the centre pockets. 'Seven points,' he said calmly, straightening.

Her mouth dropped open. Her blue eyes were wide with shock, staring at the table. 'You cheated.'

He folded his arms across his chest. 'Oh?' He raised a brow and stared down his nose. His ducal-heir-look, Robert always called it.

She flushed. 'I mean, you pretended you were not very good at this game. Only an expert can make a shot like that.'

'Are you wishing to forfeit the game?'

She stiffened, her gaze meeting his with blue sparks of anger. 'Certainly not.'

As he'd suspected, Merry Draycott did not back down from a fight. The small qualm of contrition for goading her wasn't strong enough to make him concede. 'Seven items, then, Merry.'

She tugged three hair ornaments from her artfully arranged curls. Long black silky tresses fell to her exquisite sloping white shoulders. She placed the ornaments on the table with her pearls. Her bracelet followed. Her wince said that was the last of her jewellery.

She sent him a resentful glance and he tipped his head on one side as if completely unaware of her concern.

She glanced at his bare feet, sat down on a chair and started untying the ribbons around her ankles. Her hair fell forwards as black as a raven's wing, hiding her face.

'Do you need any help?' he asked.

Chapter Three

Merry felt a blush crawl up her face. 'I can manage.' She ducked her head, untied the bow at the back of her ankle and slipped the shoe off.

Oh Lord, seven points, he only needed four to win. And what would she have left to remove if he won another seven points? She should never have let him convince her to play such a shocking game. He had cheated. He had let her think he was a hopeless player.

And then, when he'd offered her a chance to forfeit, she'd let her pride speak instead of common sense. But a Draycott never backed down, be it in a bargain or a game.

The ribbon snagged. She tugged at it. The knot drew tighter.

His bare toes appeared within her vision, which was restricted to her feet, the hem of her gown and the carpet. He dropped to his knees. 'May I help?' he asked again.

The sound of his voice was like a taste of hot chocolate, warm and rich and wickedly tempting.

'I can manage.'

He sat back on his heels. Sweeping her hair back, she glanced up at his face. His gaze remained fixed on her foot, on the knot. She let go a huff of impatience. 'Very well. See if you can untie it.'

She couldn't breathe. She had a huge fluttery lump stuck in her throat. Her mouth dried.

The wretch grasped her ankle and lifted her foot to rest on one knee. The heat of his hand, the feel of those long strong fingers taking the weight of her leg, sent ripples of pleasure through her body. She swallowed a gasp.

'Such a pretty ankle,' he murmured as he worked at the ribbon.

A melting sensation weakened her limbs. Oh, dear. If he made her feel this way with a touch on her extremity, how would she feel if he wanted to help her with her garter? She could not, nay, would not let him undo her like this. 'La, thank you, sir,' she said and was infuriated by the breathy note in her voice.

He glanced up at her face with a smile. 'No need to thank me. I speak only the truth.'

The man was impossibly handsome when he smiled like that. A dark inscrutable devil with the expression of an angel. In her heart she knew it for what it was, an act, a flirtation, but he played his part so well he almost had her convinced.

She pointed at her foot. 'The slipper, my lord.'

He bent his dark head to the task. His dark brown hair fell in thick luxurious chocolate-brown waves. She had the urge to touch it, to feel its texture. She gripped the chair arm instead.

He untied the ribbon around her ankle and slid the shoe from her foot, his palm caressing the arch. Delicious. Intoxicating. She wanted to wriggle her toes. She kept a bright smile fixed on her face. Bright and teasing, when inside she wanted to weep at the tenderness in his touch.

Gently he placed her foot on the ground. She wished she had a fan close at hand instead of a cue. She was glowing from the inside out. How could this be? She wasn't some innocent schoolgirl to have her head turned by a handsome man. Particularly not one with a title. And yet she wanted to melt into this man's arms. Feel that broad chest pressed against her breasts. Run her fingers through his hair and feel his strength beneath her fingers. Utter foolishness.

'I don't need your help with the garter.' Her voice sounded strangled.

His head snapped up. 'You disappoint me.'

She managed a quick calming breath and a light laugh. 'Intentionally, sir. To allow such familiarity would be more reward than you have earned. Turn around.'

He stood. His rueful gaze made her heart beat just a little too fast. 'Saving your life is worth so little, then?'

'Unfair,' she cried, laughing a little herself at the neat way he'd tried make her feel guilty. Oh, this man was a rake indeed and she was a fool to continue their game. 'Am I not feeding you and giving you lodging as well as helping you wile away the hours before bed?'

His lips twitched, but he bowed and turned his back.

The clock on the mantel struck midnight. She glanced at it to make sure. She could not believe so much time had passed so quickly.

She leaped out of her chair, turned her back, in case he should decide to peek, and untied her garter, a pretty thing made of the finest lace from Nottingham she'd bought on a visit to look at their mills. She walked to the chair and laid it on top of his cravat. The rug felt odd under her stockinged feet, the silk no barrier to the rougher nap of the woollen tufts.

'Let us finish our game,' she said, trying to sound as if it didn't matter that one of her stockings was slowly sliding down her calf, or that the heat inside her seemed to have reached the temperature of a furnace. He'd been right when he said their blushes would keep them warm.

Or her, anyway. He seemed remarkably unaffected.

'It is my turn.'

He bowed and gestured for her to continue.

She inhaled a deep breath, forcing her unruly thoughts back in control. She needed seven points to have any hope of winning this game. She had done it in the past. Not often. And not for a very long time. She looked at the table, the balls back in position. It would not be an easy shot.

She steadied herself against the table and lined up her cue. Her mouth felt terribly dry and her hands were shaking. The hit on the red was clean, it cracked nicely and shot across the table spinning, while her cue ball downed his ball in the nearby corner. The red ball hovered at the edge of the centre pocket…and stopped.

It stopped. Surely it would topple over. She stared at it. Willing it to move. A fraction.

She could not believe it.

'Oh, too bad,' he said and sounded sincere.

She shrugged. 'I won four points.' She'd wanted seven.

'We could take it as potted. It is so close.'

Her back stiffened. 'I'm not a child, sir. I haven't lost yet.' She brushed her hair back from her shoulders. 'You have four items to remove, remember?'

He smiled and shrugged. He took off his waistcoat and watch, then slowly released the buttons of his shirt, all the while keeping his gaze on her face.

Heat blazed in her cheeks. She was having trouble breathing and she couldn't look away.

He tugged the shirt free of his waistband and pulled it off over his head, tossing it on his growing pile of clothing.

He was beautiful. 'Oh, my,' she whispered.

Merry had never seen such a virile gorgeous male. Not out in the fields at haymaking or in the mills, where the men often discarded most of their clothing in the heat of the summer. And certainly Jeremy had looked nothing like this. Although she'd been fascinated at the sight of his body, she'd not been in awe.

The lean and heavily muscled Tonbridge, with his skin of pale gold as if he sometimes exposed it to the sun, left her breathless. The scar, puckered and white, ravaging tight sculpted flesh from breast to hip, emphasised the perfection of his form.

She felt a strange urge to touch the scar, to run her fingers along its length, to press her lips to it as if somehow she could make it disappear. A little shiver ran down her spine. Pleasure. Lust. She knew it for what it was, but had it firmly under control. Didn't she?

She raised her eyes once more to his face. He was watching her closely as if trying to read her reaction. Perhaps other women were repulsed by the sight of his ruined flesh. A tension that had not been there before invaded the room.

Oh, there had been tension, between them. The sort of electricity one felt before thunderstorms as they fenced verbally. She had found it quite exciting. This, however, felt more like the undercurrent in a fast-flowing river. An irresistible tug of unseen emotions.

She forced a bright smile. 'What will you remove next?'

He chuckled. A deep sound in his lovely broad chest. 'Not much left for either of us.'

And it was his turn to play. This was going to be very embarrassing. Four points would be bad enough. Seven would have her completely disrobed.

'Do you want to stop here?' he asked.

Why did he have to be so gentlemanly? And yet there was a knowing look in his eyes as if he guessed she would never forfeit a game. 'That would be cowardly,' she managed.

Her gaze darted from his face to his chest. 'What happened to you?'

'A sabre.'

'Duelling?'

'Something like that.'

'I think duelling is a foolish pastime,' she said, frowning at the scar. 'Real men resolve their problems without hacking each other to pieces.'

The hobnail-booted grasshoppers had returned. This time they were running around in a frenzy. Out of self-defence she turned her attention to the table. It didn't help, because he walked around retrieving the balls from her last shot, his upper arms bulging and stretching as he replaced them on the table.

She took a deep breath and realised with horror her hands were shaking and damp.

He leaned a hip against the edge of the table. 'My shot.'

His shot. This was going to be a disaster.

He leaned over the table and his elbow slid smoothly forwards, but he dropped his shoulder. His ball missed the red by such a small fraction, for a moment she was sure he was about to get another seven.

Relief flooded through her body in a hot wave.

He stood staring at the table as if he didn't quite believe it himself. 'By Jove,' he said, frowning.

'You lowered your shoulder at the last minute,' she said.

He grimaced and removed his signet ring. It tinkled against the other jewellery as he set it down with a snap.

He took a deep breath and the underlying bones in his chest expanded, drawing attention to the narrowness of his waist and lean hips, though she tried her best not to let him see she had noticed.

She was going to win. He had almost nothing left to remove. She wiped her hands on her gown. She ought to stop now. She really ought to.

But he needed taking down a peg or two.

And she wasn't going to look when he removed the last of his clothes.

Not one peek. He would remove them and leave.

'Your turn, Merry.'

For some reason, she loved the way he said her name. It was as if he savoured each syllable and consonant. As if he tasted them on his tongue.

'Yes,' she said. Her hands trembled. She didn't need to do anything fancy. Put his ball in the corner pocket.

'Whenever you are ready,' he said quietly.

She jumped. Desperate to have this over and done she took her shot quickly, neatly caroming off the red, the ball ricocheting into the pocket at the end of the table.

He made a sound like a laugh quickly stifled.

A second later she realised why. She'd downed her own ball.

'Hell,' she said.

'Oh, dear. I believe that is three points to me.'

'I know that,' she said, staring at the table where his ball happily rested to the right of the red. Blast. She hadn't made a mistake like that since she'd been a young girl.

She looked up at his face and saw his broad grin. Damn it. The sight of him half-naked had scattered her wits.

A smile pinned on her face, she let her eyes sparkle and fluttered her lashes. 'Might I ask if you have a preference?'

His look of astonishment, quickly followed by a flare of heat in those dark eyes, was all the reward she needed for her daring.

Her satisfaction didn't last long, because he was eyeing her like dinner had finally arrived. What on earth had made her give him the choice?

'The other garter, I think, and both stockings. And then it is my turn to shoot.'

And she would be the one who was naked. Her stomach dipped down to her feet.

'I will forgo the rest of the game,' he said, his eyes gleaming wickedly, 'if you will permit me to remove those items.'

Her stomach sank even further, dropping away in a rush. As if she'd fallen from a high place, or dropped into a well.

He raised his brows.

Dash it all. It was the only way to retain a shred of propriety and honour. Letting him take off her stockings and feeling those wonderfully strong warm hands on her naked flesh all the way to her knee sounded dreadful. Dreadfully delicious.

And not nearly as awful as being required to undress, should he down his next shot. He had missed once. He might miss again. Her mind went back to that odd drop of his shoulder, when usually he moved with such elegant grace and surety. He'd done it on purpose. Missed his shot. To give her a chance to win. And she'd muffed it.

No wonder he'd laughed.

She closed her eyes briefly. Then he deserved his reward. Her insides quivered. Excitement. Anticipation. Wicked. She was nothing but wicked.

She nodded.

She sat on the nearest chair. 'Your hands must go no further than the top of my knee, nor your gaze.'

The corners of his mouth curled in a sensual smile. 'Do you play the part of Portia, now?'

She lifted her chin. 'And will you play the part of fair Antonio or be the lesser man?'

'A hit,' he said and bowed. 'I will abide by your rule most cheerfully.'

She carefully arranged her skirt so that no more than the top of her left stocking showed below the hem. It had slid below her knee.

He dropped to his knees in front of her and sat back on his heels. 'A delectable sight.'

'I trust you to keep your word.'

She could not see his face, but his shoulders shook a little as if he was trying not to laugh. She saw no humour in the situation, for he had cheated. She was sure of it.

Her skin tingled with the anticipation of his touch. She bit her lip as he hooked one finger into the fine silk and rolled it down over her ankle. He eased it over her heel and off. 'That is one.'

There. Not so bad. No caresses or touches driving her mad.

His fingers went to the hem of her gown, gathering up the fine material until he reached her knee. She tried not to look, or to guess at his reaction. A rake like him would have seen lots of ladies' limbs. Her legs were long and well muscled from striding about her property like a man, when she wasn't conducting business, also like a man. He would find no feminine softness beneath her skirts. He'd probably find her unappealing.

She stared at the wall opposite and gritted her teeth.

The tug on the bow of her garter was like a tug at her centre. Wicked sensations pulsed in her core. She felt naked, exposed, yet when she glanced down to watch, her hem had risen only on one side and not a fraction above the edge of her stocking. But he knelt so close, concentrated on his task with such focus, she could feel his warm breath brush her thigh through the layers of gown and chemise. It tickled unbearably.

He pulled the garter free and dangled it before her face. 'Two,' he said.

She swallowed. Resisted the urge to pull down her skirts. Ignored the fire she could feel burning on her face. She did not fear him doing anything she did not permit. She feared she might permit him to take liberties. But she would not be so cowardly as to go back on her word, not after his generosity. 'Well, go on.'

He cast a swift glance upwards. 'Your wish is my command.'

Oh, how she wanted to hit him. She rolled her eyes to the ceiling and yawned instead. But as soon as he returned to his task, she lowered her lashes, pretending to close her eyes, and watched as he ran a finger beneath the edge of her stocking. A second finger joined the first. He made great play of stretching the fabric over her knee. Her insides turned liquid as if they had melted. Her limbs grew languid. She hauled in a deep breath.

He leaned down and placed a kiss on the bared skin. A swift brush of warm dry lips.

She gasped and gripped the chair arms tighter. 'You go too far.'

'Such beauty deserves worship.'

'You tease me, sirrah.'

He looked up, his eyelids heavy, his lips sensual. 'Not about something as lovely as this.'

A warm glow suffused her skin. Her body clamoured for more

than a whisper of touch. She must not succumb to him. She'd sworn never to let a man take her for a fool. She was her own woman. Now and always. Only with him she seemed reckless. Dangerously so.

Was it reckless to keep one's word?

She bit her lip. 'Continue.'

He rolled the stocking, as neatly as any maid would, careful not to damage the cobwebby silk. Another inch of skin, another kiss. Thrills coursed through her blood. She held herself rigid against their temptation, but she couldn't stop watching.

He continued to roll and kiss every inch until the stocking reached her ankle. He shaped her calf with his palm, lingering there as if he'd exposed a treasure. Her insides tightened with desire and longing.

He sighed, a waft of warm gentle air against her skin, then pulled the stocking off. He rubbed the ball of her foot with his thumb. Her body hummed with pleasure. He massaged her arch. She wanted to purr like a cat. Her back stretched. Her shoulders loosened. Dazed, she stared down at his broad naked shoulders, the curve of his back, the movement of muscle beneath. He was lovely.

She yearned to touch him. If only she dared.

Gently he lowered her hem, and rose to his full height, smiling down at her. Clearly waiting for sign from her as to where they would go next.

When she said nothing, he gave a slight nod. 'I think it is time I bid you goodnight.' He put on his ring, tucked the rest of his jewellery in his coat pocket and slung his discarded clothing over his shoulder.

He looked just like a pirate carrying off his booty.

She half-wished the booty included her.

Her heart knocked against her ribs. Her body trembled with the urge to join him in his chamber. To enjoy his beautiful body and the pleasure he would give.

It had been a long time since she'd known the pleasure of a man. But she never expected to be attracted to a man like him, a nobleman who no doubt would mock her in his clubs and to his friends. Blast it. Pricked by her pride, she'd let him push her too far and been tempted by his beautiful body. What a fool.

Thank goodness he'd be gone in the morning and leave her in peace.

'I'll collect the rest of my winnings tomorrow,' he murmured.

Her heart lurched.

Money. He meant the money. 'It will be waiting for you,' she said with a calm she did not feel.

She acknowledged his sweeping bow with an inclination of her head.

He closed the door softly behind him. She sat still, imagining him climbing the stairs. Would he walk slowly? Lingering, hoping she might follow? Or would he run, glad of his escape? Or had it all been one great joke?

Did he know she was his for the taking had he persisted? Did he know she'd lie awake all night, reliving his touch on her flesh?

Shame sent more heat to her face. Her stomach fell away. Would she never learn? She inhaled a deep breath, pushed to her feet and looked up at Grandfather's portrait beside the hearth. A gentler one than that in the other room. 'I certainly made a pig's ear of that, didn't I?' No doubt more scandal would attach to her name when he gossiped to his friends.

Thank God, he would be gone in the morning.

Chapter Four

Voices. Female voices. As consciousness returned, Charlie lay still, eyes closed, his cold naked body rigid. One movement would be his downfall. A laugh chilled his soul.

'Do you think he tupped the missus?'

'Why else would she bring him home?'

Odd. Charlie cracked an eyelid. Peered at the two women at the end of a monstrous four-poster bed and remembered. He was in Yorkshire, not a war-torn field in Europe. He let go of his breath, relaxing his body.

The women were dressed modestly, like chambermaids, one a chubby young blonde with an inquisitive expression, the other a sallow-faced brunette past the first blush of youth. Their eyes perused his body as boldly as a farmer sizing up a bull at the market.

Flipping the sheet over his groin, Charlie sat up and smiled. 'Good morning, ladies.'

The blonde one squeaked. The other put her hands on her hips. 'Sorry, your lordship. We didn't mean to wake you. Your fire is made up and we stopped to admire the view.'

'You should draw t'curtain,' the younger one said defensively, 'if you don't want us looking.'

He choked back a laugh. Miss Draycott had the most unusual of staff. But then there was nothing about Merry Draycott that was usual.

The dark one lowered her lashes a fraction and her gaze to the sheet, which hid little of the evidence of his morning arousal. 'I could help you out with that for a shilling.'

'I wouldn't charge you at all,' the blonde said, licking her lips and smiling. 'I'd bounce on that any day of t'week.'

Good God, what sort of house was this? Charlie tried to keep his jaw off his chest. 'Thank you, but no.'

The hopeful smile faded. 'You won't say nowt to missus, will you? About us waking you. We are supposed to be quiet.'

With a sense of unreality, Charlie shook his head. 'Thank you for the fire.'

The older of the two narrowed her gaze. 'How come you left all the candles burning? Not scared of the dark, are you?'

Scared didn't come close to describing the insidious panic he felt in the hours before dawn. He grinned. 'I fell asleep reading.' He gestured to the book on the night table, placed there in case of such questions.

'Waste of good beeswax, that is,' she muttered and flounced out of the room.

The other girl followed, lugging the coal bucket and a dustpan and brush.

Charlie collapsed against the pillows and let out a laugh. There was no mistaking the sort of fires those women preferred to light and it had nothing to do with hearths and coals.

He should have guessed from the style of Merry's dress and her lapses of speech that the damned woman was a brothel keeper.

An abbess. And one with enemies? Overnight he'd been thinking about that broken axle.

Another look at her carriage was required, but this latest piece of information added to his suspicions about her supposed accident. It wasn't one.

He glanced around the room. The candles augmented by light

from the window illuminated a carved and tapestry-hung nightmare of a room in every shade of green. It looked worse than it had the previous evening.

He threw back the covers and slipped from the bed. He strode to the window. He'd left the curtains open, too, as well as the bed curtains. Unending white accounted for the unnatural light. He frowned at the sky. While the clouds seemed less lowering, he doubted the roads would be passable.

And he was stuck in a house of ill repute. A joke Robert would have loved. Charlie didn't find it in the least bit humorous. She should have told him last night instead of her pretending to be respectable—well, almost respectable.

A vision of Merry's lovely slender leg in his hand popped into his brain. The arousal that had tormented him the previous evening, and upon awakening, started anew. He cursed. He'd behaved like a perfect gentleman with a woman who kept a bawdy house. What a quixotic fool she must have thought him.

He turned away from the window at the sound of the chamber door opening. Brian with boots in hand. The lad bowed deeply. 'Good morning, my lord. Mr Gribble said to tell you the snow on the moors is really deep.'

'I guessed as much. You don't need to stay. I can manage.'

The lad looked so crestfallen at the dismissal, Charlie relented. 'Brush my claret-coloured coat and then iron my cravat, if you wouldn't mind.'

The lad touched his forelock. 'Reet gladly, my lord.'

In less than an hour, Charlie was hunching his shoulders against a wind stronger than the previous evening and holding fast to his hat brim. The drifting snow came close to the top of his boots as he slogged down a hill to the stables. Set around three sides of a square courtyard, the building offered welcome shelter from the gale. He entered through the first door he came to and almost bumped into a fellow coming out. Not a groom. Of course not. It was Miss Draycott in a man's low-crowned hat and her mannish driving coat.

Charlie raised his hat and smiled. 'Good morning. I didn't expect to see you up and about at this early hour.'

After the startled look faded from her expression, she frowned. Not pleased to see him. 'I didn't think London dandies rose from their bed before noon.'

'Mr Brummell has given us all a very bad reputation,' Charlie said mournfully. He knocked the snow off his boots against the door frame. 'I came to see how the horses were doing.' No sense in alarming her, when he had nothing but vague suspicions.

'Don't you trust my servants to take proper care of your animals, my lord?'

My, her temper was ill today. 'If I didn't trust your servants, Miss Draycott, I would have come out here last night.'

She acknowledged the hit with a slight nod.

'I also wondered about your team. How is that foreleg?'

Her shoulders slumped. 'Not good. Jed poulticed it, but it is badly swollen.'

'Do you mind if I look?'

'Not at all.' She sounded quite doubtful. Probably thought he wouldn't know one end of the beast from the other. Nor would he indicate otherwise. The fact that he liked working with horses was no one's business but his own.

They walked along the stable block. A single row of stalls built along each back wall, nice drainage, fresh straw and a surprising number of mounts, both riding and draught. He nodded his approval.

The carriage horses were in the middle block. The wrinkled wizened man who'd met them with the lantern the previous evening stood leaning on a broom, watching the injured horse eat.

'Jed, this is Lord Tonbridge,' Merry said.

He knuckled his forehead. 'Aah. Yours are reet fine animals, yer lordship. Two stalls down they are.'

'Thank you. Miss Draycott is concerned about this one. May I see?'

The old fellow ran a knowing eye down his person. 'Well, if you don't mind mucking in the midden, you're reet welcome.'

Charlie inched in beside the horse and sank down on his haunches. The groom had packed a mixture of warm mash and liniment around the injured foreleg. 'How bad do you think it is?'

'No more'n a strain, I reckon.'

'He got hooked up in the traces,' Miss Draycott said. 'I hope he didn't do any permanent damage.'

So, she'd followed him back. That was going to make his questioning of the head groom difficult.

'Have you tried packing it with snow?' Charlie asked.

Jed scratched at the grey stubble on his chin. 'Never heard of that for a strain.'

Charlie grinned. 'Nor I. My groom discovered it takes the swelling down faster than warm mash, if you want to try it. Little else to be done apart from plenty of rest.'

'It wouldn't hurt to try, would it, Jed?' Merry said quietly. 'I feel so badly. Not once in my life have I ever injured one of my horses.'

She sounded dreadfully guilty. Charlie wanted to put an arm around her shoulders and offer her comfort, then press her up against the stable wall and offer a bit more than that, she looked so starkly beautiful with her hair tucked up under her ridiculous hat.

''T'was my fault,' Jed said. 'I should have seen somat were up wi'carriage. I should never have let you drive alone.'

'No, you should not,' Charlie said. 'The carriage could have turned over. The horse's legs might have been broken rather than strained. Not to mention Miss Draycott's safety.'

The groom's wrinkled face looked grim. 'Aye.'

'It was not Jed's fault,' Miss Draycott said. 'And it is beside the point. That poor creature is in pain.'

'Nowt to worry your head about, missy.'

'I'll check again later,' she said, rubbing her upper arms.

He hadn't thought her so sentimental a woman. Yet on their drive she had kept turning back to look at the injured beast. Perhaps, beneath her hard brittle shell, she'd a soft centre. Hopefully, the head groom wouldn't let her rampage around the countryside alone in future. He'd have a word with him in private. Later. When Merry left.

'You'd be better off staying warm by the fire,' the groom said.

'I'll take a look at my cattle while I'm here, Jed.'

'Sixteen mile an hour tits, I'm thinkin', my lord,' Jed said.

'On a smooth road downhill.' Charlie patted the injured horse's rump and exited the stall. He exited further along the stable block.

'I was going too fast,' Merry said, following him. 'I was angry and hurrying because of the weather. I must have hit a rut.'

He'd seen no signs of a rut large enough to damage an axle. 'Fretting won't change it.'

Her chin quivered. 'No. It won't. But that horse is in pain. I can see it in his eyes.'

Charlie didn't quite know what to say, so said nothing. He strode along the block until he found his team. They huffed a greeting. He spent a moment or two going over their hooves and their limbs. Someone had brushed them and their brown coats shone.

'You have a good man in Jed,' he said.

'He worked for my grandfather.' She spoke as if the words answered all.

They walked side by side along the alley in front of the stalls.

'It seems you are to be burdened by my company for a while longer,' he said.

'It is no burden,' she said absently as if she had something else on her mind. 'It won't be the first time we are snowed in for a few days.'

'Thank you for your hospitality.'

His voice must have sounded just a little dry, because her head turned, her eyes meeting his gaze.

She gave a rueful smile. 'Did I sound dreadfully rude? I apologise. I meant to say that it will be an honour to have you stay as long as you wish.'

Somehow he preferred the earlier offhand invitation to this lavish courtesy, because the first was pure Merry and the second *pro forma*.

'You must allow me to perform some service for you while I am here,' he said just a little mischievously, thinking to test the waters.

Her eyes widened just a fraction as she considered his words. 'What might you have in mind?'

He grinned, and the sparks were once more hovering in the air. Attraction and interest. Not the searing fire of the previous evening, but it wouldn't take much to set it ablaze.

'How about a sleigh ride?' He pointed to the equipage stored behind her phaeton.

'In this weather?' She glanced out into the courtyard.

'When it clears.'

'All right.'

He hesitated. 'Merry, I conversed with some unusual young women this morning. In my chamber.'

She frowned. And then gasped. 'Beth and Jane.'

'I didn't get their names. However, they seemed very…obliging.'

'They didn't…' She covered her mouth with her hand.

His lips wanted to smile. He held them in check. 'No. They didn't.' But they would have, and she knew it.

'Oh. Oh, dear. I must apologise. They are…housemaids in training. I should have told them to leave your room to Brian.'

Housemaids in training. A new twist on an old profession. She must have seen the disbelief in his face. 'I will speak to them,' she said stiffly. 'And if the weather breaks, we will go for a sleigh ride. In the meantime, I have some business affairs needing attention.'

He imagined she did—but which business?

'In the meantime,' she said breathlessly, 'please make free of the library where you will find books and a nice warm fire.'

They stood in the doorway, looking out at the world turned into a white desert, the house barely visible in a sudden flurry of snow. He inhaled. She was right, snow did have a scent all of its own. Why had he never noticed?

He took off his muffler and wrapped it around her neck and up over her mouth and nose. 'Then at least let me escort you safely back to the house.'

Over the top of the scarf laughter spilled from her blue eyes. She looked like some Far Eastern princess, saucily peeping out from behind a veil. Or she would, if not for the manly driving coat and the man's felt hat.

He grabbed her hand, tucked it beneath his arm and they began the trek up the hill. He liked the feel of her leaning on him for support. She wasn't a fragile flower of a woman, but there was absolutely no denying her femininity.

And today she was acting with the propriety of a duchess. He had the strong urge to unravel the puzzle he'd found. And part of that was learning who might want to cause her harm.

He barely noticed the icy fingers of wind tearing at his coat, or the snow cold and wet on his face, because for the first time in a long time he was doing exactly as he pleased.

Chapter Five

Merry hurried along the corridor. She knew why she was hurrying. It had nothing to do with talking to the women and everything to do with escape. From him.

Not because she was attracted to him, because that part she could handle. Indeed, it was rather pleasant being looked at with desire. But it was the other part that caused her unease. Every now and then, when he looked at her with those intense dark eyes, she had the feeling he could see her innermost thoughts, whereas he seemed to hold himself very much at a distance because he really didn't approve.

The sooner he was gone the better.

She pulled the key from her pocket and unlocked the door to what had once been the nursery. Voices from an open door let her know where she would find Caro and her charges. She entered the day room. Caro faced the two women sitting at desks along with Thomas, Caro's six-year-old son, writing his letters on a slate. The women each held a book. Beth was reading, slowly sounding out the words. She stopped the moment Merry entered.

Looking at the two women, one would never guess their original profession. Their faces shone with good health and cleanliness. They wore the modest practical clothing of the women who worked at the mills.

'Good morning, ladies,' Merry said smiling.

'Good morning, Miss Draycott,' they chorused.

'Good morning,' Caroline said. Her gaze held curiosity. Wondering about last night, no doubt.

'If I could have your attention,' Merry said, to the room at large. 'Because of the snow, we have a guest at Draycott House. I gather you ladies met him this morning. I think it would be best if you remained in this wing until his departure.'

Beth giggled.

Jane frowned. 'Ashamed of us, then, are you? Is that how it's to be?'

Heat stung Merry's cheeks. Jane was not the easiest woman to deal with, despite the fact that she'd sought out Caro's help on her own account. Jane had come north from London and was far more worldly than Beth, or the other girls they had rescued. And she'd appointed herself as their leader. The other girls had fled after the fire—Jane and Beth were all that were left of the soiled doves they'd been trying to help.

'I am not ashamed,' Merry said firmly. 'It is for your protection. I don't know this gentleman very well and I do not want any misunderstanding.'

Jane curled her lips. 'She wants to keep him all to herself, that's what it is.'

'Enough, Jane,' Caro said.

Jane sniffed. 'I don't care about no fancy man. What I wants to know is when do we get a proper job, instead of cleaning your grates?'

In other words, was her meeting successful? The townspeople had called the house in town Draycott's whorehouse and had thrown bricks and stones through the windows. Finally a torch had been thrown, starting a fire and forcing them to flee. The meeting yesterday had been supposed to bring the other mill owners over to her side.

The two women looked at her hopefully. 'It's bloody awful here,' Jane said. 'No shops. Nought to do 'cept readin'.'

'I like it,' Beth said stoutly. She'd grown up in the country. Most of the other girls they'd rescued were town girls, daughters of shopkeepers and millworkers who had taken a wrong turn and been cast out on to the streets to make their way as best they could. All had turned to the oldest profession known to women.

When Caro, who had narrowly missed turning to the same calling out of desperation, had proposed Merry use her money and her influence to help some of these women, Merry had readily agreed. She hadn't expected the resentment of the community. They seemed to believe the presence of these women would taint them and their families.

They'd driven the girls off.

She glanced over at Caro, who looked sad, but offered a supporting smile. 'I wasn't able to meet with them yesterday.'

Jane's mouth turned sullen. 'Too busy enjoying yerself with yer fancy man.'

'He is a gentleman,' Merry said. 'He provided me assistance on the road and he will be leaving as soon as the snow is passable.'

'Gentlemen are the best,' Beth said, as if repeating a lesson by rote. 'They's polite and don't have no pox.'

''Course they do,' Jane said.

Caroline rapped on her desk with her ruler. 'Ladies, please. This kind of talk is not helpful.' She glanced at Thomas, who had stopped writing and was listening with a furrow between his fair brows. 'Miss Draycott will find you work and a place to live as soon as she is able. In the meantime, you are being paid to learn to read and write.'

A groan from Beth made Merry smile.

None of the girls had found the concept of reading and writing particularly relevant. Only by offering them a wage had she been able to convince them to try when they'd moved into the house in Skepton. They'd been making great strides until forced to run for their lives. Caro insisted these two continue while they stayed with Merry. If nothing else, they would be able to read a newspaper and their employment contract before they signed it.

If they could find jobs.

'What about the grocer's in the High Street?' Beth asked. Her father had owned a shop, but when he found out she was pregnant, he'd turned her out. The boy had run away to sea and left her to fend for herself. If she couldn't support herself respectably, she would never get her child back from the orphanage. 'He's got a sign in the winder for a shop assistant.'

No one in Skepton seemed willing to risk employing Draycott's whores, no matter how clean they were or how well behaved. The townspeople claimed they would be a bad influence on the men as well as the women.

Merry pressed her lips together. 'I told him of your experience, but he said he'd changed his mind.' She'd even threatened to stop purchasing from him, but then he told her his fear of the mob tearing his shop apart. What could she say?

Jane's lip curled. 'See. I told you it was all a farradiddle.'

'They think we'll steal them blind,' Beth said.

It was an outbreak of burglaries that had turned the townspeople violent, even after Caro told the constable she could account for all her girls at the time of the crimes.

'I'm leaving at the end of t'month,' Jane said. 'There's good money to be made in London. Abbesses always looking for new blood. Once the weather breaks, I can walk there in a fortnight.'

'How much does a girl make in Lunnon?' Beth asked.

'A fortune if you finds the right man,' Jane said. 'Dripping with jewels and furs, some of the girls are.'

Beth's eyes grew round.

'It is not quite like that,' Caro said. 'Very few girls meet that kind of man. And often they cast them off, the way they throw out old clothes.'

'What would you know about it?' Jane sneered.

Caroline coloured. 'I have eyes.'

Merry didn't care much for Jane. Gribble had found her slipping a silver teaspoon in her pocket. Caro had reminded her that she might have done the same, if she had been in Jane's situation.

Damn it. If Merry didn't do something soon, these two women would slip back into their old ways.

A feeling of inadequacy swamped her. Grandfather would have been able to deal with the mill owners and the shopkeepers. He wouldn't have been locked out of the meeting.

Because he was a man.

If only Prentice would stand up to them.

As a manager, Prentice had very little clout. He could speak on her behalf, but even though he was the manager of the largest mill in Yorkshire, he wasn't the owner.

The only way she would ever have a voice in those meetings was if she was married. And then that voice would go to her husband.

Which brought her right back to the mad idea she'd had this morning—and rejected before it was fully formed. How she could have let such an idea creep into her mind, she didn't know.

'I'll find a way to bring them around,' she said. 'Don't worry.' But how?

Merry squeezed her eyes shut, then looked at the document, forcing herself to read the figures again. The mill was in trouble.

How had it happened so quickly?

The door opened and Caro glided in as if she walked on air. Even on a good day, Merry galumphed around, as Grandfather always said.

But then Caro was as small and delicate as Merry was tall and big boned.

She smiled at her friend. 'Lessons over?'

'Yes. I've left them with some needlework. There are sheets in need of turning.'

'They really don't have to work for their board, you know.'

'I know.' Caro clasped her hands together. 'But it does them good to keep occupied as well as giving them a feeling of worth. They are not bad women. Only misguided.'

'Of course.'

'Although I'm a bit worried about Jane. I think she'd sell her grandmother for a shilling.'

'Probably less.'

They laughed.

'How soon can we rebuild the house?' Caroline asked. 'Is it possible?'

'Not until the snow clears, I'm afraid.'

'I suppose Mr Prentice did his best?' Caro sounded doubtful.

'I'm sure he did. Although he doesn't feel as strongly about finding the girls work as we do, he has always followed my instructions.'

'As far as you know.'

'Your biases are showing.'

'He's too nice. Too friendly.'

Merry sighed. 'He's young. He tries too hard and I wish Grandfather's old manager had stayed on. He was crusty, but he knew everything there was to know about wool. He would have known how to handle the other mill owners.'

'Did he retire?'

All the old anger returned in a hot rush. Her hands curled into fists. 'He didn't want to work for a woman. Said if I got married he'd be happy to come back.' She'd been terribly hurt.

'Oh, Merry. That is ridiculous.'

'I know.' She sighed. 'Sometimes I wonder if I'm making a mistake.'

'Why should you give up something you've worked so hard at all these years?'

'Grandfather always used to say I was just as good as a son. But honestly…'

Caroline winced. 'You are as good. Clearly you are.'

It wasn't the first time they'd discussed the appropriate roles for men and women, and in the past they'd been in accord. Merry glanced down at the figures in her book. Was she wrong after all?

'We will find a way,' Caro said. 'I didn't have a chance to ask you how your game of billiards went. You were in high form last night.'

Merry felt heat creep up the back of her neck. 'He won.'

'Then I suppose you will be wanting a rematch this evening?'

Hardly. 'Perhaps you'd care to join us for a game of cards.'

'You need four for cards,' Caro said.

'We could ask Jane.'

Caroline giggled. 'Poor Tonbridge. He wouldn't know what hit him.'

Jane had fleeced the other girls of their pin money the first night she arrived at the house in town. Merry had the feeling she would not succeed with his lordship, but was not going to put her theory to the test.

'Perhaps I'll ask him to play chess.' And there would be no removal of garments either. Her insides fluttered pleasurably as the image of his naked chest popped into her mind. Perhaps she should go straight to bed.

She almost groaned at the unfortunate thoughts that idea conjured. It would be better if she'd never known the pleasures a man could bring to a woman.

'You will join us for dinner, though?' Merry asked. 'I can hardly entertain him alone.'

'Naturally. I will see you in the drawing room at six as usual.'

Caro glided silently out of the room and Merry turned back to her accounts. It was only to be expected that the mill wouldn't be as profitable as it had been under her grandfather. The army no longer needed the number of uniforms they'd required during the wars and the clothiers had cut back on the quantities of cloth they bought from the mill. If things didn't improve, soon, she'd have to cut back on the number of workers she employed. With the price of bread continually rising, even those fully employed were barely surviving.

Nothing but problems, no matter which way she turned.

She began adding the column of figures again. The door opened. With a sigh, she looked up.

Tonbridge. The aristocratic lines of his face stark in the cold light from the window. Gorgeous. She blinked.

'Ready for our sleigh ride?' he asked. 'I have taken the liberty of requesting the horses put to.'

Oh, she had promised, hadn't she? She glanced out of the window. No help from the weather. It looked like a perfect afternoon.

'It would be good to get some fresh air,' he said, seeing her hesitation. 'I want to take a look at your phaeton. Make sure it isn't a hazard to other travellers.'

'Oh, no, really. You did enough yesterday.' The image of him heaving the carriage out of the way returned. One would never guess he hid such strength beneath the dark burgundy superfine of his coat. Why did she have to think about that now? 'Jed will see to it.'

His gaze drifted to the papers. He hesitated a fraction, then gave her a boyish grin. The kind of grin that no doubt made ladies of the *ton* swoon. And didn't do such a bad job on her either. 'All work and no play makes Jill a dull girl.'

Her heart gave a small thud of excitement. Her knees had the consistency of mashed turnip as the force of his charming smile hit her full on. Escaping from her account books sounded terribly tempting. Temptation seemed to personify this man.

'All right. Why not?' Decision made, she leaped to her feet. 'But the sleigh hasn't been used for years.'

A vague impression of the sharp bite of the wind on her cheeks and the feel of her parents' large, warm bodies on either side of her teased at her mind.

And laughter. So much laughter.

'It's been well maintained, like everything else in your stables,' he said.

'Jed wouldn't have it any other way. I know he is mortified by that axle.'

A shadow flickered over his face. 'It can happen to the best-maintained equipages, as he well knows, and so I will assure him if you wish. Would Mrs Falkner care to accompany us? The sleigh easily holds four.'

'I will ask her.'

She suddenly felt lighter, as if the problems looming over her these past few days had disappeared, or at least become less monstrous. 'It will be fun.'

Chapter Six

Cloaked in a fur-lined rug, with a hot brick at her feet and Tonbridge's large form beside her, Merry felt toasty and warm. She curled her fingers in her swansdown muff and breathed in the crisp clear air.

The snow glinted and sparkled like fairy dust. 'This was a good idea,' she said, glancing at Tonbridge.

Once he'd manoeuvred the horses between the gates, he smiled at her. 'It's a long time since I drove a sleigh.'

She'd been surprised when Tonbridge insisted on driving them, and then decided it was just as well that his hands were kept busy with the reins, since the seats were not very wide and the thought of his hands on her body was keeping her far too warm. Just feeling him alongside her sent delicious tingles over her skin.

Not surprisingly, Caro had refused to accompany them on their jaunt and Merry had blithely said a groom would go with them. So much for decorum.

The day was too lovely for such thoughts. She wanted to absorb the warmth of the sun in through her skin. Feast on the brilliance of a cerulean sky and rolling hills of pristine white. The vastness shrank her problems to nothing. She leaned back with the muffled thud of the horses' hooves and the jingle of the bridles filling her ears.

'The Yorkshire countryside is magnificent,' he murmured.

'Most days I'm too busy to notice,' she admitted. Too wrapped up in business matters.

He tipped his head back to look up into the sky, his eyes creasing at the corners as he squinted at the light. 'An eagle,' he said. 'See it?'

She looked up and saw the bird, wings outstretched to catch the wind, wheeling high above them. 'It will be lucky to find any prey with so much snow on the ground.'

'Oh, he'll find a vole or a mouse or two. Did you know one of my ancestors was responsible for the King's mews? Back in Tudor times?'

'Mine probably cleaned up the droppings.'

They laughed and the horses' ears twitched.

The tension flowed from Merry's shoulders. He'd made her feel comfortable. She didn't feel the need to hide the smile curving her lips or to say something blunt to keep him at a distance. She could be herself. She let go a sigh. 'I wish every day was like this.'

'Me, too.'

He turned at the crossroads, entering the main road. No tracks marred the snow. No vehicles had passed this way since the previous evening. The wrecked phaeton soon came into view. Snow had drifted around it, but the shafts sticking straight up reminded her of a sunken wreck.

It looked sad and lonely. 'I hope it can be repaired,' Merry said.

He frowned. 'You know, you really shouldn't be driving around the countryside without a groom. Footpads are not unheard of in this part of the country. And there are rumours of Luddites again.'

'I know everyone in the Riding.'

He shot her a look from beneath his brows that said he thought she was a stubborn foolish woman. She glared back.

He drew the horses to a halt and handed her the reins. 'I'll just be a moment.'

'You surely aren't thinking of pulling it out of the ditch?'

'No. I want to look at the axle.' His frown deepened.

'Leave it to Jed.'

He didn't reply, just climbed down and trudged through the snow. Stubborn man.

It was ridiculous. The snow had drifted well up the wheels. There was nothing to see. And what was the point of him getting soaked and cold? He was spoiling the afternoon.

She had a good mind to drive off and leave him there.

He headed back, stepping in the tracks he'd left. He went around to the back of the sleigh and grabbed a shovel.

'Leave it be.'

He ignored her. Blast the man. Merry wound the reins around a strut and jumped down. She followed in his footsteps, the snow clumping on the skirts of her coat, making it hard to walk. By the time she reached his side, she was sodden. He had one of the wheels cleared of snow.

'This is foolishness,' she said.

'Is it?' He crouched down. 'It is just as I thought.' He looked up at her, his face solemn. 'This was no accident.'

She put her hands on her hips. 'Do you suppose I drove off the road on purpose?'

'No. Look at that axle. It's been sawn halfway through from below. The rest of it snapped, but it wasn't an accident.'

Her stomach fell away. 'Why?'

He rose to his feet. 'Yes, Merry, why? Who would want to cause you serious harm? You could have been thrown from the carriage and killed, or died in the snowstorm.'

Her heart stopped. Bile rose in her throat as she stared into the concern on his face. The world seemed to spin around her head as she tried to breathe.

Slowly her heartbeat picked up again. She managed to take a breath. 'I can't think of anyone...' Her voice tailed off as she remembered the mill owners' faces at the guild hall. Angry red faces. And one very worried-looking Mr Prentice. 'Oh, dear.'

Was it possible one of them hated her so much he wanted her dead? Or all of them? Men she'd known all her life? The backs of her eyes burned. Her chest hurt. She wanted to bury her face against Tonbridge's shoulder and weep like a child.

'Who, Merry?' he demanded, his voice almost a growl. 'Who wants to hurt you?'

She turned her face from his irate gaze. 'You are mistaken,' she said dully. 'It must be an accident.'

'The evidence is clear and it seems to me you *know* who did this.'

The urge to unburden herself ached in her throat. She bit her lip against its allure and felt the chill of the air on her teeth. 'There are several people who don't like me very much at the moment.'

'People?'

He wasn't going to let it rest. 'Other mill owners. Town councillors. But, honestly, I don't think any of them would have done such a dastardly thing. They are all respectable men. Pillars of Skepton.'

'Is anyone else angry at you?'

Her teeth started to chatter. Cold. Shock. Damn it, fear, too. 'Certainly not. Next you will be telling me this is my fault.' She spun away from him. 'This is none of your concern, my lord,' she called back as she stomped away. 'Let us return home before we freeze to death.'

'Merry, wait.'

She kept walking. She couldn't stop, because if she did, she might fall down, her knees felt so weak. Because if she stopped, she might truly believe someone had deliberately tried to end her life.

He caught her by the arm and pulled her around to face him. 'Oh, hell,' he said. 'I'm sorry.' He wiped her cheek with his gloved thumb. 'I didn't mean to scare you.'

Her breath stuck in her throat at the gentle concern in his face and the softness in his dark brown eyes. 'Of course you didn't scare me. The wind brought tears to my eyes.'

He chuckled, a soft low warm sound that comforted rather than mocked. He pulled his hand from his glove and placed his palm against her cheek. Warmth infused her skin, not just where he touched her, but all over, as if he had the power to heat the blood in her veins from her head to her feet.

'You are cold,' he said. 'You should have stayed in the sleigh.'

Her teeth chattered and her body shook. 'No, I shouldn't.'

He swept her up in his arms as if she were nothing but a half-bolt of cloth. 'My dear Merry, allow me to help you back to the carriage.'

'Put me down.' But the words were half-hearted and mumbled against his coat. Somehow her arms had gone around his neck and he was walking. Beneath his hat, his dark hair curled against his temple. His ear was very nicely formed, she decided, not too large, nor did it stick out from his head. In profile against the bright blue sky, his nose was a little crooked. A very small imperfection, scarcely noticeable unless you looked closely. Somehow it made him seem less of a god and more human.

Her heart tumbled over.

Oh Lord, she really did like him. She loved the feel of being in his arms, of being held close to his chest, like something precious. She felt feminine. Cared for. Protected.

He glanced down with a smile. 'Ready?'

Dash it, they were back at the sleigh already. He lifted her up on to the seat and walked around to the other side and climbed up. He arranged the rug over her knees and tucked it up under her chin. 'Is there any warmth left in that brick?'

'A little,' she said. She had no idea, her toes were too cold.

'But not enough, I am sure.' He put his hand under her chin, turned her face towards him. 'Tell me, Merry.'

The strength of command in his voice shivered all the way down to her toes. The intensity in his dark brown gaze trapped her.

'Who would want to do you harm?'

His hands cupped both sides of her face. She looked at the firm set of his mouth, anything not to have to gaze into his searching eyes.

'You do know,' he said. 'You foolish female.' He lifted her face, then those wonderful lips descended on hers, gentle, comforting. 'Tell me, Merry,' he whispered against her mouth. 'Let me help you.'

Then his mouth firmed, it wooed and tormented until she could no longer think of anything but the delicious sensations ravaging her body. Her insides quivered with the joy of it, her heart thundered and she angled her head for better access to those wonderful lips. She pulled her hands from her muff and put them on those powerful shoulders.

His tongue traced the seam of her mouth, not demanding, sweetly requesting. Resistance had no place in her mind; the joy filling her took up every inch of space. Trembling deep inside she granted him entry and he swept her up on a tide of passion.

She clung to him, and let her senses drift where they would. Delightful waves of desire washed over her, thrilling and beautiful.

Slowly he drew back, his brown eyes smoky beneath half-lowered lids, his breathing as ragged as her own. 'Tell me.'

The man had no mercy. And she had no will. Never had she felt so weak. So vulnerable. Not since the day her parents died and she'd learned love was a fleeting thing. She shivered.

'Damn,' he said under his breath. 'You are still cold. I need to get you back to the house.' He paused, his dark gaze hardening. 'But I will have the truth of this.'

She briefly closed her eyes against the pull of the insidious weakness. Brushed his demand away with a half-laugh. 'You make mountains from molehills, my lord.' She sounded breathless. And, God help her, afraid. The moment he released her, the bone-chilling fear had returned. Someone had tried to do her harm. A warning, or had they actually intended her death?

It didn't bear thinking of.

He picked up the reins. 'Call me Charlie. Make no mistake, Merry, I will not let this rest. You will let me help you.'

The heir to a dukedom was used to getting his own way. And he wanted to shoulder her burdens. It felt good. For once having a man want to protect her felt freeing rather than constraining.

'Very well,' she said, the words spoken before she really had time to think. 'There is one thing you could do for me.'

Engaged in the process of turning the horses in the road, his head whipped around, a question on his face.

'Marry me,' she said.

Chapter Seven

Years of dodging matchmaking mamas sent Charlie's hackles rising. He hadn't expected such a trick from a woman who seemed so straightforward in all her dealings. Inwardly, he cursed. He had held her to comfort her obvious distress. And let their mutual attraction flame out of control. Idiot.

She must have guessed at his thoughts because the smile on her lovely lips died.

Outwardly, he smiled calmly, as he had on so many other occasions when a female tried to net the heir of a dukedom. 'You flatter me.'

She rearranged her expression into one of polite dismissal and shrugged. 'I didn't mean it the way it sounded.'

He urged the horses on with a click of his tongue. 'Then what did you mean?' He shouldn't ask. He should let it go. This ground was as dangerous as the quicksand in the Wash, but knowing her life was in danger, he could not walk away. Not until he knew she was safe. Once he knew who was behind this cowardly attack, he would bring all the power of a dukedom to bear on the blackguard.

The vehemence of his reaction took him by surprise.

'I meant we could pretend an engagement,' she said carelessly, but there was an undercurrent of something in her voice he didn't quite understand.

Oh, Father would really like that. And Robert, poor Robert, would continue to be left out in the cold. 'How would that help?'

'I think some of the other mill owners are angry at me,' she said quietly. 'They are opposed to my idea of providing an asylum for women who have led less than respectable lives.'

'You mean the ladybirds I met this morning,' he said, smiling at the memory.

'Yes. They need a place from which they can find suitable work.' She winced. 'Perhaps meet husbands. I asked the local mill owners to give them employment.'

'And because they are not in favour of the idea, they decided to damage your carriage?' He couldn't quite keep the incredulity out of his voice.

'Caro and I opened a house in Skepton. They called it a bawdy house. Men came one night and attacked the girls and set fire to the house.'

'Which is why they are living with you.'

'Only two of them. The rest disappeared. We need to find them. Give them a home.'

'I still don't see how a pretend engagement resolves the problem.'

She turned in her seat, a furrow in her brow, her eyes focused somewhere in the distance, as if she could see the future playing out before her.

He wanted to kiss her.

God, he ached for far more than that. If he hadn't broken free of her a few minutes ago, he might have laid the blankets down in the snow and made love to her right there in the open. And he would have been forced to accept her proposal of marriage.

Such an error of judgement would be the final straw for the duke. The disgrace at Waterloo and then Robert's scandal had been bad enough, but for his heir to marry beneath him might well kill the old man. His father had looked ill for weeks after Robert's scandal broke. Another such event would likely cause him an apoplexy, not to mention it would certainly end all possibility of Robert's return to the family fold.

'Because I am a woman, the other mill owners will not admit me to their meetings at the guild hall,' she said stiffly, as if the admission stirred more anger than she wanted to admit. 'They would listen to you, if they thought you were my future husband.'

The slight bitter edge to her words gave him pause. How would it feel to be successful, as she so clearly was, and yet ignored by one's peers?

'If you pretended to be my fiancé for a few days,' she continued. 'If you put your name behind my plan, they would be forced to give in. Then you would cry off.'

'A business arrangement,' he said. Irrationally he felt a sense of disgruntlement. An odd reaction, when he'd been ready to flee at the word *marriage*. He shook his head to clear it of such stupid thoughts.

It had taken weeks of argument to convince the duke to accept Charlie's promise to make a suitable marriage in exchange for Robert's forgiveness. To go back on his word would be cruel to his mother as well as dishonourable. He had to be practical.

Guilt weighed him down. No matter how much he wanted to help Merry, this was not the way.

Not because he couldn't see himself married to Merry, he acknowledged with surprise, but because of what it would mean for his family if he broke his agreement with the duke.

She nibbled her bottom lip and then let go a long breath with a shake of her head. 'It would never work anyway.'

'Why not?'

'No one would believe a man of your station would stoop to wed me. Not unless you were in desperate financial straits.'

He raised a brow, considering her words.

'Well, they wouldn't,' she said. 'Look at the way *you* reacted.'

He felt insulted by her quick dismissal. But she was right. He'd instantly hunkered down behind his defensive walls. Yet he could not leave any woman defenceless, especially not this one, not now when his suspicions of foul play were confirmed.

He turned the sleigh in through the gates of Draycott House—the carved words on the pillar announced the name. Beneath the name was a coat of arms. A kingly red deer surrounded by ivy. It looked vaguely familiar.

'I will speak to these mill owners on your behalf.'

She gave a small shake of her head, a wry smile twisting her lips. 'As my friend, or even as the son of a duke, you would have no real influence. They will meet you individually, agree with everything you say, but behind closed doors, they will do as they please.'

How she must hate the exclusion. 'Then I will speak to the constable. And the magistrate.'

'You are most kind.'

She couldn't have sounded more unconvinced. He wanted to throttle her pretty little neck. Or kiss her pursed lips. Neither one of which would help matters.

'Don't underestimate the force of the Mountford name.'

'Oh, I won't.'

The dryness in her voice grated. He had the feeling she felt let down, but she really didn't know the power he wielded as heir to a dukedom.

'Oh, my word!' she exclaimed, sounding shocked and amused.

Charlie followed the direction of her gaze. In front of the house, on an expanse of snow-covered lawn interrupted only by the odd ancient elm and cypress, several figures darted about with cloaks flying. Snowballs flew through the air. The sound of laughter and shrieks of joy pierced the quiet. There was a smaller figure, too. A child?

'Your ladies are out on a spree,' he said.

'I suppose Caro decided they needed some exercise in the fresh air.'

'They look like any other young women when faced with sunshine and an unexpected fall of snow.'

'I know,' she said. 'Hard to imagine how awful their lives must have been before.'

For a moment, Charlie tried to imagine what it must be like, selling your body to live. Hell, wasn't that what his father wanted him to do when he married Lady Allison in order to expand the Mountford influence? The thought left a sour taste in his mouth.

One of the women collapsed in a heap of giggles on a snow bank. Another dropped a snowball on her face. Mrs Falkner—Charlie could make her out quite clearly now dressed in dark grey—called to the small boy.

All the women were laughing and giggling. He guessed there were few times in their lives when they'd been as happy as they appeared this afternoon. Something about it felt right and good. One of them picked up the boy and whirled him around.

'Do you think they would like a sleigh ride? Around the lawn?'

Merry's face broke into a smile. 'They would love it. And it would be a terrible shame to waste all the work of harnessing the team.'

Her obvious pleasure put warmth back in a day that had grown cool after their kiss. He walked the horses across towards the small group. One girl came running when she saw the horses approach. The thin sallow-faced one hung back.

He doffed his hat and bowed. 'Ladies.'

The round-faced one giggled as she had this morning. She covered her mouth with her hand when she saw him looking at her.

He grinned.

Merry threw off the blanket and jumped down. No waiting for help for Miss Draycott; it didn't surprise him in the least.

'Clydesdales,' the giggly girl said, stroking the off-side horse's nose. 'They are beauties.'

The horse nuzzled at her hip. 'I don't have anything for you,' she said with obvious dismay.

'I do,' Merry said and pulled a lump of sugar from her pocket.

The girl's face lit up, making her look terribly young. No more than eighteen, Charlie was sure. Too fresh-faced for the kind of life she'd fallen into. The freshness would fade all too quickly in her line of work.

The other woman stayed well clear, obviously unused to such large animals.

'Lord Tonbridge offered to take the girls for a drive,' Merry said to Mrs Falkner.

Mrs Falkner eyed him a little askance.

'I won't take them out of sight of the house,' Charlie hastened to assure her. 'A couple of spins around the lawn.'

The girl petting the horse turned a hopeful expression in Mrs Falkner's direction.

'Of course,' she said. 'Thank you, Lord Tonbridge.'

'Don't thank me, it is Miss Draycott's rig.'

'Let me introduce you to the girls,' Merry said. She pointed to the giggly one. 'Ladies, this is Lord Tonbridge. This is Beth and that is Jane.'

Jane lifted her chin as if daring him to say anything about their earlier meeting.

'What about the lad?' Charlie asked. 'Would he like to go, too?'

'That is Thomas,' Merry said. 'Mrs Falkner's son.'

Charlie touched his hat. The boy bowed with a grace many men would envy.

An anxious expression crossed Mrs Falkner's face.

'Please, Mama,' the boy said.

'Tonbridge is a very good driver,' Merry said. 'I can assure you, Tommy will be perfectly safe.'

The boy looked pleadingly at his mother.

'Very well,' Mrs Falkner said. 'Stay close to Beth, Thomas.'

Charlie jumped down to help the ladies aboard, handing Beth up first into the back seat. An eager Thomas waited his turn.

'You can sit next to me,' Charlie said and lifted the boy up into the front seat, ignoring Mrs Falkner's frown. The boy's happy smile clearly prevented her from remonstrating. He pretended to notice nothing amiss and held out a hand for Jane.

She shook her head with an ingratiating smile. 'Not me, thank you very kindly, my lord. I need a good walk after being shut up in t'house for days, if it's all right with you, missus?'

Mrs Falkner nodded. 'When you return, come to the day parlour. I will ask Gribble to send up hot chocolate. I doubt his lordship will be long.'

A warning to Charlie. The woman was a proper mother hen. He hid the urge to grin.

Jane nodded and trudged along the tracks left by the sleigh, heading for the gates. Mrs Falkner watched her go with a frown.

Merry released the horses' heads and stood back. Not that the team really needed holding—Charlie had never driven more placid obliging beasts.

He flicked his whip over their heads, jingled the bridles and they lumbered forward. He glanced down at the bright-eyed boy beside him. 'Would you like to hold the reins?'

The boy stared up at him. 'Will you teach me how to do that thing with the whip?'

'Get used to guiding these beasts first,' he said. He turned and looked over his shoulder. 'Everything all right, Beth?'

'Oh, yes,' she breathed, her eyes shining.

The sleigh glided off.

Merry stood beside Caroline and watched the sleigh draw away. 'How kind of him.'

'Very,' Caroline said. 'What is he after?'

'Not me, sadly.' Dash it. Was she speaking the truth?

'Merry!' Caroline sounded shocked.

'He offered to help me with the mill owners, that is all.'

Caro frowned. 'Won't that look rather odd?'

Merry stiffened. Another person who viewed her as beneath a marquis's touch. 'Do you think so?'

'Merry, can't you see? If a man like Tonbridge takes an interest in your affairs, might they not make assumptions about why? Why does he want to help?'

'Out of friendship. Gratitude.'

Even to Merry's ears it sounded rather weak. Nothing but the truth would do. 'He thinks someone tampered with the carriage.'

Caro pulled her gaze from the slowly diminishing sleigh, her wide eyes searching Merry's face. 'Oh, no. Surely not?'

'I think someone wanted to give me a warning, but Tonbridge is taking it more seriously.'

'This must stop.' Caroline clasped her gloved hands together. 'First a fire. And now this. We will set up the house somewhere else. I will not endanger your life.'

'Do you think it will be different elsewhere?'

'I won't have your death, or your injury, on my conscience.'

'It is not your decision.'

Fists clenched, Caroline spun away. 'I will have nothing to do with it.' It was the first time they had ever argued. Merry felt quite adrift, as if she'd lost her friend.

'Caro, we can't just give up.'

Caro turned around slowly. 'Why not?'

'A Draycott never admits defeat.'

'Never is a long time. Please, Merry. We will find another way. We certainly don't need to involve a man like Tonbridge in our affairs.'

Merry stared at her friend. Perhaps she was right, but it felt galling to give in to threats.

Caro turned to watch the sleigh in the distance. 'Oh, good Lord, is that Thomas standing up?'

'Yes,' Merry said, nodding. 'Charlie seems to like children, doesn't he?'

'Charlie?'

'We are friends.' Dash it, did she sound too defensive? 'I told him to call me Merry the first day we met.'

The suspicious gleam in Caro's eyes made her skin itch as if she'd done something wrong.

'Be careful, Merry,' Caroline said, shading her eyes with her hand. 'A man with his kind of charm and wealth is used to getting his own way, and it will be for no one's benefit but his own.'

Merry's stomach dipped. Few men did anything out of altruism. He would want something in return. Caro put an arm around her shoulder. It was an unusual display of affection. 'Tell him you don't need his help. Like all men, he'll want to take control. We don't need a man to solve our problems. We will deal with it.'

Caro was right. Of course she was. What on earth had she been thinking? She'd never needed anyone's help since Grandfather's death, despite her mother's family trying to insert themselves into her business. She would tell him not to bother with the councillors or the magistrate, that she was giving up her plan. She'd wait until he left before she tackled the problem.

She and Caro would manage.

All through the dinner Caro kept looking from Merry to Charlie, acting the chaperon. Looking for signs of misconduct on Tonbridge's part, no doubt. Merry sighed. With no opportunity to tell Lord Tonbridge her decision since returning from the drive, Merry kept her discourse so carefully light that her head ached.

'Shall we take tea in the drawing room?' she said brightly, after Gribble cleared the table of all but a decanter of port. 'You could bring your port there, Lord Tonbridge, unless you prefer drinking in solitary state. I am sorry we have no other gentlemen visiting to keep you amused.'

'You do yourself a disservice, Miss Draycott. Your conversation keeps me well entertained.'

'I am a chatterbox, in other words.' She almost poked out her tongue at him, but remembered not to just in time. 'Will you join us, too, my dear Mrs Falkner?'

Caroline looked torn. 'I really should see Thomas to bed. He likes me to read a story,' she explained to Lord Tonbridge, 'before I tuck him in for the night.'

'You are truly a devoted mother,' Tonbridge said. 'Don't worry about us. I will take Miss Draycott up on her offer of conversation in the drawing room.'

A look of relief crossed Caro's face. She turned her gaze on Merry, an intent gaze, reminding Merry of her promise. She rose and curtsied. 'Then I will bid you both goodnight.'

Tonbridge's eyes narrowed, but he said nothing as she left the room.

Merry popped to her feet. 'No time like the present,' she said, heading for the door.

She hoped they could have their discussion without the tingle of attraction, the incendiary sparks that filled the air.

She strode into the drawing room. The tea tray awaited them, just as she'd arranged with Gribble. She had no wish to end up playing billiards again.

She sat in front of the tray 'Tea for you, my lord, or will you stick to port?'

He looked down into his almost-empty glass. 'A cup of tea will do very well, Merry.'

He sat on the sofa opposite her. She poured the tea. 'Milk and sugar?'

'Yes, please,' he said. He crossed one ankle over the other.

He looked every inch the dandy tonight. The deep blue coat hugged his form. The high cravat was tied in a complex knot, its creases perfect. How Brian had managed it she didn't know. And his cream waistcoat embroidered with lily of the valley was a work of art.

She handed him a cup.

'So, have you thought further about my offer?' he asked. 'I feel strongly that the person or persons responsible for this crime should not go unpunished. Who leads these mill owners? I will speak to him.'

She smiled politely. 'By gum, I've been doing some thinking since last we talked.'

A frown furrowed his brow. 'Why do you speak like a common labourer when I try to offer a suggestion?'

'Common is what I am. Listen, Charlie, I've been talking things over with Mrs Falkner. We do not need your help.'

His expression darkened. 'Now you really surprise me.'

'Full of surprises,' she said lightly. 'There is no need for you to speak to anyone. We are giving up on the idea.'

A hard intent gaze searched her face. She tried to look calm, unaffected. 'I don't believe you,' he said finally. 'You are not one to give up, Merry.'

The way he made her name sound like a caress caused her breath to catch in her throat. But worse yet was his correct assessment of her nature. It wasn't like her to give up. She made a desperate bid to unscramble her thoughts. 'What I do is nowt of your business, my lord.'

His lips tightened. 'Because I won't engage in trickery.' He curled his lip. 'I am shocked, Merry. Draycott's is known for honest dealing, in word and deed. Would you compromise your good name?'

His accusation struck her on the raw. She held on to her rising temper, a hot fizz in her chest. 'It is precisely because I treasure my good name that I am refusing your offer.'

He blinked. 'I do not see the connection.'

'I am sure you do not.' And she wasn't going to tell him. 'Let us be quite clear on your position: while the Draycott name may be known for honest dealing, I certainly understand why it is not good enough to be linked with that of Mountford.'

'Blast it, Merry, I didn't mean that.'

But he did. She could see it in his eyes. Rich Merry Draycott. Low class and unacceptable, unless someone wanted her money. She folded her hands together in her lap and tried not to show the ache in her heart. 'You are leaving tomorrow. None of this is your concern.'

He got up and threw a log on the fire. The scent of burning apple-wood filled the room. 'So you are refusing my aid?'

'Yes.' She put up her hand, when he opened his mouth to speak. 'The matter is closed.'

He turned to face her, his eyes hard. 'You expect me to walk away when your life is in danger.'

'Do you think that words falling from your lips will change that? You faffing in my business will only make things worse. I will speak to the constable and the magistrate myself.'

She didn't see fit to add that the local magistrate was also a mill owner or that his wife had been among the most vociferous in her objections to the house in town.

He clearly wanted to distance himself from her and she'd offered him the perfect way out. She certainly had no reason to feel hurt by his rejection. He owed her nothing.

Nor did she need his approval. She didn't need anyone's approval.

'Let us not talk about this any more. It is a storm in a teacup. Would you like me to play for you?'

Without waiting for an answer she went to the pianoforte and lifted the lid. She arranged her skirts around her on the seat and began to play.

A look of frustration passed over his face.

Well, it would. He could scarcely interrupt her. It would be very rude indeed. The one benefit of attending a select academy for young women was that she knew all the rules of polite society. Grandfather had been so proud of her accomplishments. If he'd any idea how she had suffered in that place, it would have broken his heart.

As well as teaching her social niceties, to paint and play the pianoforte and the harp, her time there had taught her to survive all the meanness the world could toss her way. She'd also learned something about men.

Charlie wanted to strangle her as she played one piece after

another. The moment he began to applaud a piece, she started another. Her playing was excellent. Not a single note did she miss,
and she played without music. The pieces were all about lost love.
Positively heart-wrenching, if one had a heart to wrench.

An hour had passed and the punishment continued. Though what
he had done, he couldn't imagine. Unless it was his sensible alternative to her madcap plan.

Clearly the headstrong wench was too used to getting her own
way. And while he could see a kind of logic in her devious plan, it
put him in a hell of an awkward position, when he was on his way
to make overtures to Lady Allison.

Not to mention that the men she planned on duping, if they didn't
want her blood now, would once they realised her trick. If she refused to accept his offer of help, there was little he could do. He'd
have to accept her decision, much as it went against the grain.

He leaned back in his chair and let his mind drift. She looked
beautiful tonight and completely different from the previous evening. Her modestly cut gown only hinted at the lush figure beneath.
Her black hair, pulled back severely from her face, showed off her
high cheekbones, vivid blue eyes and unblemished milky skin. It
also revealed the faint blue lines at her temple and tracing down
her long elegant throat. If anything, she looked more alluring than
she had in her seductive attire. Unattainable and therefore utterly
desirable.

Beautiful. Cool and closed off. And brittle. The tension from
their earlier kisses vibrated in the air. Whatever was happening, he
feared if it went on any longer, she might shatter.

The closing notes of the piece she was playing brought him to
his feet. He clapped loudly at the same time as he strode to the
piano. He took her hand and kissed the back before she could start
again.

'That was lovely, Miss Draycott; however, I think it is time I
retired.'

She glanced at the clock. 'Eleven already? I had no idea. Still, I am sure that is not all that late for a man such as you.'

Ah, still angry then. He smiled wolfishly. 'And what sort of man would that be?'

Her lips parted. Her face flushed. 'A man who spends his time in London, I suppose.'

'Have you ever been to London?'

The blush deepened. 'I visited once. As a child.'

'Perhaps it is time you visited again. And when you do, let me know, and I will be delighted to show you the sights.' He took her hand again, held it in his and had the urge to bring her to her feet and kiss her again, recapture that moment of blissful mindlessness in the sleigh. The moment before she made her outrageous proposal, which now hung over them like a storm cloud. Kissing her would be a mistake. She would think his resolve was weakening.

He would not be twisted around any woman's finger.

He raised her hand to his lips one more time and dropped the tiniest of kisses on the back of it, felt the tremor in her fingers in response and his body clenched.

He released her hand. 'I bid you goodnight.' He bowed and strode for the door before he changed his mind.

Why did doing the right thing feel so completely wrong?

Merry paced her chamber; her nightdress swirled around her ankles each time she turned and the rug was rough beneath her bare feet. Two hours has passed and she still couldn't settle. She just wished she could clearly see a path.

Caro *was* right. She was. They must find a way to accomplish their goals and vanquish their opponents. She certainly didn't need the help of a husband. Not even a pretend one. A woman with a husband wasn't a person. She had no rights. No freedom of choice or of decision. Until Caro came, she had never thought of it that way. She'd always thought that one day she would have a husband and children. Men married for money and power. A man would absorb her money, wield her power, without consultation. Grandfather had trusted her enough to leave her his hard-earned business; she would never hand it over in exchange for a ring. Or companionship in bed.

She kicked her gown out of the way and turned. Tonbridge had no place in her life.

The thought left her with a deep sense of loss. Because her body was yearning for the pleasure it knew could be hers? Was that the reason she felt restless? On edge. She kept remembering his beauty as he left the drawing room. Virile, powerful and unbelievably handsome.

And that was the problem. She glared at her empty rumpled bed. The flare of heat in his gaze and the intensity of his kiss this afternoon had called to long-repressed desires and longings.

It had been years since she felt the warmth of a man. And this one knew how to seduce a woman's senses. When his mouth had plied her lips, her body had been overjoyed.

She missed it.

She clenched her fists until they stung from lack of blood and lifted her gaze to the portrait above the mantel. Her mother. Daughter of an earl, beloved wife of her father—what would she think of the wicked thoughts going through her daughter's mind, the hot fires of lust burning in her loins?

They burned within him, too.

Merry turned away from the gentle face looking down. No doubt her mother would be ashamed of her along with the rest of the fashionable world.

Tonbridge lay nearby alone in his bed and she would lie alone in hers. This was her future. She and Caro would live together, helping each other while she remained a spinster in name, if not in truth, forever.

Why not take advantage of the chance that brought him into her house? a voice whispered in her mind. *Why not?* A night of pleasure they would both enjoy. It would only be one night. No ties. No obligations. No tit for tat.

She'd kept him at a distance this evening, despite the way her body hummed each time he came close. Was still humming with the after-effects of his kiss this afternoon. Oh Lord, and the pleasure of his touch last night.

In spite of her coldness toward him tonight, there was no doubt of his desire when he kissed her hand. She rubbed the back of her hand as if she could erase the feel of his lips against her skin.

Lust.

Unrequited passion.

What if he rejected her? But if she didn't ask, how would she know?

Chapter Eight

Tired! Hah! Charlie hadn't felt less tired in his life.

Used to awakening in the smallest hours of the night, he always kept the candles alight to ward off the hated sensation of suffocation brought on by total darkness.

At home, when it got really bad, he'd go for a ride. His servants were used to his odd ways. But here, there would be questions he wasn't prepared to answer.

He rarely had trouble falling asleep. Only when the dreams started did he feel the need for escape. Tonight was different. He tossed off the brandy he had poured. It added to the heat in his blood, increased the thud of his heart.

Desire for Merry.

An urgent pressing lust.

Never had he felt like this about a woman. Naked, with the fire almost dead, he didn't feel the least bit cold. The vaguest thought of the woman had his blood running hot, had him rousing.

She'd certainly taken him by surprise this afternoon, asking him to pretend to be her betrothed. God, he'd like to pretend to be her husband.

His shaft jerked with pleasure at the thought. He could bring himself to release. A youth's trick, something he'd given up long ago in favour of control. If a man couldn't control his own base urges, what hope did he have of controlling his life? Or his bloody dreams?

He got up and strode to the window, thrusting back heavy brocade curtains glinting with gold bullion knots and twists. The cold permeating through the casement seared his overheated skin. He breathed in the smell of old wood and frost on the windowpane.

He placed his palm on the glass and thawed the ice.

The world outside looked ghostly. Snow glittered where the moon cast its path. Here and there, dark patches ruined the purity. A thaw well under way. Tomorrow he would leave.

Drive away from temptation.

Slowly, painfully slowly, his erection subsided, chilled by the cold air, or the thought of departure.

It didn't matter which.

Sure he would now sleep, he let the curtain fall and returned to the bed. The candles had hours of life left. They would last until dawn.

Stretched out on top of the covers, he closed his eyes, kept his mind deliberately blank and breathed deeply.

A sound by the door.

A mere whisper of noise. His gut clenched.

Nothing. It was his mind playing tricks. He forced himself to ignore it, the way he had ignored far worse indignities after Waterloo. He would sleep. He must.

He resisted the urge to toss and turn. Forced his limbs to remain quiet and once more emptied his mind.

More rustling.

The bed sank in one corner.

Heart drumming, he shot upright, staring wide-eyed at the foot of his bed.

Merry? 'What the hell are you doing here?' He scrubbed a hand over his face. 'I beg your pardon.' God damn it, he was naked. He flipped the edge of the counterpane over his hips.

Her gaze remained on his face, but she must have seen, when

she walked in, that he was stark naked. Once more, blood headed for his groin. Damn the woman. 'What did you want?'

'I couldn't sleep.'

That made two of them. 'So you thought you'd wake me to share in your lack of rest. Hand me my robe.' It lay beside her across the foot of the bed.

She bit her lip and handed it to him. 'I'm sorry.' She slid off the bed and walked to the hearth, looking down at the fire, while he pulled the banyan around him.

She spun around as he finished tying the knot. 'I did not intend to disturb you.'

Disturb. Hah! He couldn't be more pleased. Or at least one part of him couldn't. The rest of him wasn't so sure. He waved off her apology. 'How can I be of service?' A bad choice of words. The low thrum in his blood had become a steady pounding beat. He could smell her, the scent of lavender and soap, and a woman fresh from her bed. He wanted to carry her to his. He wanted to lay her down amid his sheets. He wanted all she would give. But only if she gave it freely.

She looked at him, her head tilted on one side, her full lips parted. Lips he longed to take with his own. He clenched his jaw.

'I came to apologise,' she said and pressed those full lips together as if trying to decide what to say next. She clasped her hands at her waist. The firelight behind her shone through the flimsy nightgown and wrap. Outlined in the faint glow, her legs were long and slender, the dark triangle at their apex more imagined than seen. Black as night to match her hair, no doubt, and a delightful contrast to her pale skin.

His teeth ground together. He picked up a candle. 'Let me escort you back to your room.'

She backed away, thankfully into the shadows beside the hearth. She looked nervous. 'You cannot deny the attraction between us.'

The clenching of his groin anticipated what might come next, but at what price? 'I won't change my mind, Merry, whatever coin you use.'

She flinched. A mere flicker of an eyelash, a minute tightening of her jaw. He'd hurt her. He wanted to apologise and grant her wish. He couldn't. It had taken all of his powers of persuasion to convince Father to let Robert return. One misstep and all would be ruined.

Yet she did not retire in defeat. It wasn't in her to give up. Her gaze did not shift away. Instead her bright blue eyes held his gaze boldly. She licked her top lip, leaving it moist and pink. It held his attention as she spoke again.

'It has nothing to do with...' she gestured vaguely with one hand '...that. No one would believe you would offer for me anyway.'

Truth was a bitter brew. He wished she wasn't right. But if she wasn't here to convince him to follow her plan, then why had she come after her coolness this evening? A bubble of something light and airy restricted his breathing. Hope. Damn it. When he should really be turning her around and sending her out of the door, he nodded for her to go on.

'I enjoyed our kiss today. I would like to repeat the experience.'

His groin gave a pulse of approval. Why not, indeed? The urge to say yes filled his throat.

He walked to the window, before the words left his mouth. Before he did something he'd regret. 'You are a beautiful woman. I cannot deny I find you alluring, but I no longer believe the impression you gave me on my first night here. Or my conclusion this morning that you might be an abbess.'

She gasped.

He turned with a smile. 'Finding two very bold females in my bedroom this morning led me astray.'

A small smile of acknowledgement touched her lips. 'I see how it might happen.'

He forced himself to say the next words. 'I certainly recognise the spark of attraction between us, it was there from the first, but you are unmarried and therefore out of bounds. I'm sorry.'

Hades. How utterly priggish he sounded. But it was the right thing to do.

Her fingers played with the tie at her waist.

Bloody hell, if she didn't take him at his word and leave he'd have that small knot untied and the whisper of silk covering her form puddled at her feet.

Randy bastard.

She glanced at him from beneath half-lowered lashes. 'You are indeed a gentleman. But we are both adults, are we not? Both experienced in the ways of the world and capable of making our own decisions. Why should we not have one night of pleasure before you leave?'

He strode to face her toe to toe. She didn't flinch. Her gaze didn't drop from his as he held her chin between forefinger and thumb, tilting her face up, bringing her lovely mouth within reach of his own.

He wanted her.

More than he wanted to give her aid, he wanted her in his bed. Had wanted her since the moment she gazed at him on the road.

And here she was offering herself to him. Not a virgin, the kind of woman he must marry, but a bold sensual woman who knew what she wanted.

A groan rose in his throat. He forced it to silence. Closed his eyes briefly against the urges riding him hard and forced himself to speak. 'Are you sure?'

'Yes,' she whispered, her body swaying towards him, her lavender perfume rising like incense to his senses, sweet and heavy.

He bent his head and claimed her mouth.

Merry sank into his embrace, clutched at the front of his robe with desperate fingers in case she collapsed to the floor on legs weak with relief.

She let her senses drift on the pleasure of his kiss, the lovely feel of his body hard against hers, the intruding thigh between her legs, the large hands roaming her body at will.

Ever since he had caressed her feet in the billiard room, her body had been on fire, her mind a senseless mess of conflicting and confusing thoughts. She wanted this, even if she was beyond the pale to him except in this most basic of passions.

Tonight she would have her desires fulfilled and out of the way, so she could plan how next to proceed without regret for what might have been.

His tongue licked her lips and pressed against the seam of her mouth. She opened to him, tasted brandy smoky on her tongue.

Her breasts felt heavy and full, the place between her thighs moist and tingling; she tilted her hips, increasing the pressure of his thigh and was rewarded by his brief indrawn breath.

She uncurled her fingers from the fabric of his robe and slipped them beneath, to run her hands over his broad expanse of chest.

She'd seen much of him in the billiard room and again as he lay naked on his bed with his eyes closed.

She'd been surprised but grateful for the candles' revealing light. His body was gorgeous, his male member thick and large; she could feel it now pressing against her lower abdomen as his hand brushed up from the indentation at her waist to cover her breast.

She let go a long sigh of pleasure and a satisfied sound of male approval rumbled in his chest.

It sent a shiver down her spine.

Her fingers splayed across the warm silken skin of his chest, felt the roughness of hair and the puckered skin of his scar.

She longed to touch it with her tongue, taste it with her lips, but right now his mouth was taking her senses to new heights of arousal. She slipped her hands up to his shoulders and thrust her tongue in his mouth.

He groaned and swept her up in his arms, breaking the kiss. She looked up into his face.

'My bed or yours?' he asked.

'Yours.' She laughed. 'It is closer.'

'A sensible woman indeed,' he murmured, his dark eyes hazy with passion and glinting with amusement.

He was so bloody handsome. It wasn't fair.

But he was hers for now. And she would make the most of the one night he'd granted.

He frowned.

Had he sensed her regrets?

She smiled and licked her lips. 'What now, you great gormless statue?'

At that he threw back his head and laughed out loud. He strode for the bed, pressing her back against the mattress, and gazed into her face. 'Did I tell you how much I adore that tongue of yours?'

'For what it says?' she asked, fluttering her lashes. 'Or what it can do?'

'Hades,' he muttered under his breath and swooped down for a kiss. Their mouths melded, blissfully fitting together. Her thoughts scattered as he plundered her mouth and she clasped her hands around the back of his neck, holding him tight, as she devoured the slick silkiness of his tongue in her mouth. She sucked.

He stilled.

Had she been too bold? Gone too far? Would he think her completely wanton? Her heart beat hard against her chest as he broke the kiss. She let her hands fall away as he drew back, his low-lidded gaze sweeping her body, his lips curving in a sensual smile of approval. 'You are a feast for the senses.'

The words struck a chord low in her belly. Flutters tormented her feminine core. What was he waiting for? Suddenly shy, she twisted her fingers in the curls falling over her shoulder, staring at the strong column of throat emerging from his robe, at the rise of his angular cheekbones. In daylight they made his face look hard and stern, but now they made him look like a fallen angel.

Her angel. For one night. A yearning she did not expect pulled at her heart. Such yearning had no place in her life. She pushed it away and opened her arms to him.

He untied the cord at his hips, and discarded his robe in one easy movement. The scar across his chest gleamed white in the candlelight. It crossed sculpted muscle and striated ribs, missed his navel by an inch where it sliced a path across a stomach ridged with tight muscle to come to rest at his hipbone.

And below, the evidence of his desire, the engorged member jutting from wiry black curls, a dark tip. Proud and very male.

She sucked in a breath and raised her gaze to his face. His expression was dark, harsh and full of seduction.

She reached up and traced a finger down the scar's length, from just above his left nipple to his right hip, where the skin jumped beneath her touch.

'Ticklish?' she asked.

Mischief gleamed in his dark eyes. 'If so, be prepared for repayment in kind.'

Her skin tingled as his hot gaze seared every inch of her body. In a moment of weakness, a slight edge of fear that this dark angel would steal more than she was prepared to give, she covered herself, her breasts, her groin.

His brows lowered. 'Unlike you to be shy, sweet Merry.'

What could she say? She hid behind rough words, yet none came to her tongue. She felt weak with yearning.

'Will you stand there all night looking, then?' Perhaps not completely undone. She brought her arms up, stretched like a cat, feeling the peaks of her breasts against the soft muslin of her nightgown.

He grinned. 'Ah, sweet tormenting witch.' Leaning over her, a hand each side of her head, he brought one knee up on to the bed, a tall man, with no need for the step. He nudged his knee between hers, a gentle insistent pressure of warm skin and hard bone.

No going back. She opened her thighs. Gave him room. Gave him leave. Her breath left her in a rush of anticipation.

Half-on, half-off the bed, he hung over her, his dark eyes searching hers, seeking assurance? Permission? She raised her hands, cupped his cheeks, felt the roughness of beard and drew him down.

Blissful kisses rained from his lips, a touch on her mouth, her chin, her cheekbone, her eyelids, between her brows. Each kiss fired heat low between her legs, her body ached to feel him within her, her breasts longed for his touch and all the while featherlight kisses seared her face.

'Lovely, Merry,' he murmured in a low growl at her ear. His tongue traced the swirls. Her skin thrilled and her insides shivered. Never had kisses felt so sweet, yet the brush of his lips promised so much more.

Panting, she tugged at his shoulders, wanting him closer, hard against her, his bulk weighing her down. She ached.

The strength in his shoulders resisted her feeble attempts to drag him on top of her. She raised herself up to press against him, feeling the prod of his erection against the softness of her belly, the press of his chest against her breasts. 'Charlie,' she moaned.

'Yes, love?'

The amusement in his voice flared her temper. She struck at him with her fist and fell back against the pillows. She glared up at him. The muscles in his upper arms bulged with the effort of holding his weight. She shoved at his arm. 'Don't tease.'

Dark lashes swept down and rose again, revealing wicked laughter in their depths. His mouth curved in a smile so sensual her insides tightened beyond bearing. 'What, Merry? Is this to be naught but a hurried encounter, a quick nibble, when I would savour the banquet before me?'

'Sometimes,' she whispered in sultry tones, 'the table is cleared before you can taste.'

'A threat, Merry? Are you playing the tease?'

The edge to his tone gave her pause. This was not a man she could manipulate. He liked to be the one in charge as much as she did. Mayhap more.

If she wanted him, she would have to take what he offered.

She clawed her fingers through the rough hair on his chest and tugged. His jaw flickered. Curving her lips in what she hoped was a smile as seductive as his own, she peeped up at him from beneath lowered lids. 'This is a banquet for two, is it not?' She lightly pinched his nipple between her fingernails.

His eyes glazed. His chest expanded on a quick breath. 'It is.' His voice sounded ragged.

'Then I would taste, too.' She let her hands wander over the smooth contour of his shoulders, felt the slight tremble deep in his bones as he held himself still, looking down at her face. Desire warmed his eyes, while restrained power tensed his jaw. Control.

A man with a will of iron.

Her fingers traced the contours of the arms bracketing her head against the pillows; her palms warmed to the heat of his blood beneath the satiny smoothness of his skin. A pulse beat in his strong neck, a hard beating throb that echoed in her own veins.

Once more she raised herself up, but not to take, to give. She licked along the artery. Blue blood for the son of a duke. She nuzzled against his neck, sweeping her tongue across the salty skin, sucking and nipping. His breathing roughened. Not so much in control as he would have her think.

She nibbled his earlobe and breathed into his ear.

He groaned and pressed closer, encouraging her tongue deep into the orifice. Controlling again. Demanding.

She pulled away.

'Witch,' he muttered. 'Will you torment me?'

'No more than you torment me,' she whispered.

He took her mouth in a hungry plundering kiss.

Strength surrounded her, his body a wall she could see nothing beyond. It filled her vision, and her mind. He was powerful male. Beside him, she seemed feeble.

Vulnerable. Her heart picked up speed. Trickles of fear rose up from her belly. Her wanton yearnings had almost destroyed her once; she should not let it happen again. Even so, the kiss overwhelmed her senses, carried her upwards on currents of air, rising in twisting strands of pleasure and the pain of need.

A hand, large and firm, cupped her buttocks, caressed the curve. A finger dipped lightly into the crease. A titillating sensation through the fabric. She gasped into his mouth.

He squeezed and kneaded her bottom, while his erection pressed against her.

The teasing fingers travelled down her thigh to her knee. They bunched the gown, easing it upwards. Yes. Now they stroked the bare flesh above her knee, little circles travelling up her thigh, bringing her gown higher, while his kisses numbed her mind to all but his touch.

The fresh scent of his soap and the musk of male arousal dizzied her senses. The longing to submit to his greater will made her limbs languid and heavy. She was pliant in his arms, a shadow of herself. Overpowered by his skill.

His to mould and to shape. It felt lovely.

Chapter Nine

Charlie longed to see her naked. The fine lawn of her shift, the satin of her robe, hid little, yet veiled enough to send his imagination wild. The torment of not possessing her left a growl low in his throat.

He slipped the robe off her shoulders and down her arms. Long, slender, white-skinned arms. He kissed the inside of her elbows, one at a time, smelled the scent she'd placed there earlier, lavender, inhaled it to the depths of his lungs, knowing he would never smell that scent again and not think of Merry.

Eyes half-closed, she lay with her black hair spread over the pillow. He lifted her hand, kissed each finger. The pulse in her throat beat hard and fast. Her breathing quickened.

So sensual. So feminine. So desirable.

He tugged the hem of her nightrail free and she raised her arms to help him lift it off. Her breasts, full and round and high, left him in awe. He filled his hands with their bounty, marvelled at the whiteness of her skin and the firmness of the beautiful flesh.

Beautiful. Rounded. Firm and proud. The peaks were dark, a soft shade of brown, puckered and tight from the exposure to cool air.

He puffed out a breath.

She wriggled.

'Not yet,' he said. 'I have been waiting to see these all night.'

He swirled his tongue around first one tightly budded nipple and then the other.

She moaned.

He felt her dampness on his thigh pressed between hers. Oh, yes, she wanted him as much as he wanted her. Desire shone like a bright flame between them, glowing on their skin and heating their blood. The pulse at the base of her throat urged him on, yet he was loath to let it flare and all too soon die.

He suckled.

She speared her hands in his hair, pressing his mouth to her breast. He caught her by one shoulder, supporting himself and holding her trapped, teasing her other breast with a flicking thumb.

She cried out her pleasure. The shudder of her body as the shocks of pleasure held her in their grip drove him beyond control and into the darkness of his own urgent need.

He widened his knees, opening her thighs. Her dark curls were damp. He guided himself to her entrance.

'Merry,' he commanded. 'Look at me.'

She lifted her eyelids. Her full lips smiled. There was yet one more thing he needed. One thing he needed to know.

'Say my name.'

She licked her lips. 'Charlie,' she breathed.

He slid deep inside her. Knew her as only a lover could know a woman.

Her heat closed around him in welcoming warmth. He kissed her mouth, probed with his tongue as he moved his hips. She clutched at his shoulders, digging her nails into his skin, tilting her hips, rising to meet his every thrust as he stroked her insides. He watched her submit to the pleasure.

The urge to drive into her, to bury himself deep and simply let go, jolted through him.

He fought for command. Battled for the will to lead her from one little death to the next without taking his own. He was known for it. Anything else was unacceptable.

He slowed his breathing.

Clung to control by a thread with each warm slide into her depths, each slow lingering withdrawal.

He breathed deep and slow, the body and the mind in perfect harmony. Energy building to peaks, then rippling away in muscle and bone.

'Charlie?' She ran her fingers over his chest, tweaked his nipples, raised herself to suckle.

His breathing faltered, distracted by the sight of her glorious black tresses against the whiteness of her shoulders and the generous exploration of his body.

Her touch felt wonderful. Not giving or taking, but delightfully shared.

She lifted her legs high and took him deeper.

The pleasure hit him hard and fast. A breath caught in his throat. Breathe, damn it. He twisted his hips, grinding himself hard against the yielding heated flesh.

'Oh, Charlie.'

The sound of his name on her lips, the feel of her luscious body around him, her legs tight at his waist, sent him over the edge. He succumbed to the urges beating in his blood.

He pounded into her. Mindless. Feral.

The climax built. Hit him hard. 'I can't... Merry you have to...' He pumped his hips and caressed with his thumb.

Her eyes widened. Her body trembled. Her inner muscles tightened around him. Gripped him, as her fingers gripped his shoulders. He gazed into her face, saw the strain and the reach. Her eyes opened wide. She let out a cry as she fell apart.

Undone by the glory of the utter bliss on her face, unable to contain his own race to the finish, he pulled clear and spilled against the covers.

Oh, what did she do to him? He felt like an inexperienced lad.

Vulnerable. Without control instead of bringing her to greater heights, keeping her in a state of ever-increasing arousal, until he decided to let her go.

Dear God, he'd almost spilled inside her body.

Aware of her laboured breathing, he turned on to his side and gazed into a face dreamy with satiation. Eyes closed, she lay utterly relaxed, her face still flushed; the scent of their lovemaking perfumed the air.

Her eyes drifted open. 'Mmmm,' she murmured, her chest still rising and falling. 'That was…good.'

Bloody hell. He was leaving in the morning and one night with Merry was not nearly enough.

'You are glorious,' he said and pulled her into the cradle of his arm, let her head rest on his shoulder. His pounding heart slowly quieted, her breath tickled his chest and his own breathing slowed to match hers.

Cosy and warm and deliciously replete, Merry woke to light filtering through her eyelids. It must be morning.

Time to get up. She opened her eyes.

The room was ablaze with candles. They burned on the tables each side of the bed. And on the mantel. Beside her the sound of another's deep breathing. The gentle inhale and exhale from Charlie. She glanced over at the window. Still dark outside.

The last thing she remembered was him saying he wanted to watch her sleep when she suggested they snuff the lights. Carefully, she eased on to her side and gazed at the man sprawled beside her on top of the covers. He lay on his stomach, his flanks and broad back gilded by candlelight. She reached out to run a hand over the beautiful skin, then whipped it back, touching her lips with a fingertip. He looked so relaxed, it seemed a shame to disturb him. Even if the little flutters low in her abdomen suggested he might very well like it.

She glanced at his face, at the full lips, relaxed in sleep, the dark crescent of eyelashes, the slash of brow, the rugged features.

Delicious. A gorgeous man.

She raised up on her elbow. He looked younger in sleep. Less world weary. Less drawn. Less severe. Closer to her own age than she'd thought.

The clock on the mantel struck the quarter hour. She glanced over and saw it was past five o'clock. Very soon Brian would come to make up the fire and find her here. She'd asked him to take over the task from Beth and Jane. She didn't want Tonbridge propositioned again. Not by them, anyway. She quelled a small smile.

Nor did she want to start any gossip.

The ripple of concern over the bourgeois Miss Draycott and her brief girlish love affair in those long-ago schooldays would be nothing to the scandal of being caught in a marquis's bed.

Her first indiscretion had been with a boy. Charlie was a man. A beautiful, wonderful man who knew how to please a woman.

She stretched. She really should return to her own room.

Their mutual passion had been nectar from the gods to her, but might have seemed passing ordinary to him. A sow's ear, rather than the silk purse in her mind. Hopefully, Tonbridge wouldn't betray her indiscretion. He was much too much the gentleman.

What did it matter? After today, she would never see him again. A pang beneath her ribs halted her breath.

Sadness, when she should be feeling nothing but sated. A longing for what could never be. How futile. How unlike her since she'd grown up.

She retrieved her robe from the floor beside the bed.

Charlie sighed, but didn't waken. Just as well. He only had to look at her with those dark eyes and sweep away any semblance of reason.

She slipped on her nightgown, thrust her arms into the sleeves of her robe and knotted the tie. She glanced around the room. It was dangerous to leave candles burning unattended. The thought of a fire made her skin crawl. The house in Skepton had taken but minutes to burn. The girls had been lucky to escape with their lives. She took the snuffer from the mantel and tiptoed around the room, quickly extinguishing them all.

Unfortunately, Charlie didn't seem to notice her departure. With a rueful smile at her continuing feeling of regret, she opened the door and peeped out into the corridor. All quiet. And dark. With no sound from her bare feet on the runner, she ran lightly back to her own room at the end of the hall.

She jumped between the cold sheets and shivered.

It would have been nice to stay next to Charlie. For them to wake up together. Like husband and wife.

The faint memory of sitting on her parents' bed in the early mornings, drinking chocolate like a real grown-up lady slid into her thoughts. They'd been so happy. Before the fever had struck.

Afterwards, everything had changed. Poor Grandfather had been so sad, so worried about what to do with her.

She snuggled deeper beneath the sheets and closed her eyes. If only things could have been different. If only she could have been a lady like her mother, as Grandfather had hoped, Charlie might have gone along with her proposal. Betrothed to a marquis. Merry Draycott. What a thing. She couldn't help but chuckle beneath her breath. She hugged her arms around her body. Imagine meeting such a gorgeous man on the road across the moors.

The vision of her phaeton, shafts upright in the ditch, brought her upright. Deliberately damaged.

Her stomach roiled. Her heart raced, rising in her throat to shorten her breathing. Fear.

Saints above, she'd never sleep now. She couldn't go back to Charlie, admit her terror. He'd use the knowledge to impose his will.

Shivering, she got up and lit a candle to keep the dark thoughts at bay. She stared at the flickering flame. Was that why Charlie kept his candles alight when he slept? To keep away evil?

It would have to be something terrible to trouble such a powerful man.

Numbers were her escape. She picked up the accounts ledger she'd put aside earlier in the evening. It would either put her to sleep, or she would get her morning's work done before first light. She must find a way to increase production, or she would have to let employees go.

Why was everything going wrong now? Were all the naysayers who had wrung their hands in horror at her inheritance of the mill right after all? Was it impossible for a woman to run such a large enterprise as Draycott's? Should she have abided by her uncle Chepstow's wishes and put everything in his hands?

She sighed. Grandfather would have solved the problem in an instant. *Look out for t'coppers* was his motto. Was that what she was doing wrong? Looking out for the pounds?

Dash it all, she would not be beaten.

She opened the ledger at the beginning. The answer had to be here.

Cold. Alone. Charlie opened his eyes.

Darkness assaulted his gaze. Silence his ears. A band tightened around his chest, cutting off air. Sweat trickled down his back. His heart thundered. He lay rigid. Still. Suffocating.

In a bed?

Why the hell was it dark?

The candles must have gone out. Darkness had woken him. He threw back the covers and drew back the curtains from the window. It didn't help.

He gathered the supply of candles he'd left ready with shaking hands. He brought down the candelabra and struck the flint. A candle flared. He inhaled a deep calming breath.

He held the flame to the candelabra. Its candles hadn't burned down, they'd been snuffed. Some time ago by their length.

He glanced at the rumpled bed. Merry must have doused them when she left.

Why hadn't he awoken then? He had slept through her departure. Were the nightmares finally gone?

He rubbed at his breastbone and stared at the window. A faint trace of grey in the darkness of the room. He wanted to cheer. He felt rested. For the first time in years, energy coursed through his veins at the thought of a new day.

He'd made love to Merry, wonderful passionate wild love, and fallen asleep. God, he'd lost complete control with her, behaved like a green boy with his first woman.

She had climaxed deliciously. He hardened, wanting her again.

It wouldn't happen.

Their lovemaking hadn't changed her decision. The two things were not connected. She wanted him gone. He was to drive away and leave her to face the danger alone. Impossible. Yet what choice did he have…unless he agreed to her suggestion that he pose as her future husband.

He groaned. If his father ever learned of this new adventure of his, Robert would be outcast forever. But leaving Merry in danger was out of the question. He already had enough guilt to carry. What he'd done to Robert. His failure at Waterloo.

He would not fail Merry.

He stilled. Was he once more being reckless, endangering others to satisfy his own ego as his commanding officer had accused?

He went hot, then cold. Damn it all, what else could he do? If he left and something happened to Merry, he would never forgive himself.

A knock sounded at the door. He grabbed for his banyan as Brian stepped in, carrying hot water in a jug. 'Ready for your shave and a bath, my lord?'

Ready? Yes, indeed. Because he needed to see Merry as soon as possible. Not that he expected the conversation to be easy.

Chapter Ten

The account books didn't look any better now than they had in the early hours of the morning. One thing was obvious—while costs were rising at the mill, income was falling. Clearly, she would have to deal with the other mill owners' enmity quickly or face ruin.

Merry raised her gaze from the rows of numbers and stared out of the window. No blue skies today. The moor looked particularly bleak, a wasteland of white patches amid the brown grass.

A brief knock and the door opened to admit Charlie. He looked wonderful. Refreshed. And, damn him, more handsome than ever.

An odd feeling of shyness tensed her stomach. Warmth stung her cheeks. He'd think her such a naïve fool for blushing after her wantonness in the night. She kept her smile cool. 'Good morning, my lord. Ready to leave?'

He grinned. 'Forgotten my name so soon, my sweet? How are you, Merry? Did you sleep well?' He strode to the desk, gathered her hands in turn and kissed each palm. 'You look beautiful.'

Right, beautiful in her plain brown gown and ragged grey wool shawl. Her working clothes. The man was a flirt. 'I am well, thank you, *Charlie*. Is your carriage at the door? I will come and bid you farewell.'

He wandered around the room, looking at the neat rows of ledgers on the shelves lining one wall, each one neatly dated. 'So this is where you spend most of your time?'

'Yes.' She pulled her old shawl closer around her, not because she was cold, but because having him prowling around her office seemed to make the room smaller.

'I'm not leaving,' he said.

'What?' Her mouth fell open.

'I'm not leaving while your life is in danger.'

Why did men always think they were the only ones able to solve problems? 'I don't need your help.'

He sat down in the chair opposite the desk. His jaw set in a stubborn line. 'Yes. You do.'

She squeezed her eyes shut. 'Do you know what they will think if you run around town standing up for me? They will think I am your mistress.'

His dark eyes gleamed, but his face remained deadly serious. 'After last night, you are.'

'Well, it won't matter what you say in that case. They will listen politely and once you leave they will do as they wish. As my... my...'

'Lover,' he said, raising a brow.

'Very well. As my lover, you will have no influence at all. And my reputation will be ruined into the bargain. I have to deal with these men every day. I need their respect. This will only garner ridicule.'

He leaned back in the chair, kicked out his legs and folded his arms across his chest. 'Not if I pose as your fiancé.'

She stared at him. 'Why? You were vehemently opposed to this idea barely a few hours ago.'

'I won't leave you to face this alone. It wouldn't be right.'

She blushed. 'You owe me nothing. No. I don't need your help. Caro and I can manage this for ourselves.'

He shrugged a shoulder. 'Your choices are fiancé or lover. Either way I will speak to them today.'

Blackmail. *Brass makes t'wheels turn.* Only he didn't lack for money, and, unless she was completely deranged, he still wanted her.

'It's a mickle for a muckle, then,' she said.

He stared at her blankly.

'Is't not plain as the nose on your face? I'll be your mistress while you play the fiancé. 'Tis a fair bargain and when it is done, there's no obligation on either side.'

His eyes flashed. 'There you are with the outrageous statements in that dialect again. I'm not looking for damned payment. What kind of man do you think I am?'

She glared at him. 'What? Is it beneath you to make an honest bargain? Smell too much of the shop?'

A blank look crossed his face. He took a deep breath. 'It's a matter of honour, Merry. Surely you understand?'

Unfortunately she did. A man who thought his honour was at stake would never give in. Her heartbeat quickened. Her pulse raced. The thought of him remaining here for days, no doubt. The temptation of having him close by.

Caro would be furious.

She glared at him. 'You said you were in Yorkshire on business. I suggest you continue on your way.'

A dark brow flicked up. 'Suggest all you want, I am speaking to these men and that is final.'

He meant it. This man was as stubborn as she was. And if he succeeded, she would be beholden to him. *Every good turn deserves a reward.* Asking him to tie his name to hers deserved a far greater reward than one night in her bed.

'And you won't accept payment.'

A muscle flickered in his jaw. Anger. Pride. Well, she had her pride, too.

'But you won't turn me away if I come to your bed of my own free will.'

He closed his eyes briefly as if he battled demons of his own.

She half-expected him to back down. The other half waited desperately for his answer. Because if he rejected this offer, she would know he despised her indeed and his offer of help was out of the question.

A long sigh escaped him. 'No, I would not turn you away if you came to me of your own free will. I'm damned well not made of stone.'

She let go a breath of her own. She'd actually been holding it while she waited for his answer. 'Then we have a bargain.'

Dear God, what would Caro say? She'd be angry, and disappointed, but she'd have to admit, eventually, it was the best solution. She'd have to forgive her, eventually.

Her insides trembled. He was staying. He would be hers tonight and tomorrow and into the future. The pen dropped from fingers weak at the thought of nights in his arms.

He leaned forwards, elbows on his knees, gazing at her intently. 'Now that is settled, let us start with who you think might have tried to damage your carriage.'

Merry could quite happily drown in those dark brown eyes.

Concentrate, Merry. She shook her head. 'I've gone over and over it in my mind. I know some of the mill owners and clothiers hate dealing with a woman, but they were Grandfather's good friends. I can't believe any of them would do me harm.'

'Businessmen are notoriously ruthless,' he said reasonably.

She rose to her feet. 'But they are not murderers. I won't believe it. I've known these men all my life.'

He held out a hand. She walked around the desk and took it, feeling its strength. He enclosed her hand in warmth. 'You can't let soft emotions cloud your thinking.'

'I'm not one of your sentimental women who doesn't know about harsh realities.' She pulled at her hand. He gave it a tug and somehow she ended up sitting on his knee, enfolded in his arm, resting against his chest. It was so easy to lean against him.

He placed a warm hand on her thigh. His heat scorched her leg through the wool. 'Merry, listen to me. Someone tried to kill you, no matter how you look at it.'

'But why? I've done no one any harm.'

A finger toyed with the fine hairs at her nape. A shiver ran through her, not cold, searing hot. Her insides turned to liquid.

His voice was a gentle murmur when he spoke as if he, too, felt the rise of passion. 'Let us think it through together. What is the reason behind their dislike of the asylum you established? It is not unusual for towns to help those less fortunate. Indeed, every parish is obliged to help their poor.'

'It might be their wives egging them on. Because of the kind of women we sought to help.'

'Ah,' he said.

'What do you mean, "Ah!"?' Indignant, she pulled away.

He hauled her back against his chest. His chuckle vibrated against her shoulder. 'Nothing like an angry woman to move a man to action.'

His hand caressed the underside of her breast. Oh, heaven help her, was that his...his erection against her thigh? Desire flooded through her. She turned her face up. His dark eyes were glimmering with light, yet his expression contained concern. For her. As if he cared.

The door burst open.

Merry tried to jump to her feet. She found herself restrained as she looked into the startled face of her manager. 'Mr Prentice?'

The short stocky man reared back as his pale blue eyes took in the scene. His ruddy face flushed a deeper shade.

'Miss Draycott,' he gasped, shock writ large on his face.

Merry winced. More grist for the gossip mill. She pried Charlie's hand free and stood up. 'Mr Prentice, let me introduce you to the Marquis of Tonbridge, my betrothed. My lord, this is Albert Prentice, my manager.'

Charlie rose easily to his feet. He stuck out a hand. 'Prentice,' he said easily, with just the right amount of friendliness and condescension that would put the man at ease without being effusive.

Prentice's eyes goggled. His jaw worked, then somehow he managed to take Charlie's hand and bow. 'My lord. A pleasure.' He turned his eyes to Merry. 'I'm sorry for interrupting. I wasn't expecting...'

'I am glad to see you. I hope you had no trouble on the roads?'

'I...no. I came along just as they were removing your carriage from the ditch. For a moment I thought... Jed said you had an accident. Are you all right?'

She saw Charlie narrow his eyes, watching Prentice's reaction. Good Lord, the man suspected her manager.

'I'm fine,' Merry said quickly. 'Luckily his lordship arrived in time to rescue me.' She shot him a look. 'Although I had things well in hand.'

Prentice's gaze swivelled to Charlie. 'I didn't know you were expecting company.'

'No reason why you should, is there, old fellow?' Charlie asked.

Merry's gaze flew to his face. His expression was dark. Stern. Questioning.

'Mr Prentice is my trusted adviser in all aspects of Draycott's,' she said quickly. 'I wasn't sure his lordship would come so early in the New Year, Mr Prentice, but negotiations regarding our betrothal have been under way for some time.'

Prentice swallowed and tugged at his neckcloth. 'Oh, aye.'

'You have no cause for concern, Mr Prentice,' Merry said firmly. 'Nothing at Draycott's will change.'

'Except my assistance with Miss Draycott's problems,' Charlie said in rather a dangerous-sounding voice. It was almost as if he mistrusted the man. Dash it. She wouldn't have him upsetting her manager.

She smiled at the young man. 'Albert, Lord Tonbridge is going to help with our plans for the Skepton Asylum. He and I are going to speak to the other mill owners. Who do you think we should approach first?'

Prentice twisted his hat in his hand; expressions chased across his face: chagrin, worry, doubt. He forced a smile. 'Mr Broadoaks would be best, Miss Draycott.' He took a deep breath. 'All t'other owners listen to him.'

'Is he married?' Charlie asked.

'Aye. Got four sons and three daughters, too.'

Charlie gave her a significant look. 'I suppose the sons are out of leading strings?'

'Aye. Two of them already help their Pa at t'mill.'

'Benjamin Broadoaks was Grandfather's best friend,' Merry added. 'He has been the most receptive to my ideas. He will help us.'

Prentice looked unconvinced. 'Shall I speak to him?'

'No,' Charlie said, before Merry could answer. 'Mr Broadoaks will receive a visit from me.'

Merry bridled at the tone of command. 'From us,' she said. 'Mr Prentice, I have here a list of instructions for the mill. I think it will reduce production costs appreciably. Would you see to it, please?'

Prentice ran his eye down the notes she had made. 'It might help,' he said. 'I'll take it right away.' He hesitated. 'You are sure you were not harmed yesterday?' His gaze darted to Charlie. 'You were lucky out there on the moors with a snowstorm coming on.'

'Very lucky,' Charlie said.

'I am fine, Mr Prentice. Thank you for your concern. Please give my regards to your mother.'

A muscle in Prentice's jaw flickered at the obvious dismissal. 'Mother will be most glad to know of your kind wishes, Miss Draycott.' He bowed and went out, closing the door behind him.

'Shifty-eyed bastard,' Charlie said. 'I don't like the look of him.'

Merry blinked.

'Bursting in here as if he had the right,' he continued.

'He's a friend and an employee.'

Charlie rose to his feet. 'You may think of him as a friend, but do not be surprised if he has other designs.'

Had she been too friendly? Let the young man jump to conclusions? 'Nonsense,' she muttered. Dash it. Yet another problem to resolve. She couldn't afford Prentice going off in a huff.

'Time to visit Mr Broadoaks,' Charlie said.

'Not without me.'

He grinned. 'Now why would I miss an opportunity to drive a lovely young woman out in my curricle?'

She wrinkled her nose. 'I have a better idea. We'll take the closed carriage. More private. And warmer.'

He smiled. 'Why, my dear Merry, you are a naughty puss.'

She hadn't been expelled from school for misbehaving with a gardener's boy without learning a thing or two about taking chances when they came along. She cast him a sideways glance. 'You don't know the half of it.'

'Regretfully, I must decline.'

Dumbfounded, she stared at him.

'My horses need exercise.' It was a lie. She could see it in his face. But why? She tried not to care, not to feel rejected, but it didn't seem to be working.

They were admitted into the courtyard of Broadoaks Mill, at the edge of town, by a child of about ten with a runny nose and a ragged jacket covered in white fluff.

There but for the grace of God, Charlie thought. Only an accident of birth separated him from the masses. He certainly didn't believe in divine right. Charlie tied his horses to a post.

'Master's in t'office.' The boy pointed to a set of wooden steps up the outside of the building.

Charlie gestured for Merry to go ahead and enjoyed the view of her shapely ankles and the sway of that deliciously curved bottom as she climbed. No wonder men had invented this bit of courtesy. Ready to catch them if they fell, indeed. It was all about the view.

To his chagrin, his body responded with enthusiasm. He hadn't expected her to offer to be his mistress, and he'd had the devil of a time refusing. Not that she'd listened. The determination had been clear on her face. And damn him, he was looking forward to tonight with impatience.

He ought to be ashamed.

When they reached the wooden landing at the top, Charlie rapped his knuckles on the peeling green paint on the door on the narrow landing.

'Come,' a deep voice said.

Charlie ushered Merry inside. The room overlooked the mill floor on one side and the courtyard on the other. The elderly man behind the desk with red cheeks, a nose covered in broken veins and a full beard sprinkled with grey covering most of his lower face, hauled his bulk to his feet. 'By gum, Miss Draycott. I weren't expecting you! Not so soon after the meeting.'

If ever again, Charlie thought, searching the other man's face for signs of guilt or disappointment. He looked genuine pleased to see them.

'Come in, lass. What can I do for you? My word, young lady, don't know when I've seen you looking more gradely.'

Bliss had that effect. She glowed with it. Charlie felt more than a little pride, though he kept his face completely expressionless as the mill owner turned to him with curiosity in his gaze. 'I don't think we've had t'pleasure, sir.'

'Tonbridge,' Charlie said. He put out a hand.

The older man's eyes widened. 'Mountford's heir, if I'm not mistaken.' Curiosity deepened in the muddy brown eyes.

'Miss Draycott has done me the honour of accepting my offer,' he said. Not a complete lie. The offer was merely not the one this man would expect.

He hoped. He was none too sure what the townspeople thought

of Merry Draycott. He wasn't quite sure what he thought of her himself.

'By gum, lass,' Broadoaks said, grinning. 'Your grandfather would be in alt. My heartiest congratulations.' He took Merry's hand in his big rough one and patted it. Charlie had the urge to snatch it away, but held still. Finally the elderly merchant stuck out his hand to Charlie. 'By thunder. A Mountford. Congratulations.'

Beneath the older man's assessing gaze, Charlie felt a bit like a prize Arabian stallion. It wasn't the first time he'd been accorded that kind of inspection, but usually it was the mothers who looked at him that way.

He managed a grim smile and shook the meaty paw. 'Thank you, sir.'

'Ah, you are a Mountford, all reet. By gum, a chip off the same block as your father.' He rubbed his hands together. 'I'll wager Chepstow is crowing from the rooftops about this.'

A cold weight settled in Charlie's gut at the sound of the familiar name. He glanced at Merry.

She winced and shook her head.

Charlie's bad feeling travelled up to his chest. 'Chepstow?'

'The earl. From over York way,' Broadoaks said, oblivious to the chill sweeping the room. 'The Purtefoy family are her ma's family. Not pleased with the marriage they weren't. Always was a thorn in your grandpa's side, lass, the way they treated your poor ma. But you showed them.'

'You are related to the Earl of Chepstow?' Charlie asked, hearing the growl in his voice, the building anger, but didn't care to hide it. The earl was a crony of his father's. A man with political clout of his own. And Lady Allison's father.

'He's my uncle,' Merry said, looking decidedly uncomfortable. Guilty.

Charlie's anger rose from his chest to the skin at the back of his neck. Had she played him for some sort of dupe? The hart in one quadrant on the shield on her gatepost came from Chepstow's coat of arms, he realised. The rest of it, some sort of puffery. Hell. Why hadn't he recogised it?

Broadoaks's bushy eyebrows shot up. 'Something wrong, my lord?'

Charlie stared at him. Wrong? It couldn't be worse.

Merry shot him a pleading look. 'We can talk about this later, Tonbridge. We came to ask Mr Broadoaks a question.'

Charlie gave the old fellow a smile that said he was about to impart a secret. 'If you'd keep the betrothal between us for now, we'd be grateful. The settlements are not yet final.'

'Aye, certainly, my lord. Business comes first.' He winked at Merry. 'Make sure you drive a hard bargain, young lady. Do your grandpa proud.'

Merry blushed, as well she might, the sly little baggage.

Charlie took a deep breath, reining in his temper, tamping down the suspicion he'd been gulled from the first moment they met. If it wasn't for the fact that there was no way she could have known he'd be travelling along that stretch of road two nights ago, he might have thought she'd planned the accident herself.

She couldn't have known.

While some of the glow seemed to have gone out of Broadoaks's smile, he waved expansive hands. 'Even so, this news calls for a celebration. A glass of wine? Some brandy?'

Merry smiled. 'Not this early in the day, Mr Broadoaks.'

Making the decisions again. Ruling the roost. Indicating he was under her thumb. Charlie gritted his teeth. 'Perhaps another time. Our business is pressing.' Not nearly as pressing as the words he had for Merry after this meeting. 'Let me explain.'

Merry looked startled, no doubt surprised he had taken charge of the conversation.

The old man's eyes sharpened. 'Aye. Sit ye down, both of you. Tell me what service Benjamin Broadoaks has in his power.'

Charlie gave Merry a warning glance. 'The matter of a home for women in need.'

Broadoaks's face turned the colour of puce. His gaze swivelled to Merry. 'Now then, lass. The matter was put to rest the day before yesterday.'

'I think not,' Charlie said. 'You know as well as I, Miss Draycott has no intention of letting the matter die. The real question is how did you and the other mill owners plan to stop her if setting light to the house didn't work?'

Broadoaks recoiled. His chair creaked in protest. He stared at Merry. 'That's a terrible thing to say.'

Merry bit her lip. 'Someone put those men up to it.' She looked at Charlie. 'And now—'

'Someone tampered with Miss Draycott's carriage on her way back from her meeting with you and the other mill owners. She was lucky she wasn't killed.'

Broadoaks lunged forwards, his beard stiff with indignation. 'Now wait a minute, your lordship. I won't say I like the idea of a flock of whores setting up shop in the middle of town as bold as brass, but it ain't a matter to kill someone over. Nor did I have owt to do with t'fire. Were some of the lads from the Muddy Duck got fired up about t'women taking their work.'

'They are not whores,' Merry said. 'Not any more. How will they ever get free of that life unless someone gives them a chance?'

'Hmmph,' Benjamin Broadoaks replied. ''Tis same old argument. We don't want them here.'

'Not quite the same,' Charlie said, before Merry could speak again.

Broadoaks eyed him warily. 'Now, young fellow, surely you see the right of this. Miss Draycott here has a soft heart, but we are men of the world. We know—'

'The Durn estate will pay for the rebuilding of the house. The asylum will be named for the duchess. I will act as her agent in this matter and Miss Draycott will head up the Board of Directors.'

Merry's look of gratitude was like a knife to the gut, because it was a bloody lie. He wanted to throttle her. He flashed her a charming smile. 'That is all you want, isn't it, my dear?'

From the way her face stiffened, he was pretty sure she heard the sarcasm in his voice.

Broadoaks didn't seem to notice. He sank back in his chair with the look of a man about to be hung. 'That puts the cat in with the pigeons.'

'You have a problem with the plan, Mr Broadoaks?' he asked quietly.

The old gentleman fought through his beard to tug at his shirt collar. 'No, my lord. The wives won't be best pleased, I'll admit to that, but they'll come round once they know a Mountford's behind it.'

His father would know nothing of the matter. Or at least he wouldn't have known, if Merry wasn't related to the Purtefoys. Now Charlie wasn't quite so sure if he could bring this off without the betrothal becoming common knowledge. He'd been well and truly caught. Just as Robert had. An ironic smile formed on his lips. 'Good.'

'How is Mrs Broadoaks?' Merry asked a little breathlessly. Fearing his wrath now she'd been found out, no doubt. 'Well, I hope?'

Broadoaks's eyes twinkled a little. 'My missus doesn't change, Miss Draycott, but she is well, thank you for asking.'

Merry grinned.

Charlie glared at her and then at Broadoaks. 'I still want to know who is behind the threat to Miss Draycott's life.'

The old man closed his eyes briefly. 'I know nowt about it. Nor do any of the other owners, I'd vouch my life on it. Aye, no good looking down your nose at me, my lord. Why would we be involved? We had her set to rights. No. You look elsewhere. I've not heard any gossip neither.' He looked at Merry. 'Only you know who might want thee feeding t'worms.'

Right now Charlie wanted to do a bit of worm feeding himself. 'Who *would* know?'

'Beyond me, my lord.' He shook his head. 'I'd try talking to the innkeeper at t'Muddy Duck. He might know what set them off.'

'The Muddy Duck is in the Skepton Town Square,' Merry said.

'Not a place for a woman,' Broadoaks said heavily. 'You know, lass,' Broadoaks went on, 'if you'd put that house of yours on t'other side of town, people might not have been so fratched by the idea.'

Apparently, Merry didn't care who she angered, as long as she got her own way. Damn her. 'Do you have a suggestion, Mr Broadoaks?'

Merry gasped. Charlie shot her a warning glance.

She pressed her lips together. At least sometimes she showed a little sense, because he was in no mood to tolerate an argument.

The elderly gentleman pulled a large handkerchief from his pocket and mopped at his brow. 'There is a house, a small one, over on west side of town. Regular folks live there. It would do for two or three women.'

'To keep the numbers down,' Merry said with a marshal light in her eyes.

'Within reason, I'd say,' Broadoaks said.

'I—'

'We will think about it, Mr Broadoaks,' Charlie said. He smiled at Merry. 'Won't we, my dear? Advice is always appreciated.'

'Well—'

'We won't take up more of your valuable time, Mr Broadoaks. I believe I have business at the Muddy Duck.'

Broadoaks rose to his feet. 'Tell t'innkeeper I said for him to tell you all he knows.'

In those few words, the old man had admitted Charlie to the inner sanctum. The local gentlemen's club. He knew it from the chagrin on Merry's face. He shook hands with the fellow. 'It has been a great pleasure, sir. I hope we meet again soon.'

'Ah, and good luck to you, my lord.' He darted a glance at Merry. 'Needs a strong hand on the bridle, a woman like her do.'

So she might, but that hand wasn't going to be Charlie's. Finally he'd seen right through the scheming little wench and he felt more than a little foolish. Not to mention angry.

He ushered her out of the office and down the steps.

She turned to him. 'I—'

He grabbed her by the arm and pulled her along, not hard enough that anyone would notice, but firmly enough so that she knew he meant business. 'We will talk in the carriage.'

Several times in the past few days, Merry's escort had looked less than pleased. Now he'd withdrawn into a cool remoteness that put the distance of miles between them.

The distance of a duke-to-be from a lesser mortal. She had no trouble recognising it, since she'd seen the same kind of look on her fellow students' faces at school when she was intemperate or bold enough to express her opinions or join their conversations. The reason she'd sought solace with Jeremy.

She lifted her chin as she'd done in those long-ago days. 'What bee's bustling in tha's bonnet then, lad?'

'Oh, for God's sake, you don't think I'm fooled by that rubbishy accent, do you?'

She stiffened. 'There is nothing wrong with the way I speak.'

'Isn't there? Perhaps the names of Purtefoy and Chepstow might give you a hint as to why it doesn't ring true.'

She shrugged.

Anger flared in his eyes. Anger she could deal with. Better that than indifference. 'My mother's family has nothing whatsoever to do with me.'

A muscle flickered in his jaw. His lip curled in derision. 'I'm not green, Miss Draycott. Or wet behind the ears. Nor do I have my mother's milk still on my lips, my dear. I know exactly what you are up to. And it won't wash.'

Inside she shrank from the bitterness in his quiet voice; on the outside she kept her back straight and her expression disdainful. 'Doing it rather brown, Charlie. You forced your way into my business uninvited, you know.'

'You asked me to pretend to be your fiancé.' He said the words as if they tasted of poison.

'For a few days,' she said warily.

'Let us hope Broadoaks is good to his word and keeps a still tongue in his head or Chepstow will be on my father's doorstep tomorrow morning. And won't that stir up an ant's nest?'

What on earth was he raving about? 'The Earl of Chepstow barely acknowledges my existence.'

'Believe me, that will change if this betrothal comes to his ears. He'll care enough to learn I have been living at your house. A house full of prostitutes, no less.'

'They are not prostitutes.'

He raised a cynical brow. 'I know when I am being propositioned.'

She gave him a slit-eyed look. Did he mean her?

'I'm talking about Jane,' he said.

'I told you, I don't think she is going to stay. In fact, I had already decided to talk to Caro about her leaving as soon as we get back.'

'Stop avoiding the issue at hand.' He leaned against the seat back, a hard smile thinning his lips. 'Oh, Merry, I'll admit you are good. Chepstow's niece, for God's sake. All that straightforward honest stuff really had me fooled. But I'm wise to you now. So let's just deal with the business at hand and we can end this farce and go our separate ways.'

Chapter Eleven

It was if a hive of bees had stung her all over. The hot and itchy feeling was swiftly followed by a sweep of cold. She inhaled a few deep breaths through her nose and the cynical twist to his mouth became more pronounced. She wanted to hit him. Scratch his face. She curled her hands inside her muff and bit down on her tongue. The old hurt and misery boiled in her chest, the memory of things she'd never told Grandfather, knowing he would be cut to the quick. Not for himself, but for her.

A burning sensation scoured the backs of her eyes and bile rose in her throat. Damn him. She would not let him make her cry the same tears she had shed as a lonely schoolgirl in the gardener's shed.

There, someone had cared to offer comfort. Here she was on her own.

Glad of his need to focus on his horses as they passed a cart, she forced a smile, even managed a couple of flirtatious bats with her eyelashes and turned in her seat. 'Ah, I see your problem.'

He shot her a quick dark glance.

Her smiled broadened. 'It is all right to seduce a woman of the lower classes, but a noble-born wench requires a different set of rules. Not because she is any better, but because her family has the power to do something about it.'

He stiffened. 'You go too far, madam.'

'Do I? Well, rest your mind easy, your lordship. I wouldn't marry you, if you were the last single man on this earth. What would I want with some useless nobleman, only interested in horses and gambling and the cut of his coat?' She glared at his exquisitely cut driving coat with its layer of capes and gold buttons, at the artfully placed whip points in the lapel, and did a bit of lip curling of her own. 'All right for a bit of fun in bed, but about as much use as tits on a bull, as Grandfather would say.'

His jaw dropped. 'Good God, woman. Your grandfather should have been shot for talking like that to a gently bred female.'

Smile fixed, she straightened in her seat. 'Get it through your thick skull. I am not gently bred just because I am related to the Earl of Chepstow. Draycotts are common hard-working people. My grandfather watched sheep from the age of four until he was ten. My father worked in the mill all his life. If I had been a boy, I would have worked there, too.' Instead of going to Mrs Driver's Academy for the daughters of gentlefolk and finding out exactly how unacceptable she was to the upper classes of England.

'Don't act insulted,' he said stiffly. 'You know you should have told me.'

She pulled all the pieces of her that seemed to have scattered themselves in the air around her—the pride, the hurt, the anger— and settled them back where they belonged with one deep breath. She clenched her hands together inside her muff and willed herself to feel nothing.

'I am not acting insulted,' she said, her voice deadly calm. 'Angry, yes, but since we are almost at the Muddy Duck, I suggest we make our enquiries and then return to Draycott House. You may continue your journey to Durn immediately.'

He frowned. 'You will wait in the carriage. I will make en-quiries.'

'Certainly not. If someone is out to harm me, I want to know who it is.'

The curricle pulled under the arch and into the small courtyard. An ostler ran out to take the horses' heads.

'If we are to carry off this *betrothal*,' he spat the word, 'in the eyes of the world, you will remain in the carriage. Any inn laying claim to the sobriquet of the Muddy Duck is no fit place for a respectable woman.'

'I thought we had already agreed I am not the slightest bit respectable,' she said. Blast. That sounded bitter when she had intended it to be simply sarcasm.

Tonbridge frowned at her. 'If you are my fiancée, then you are respectable. Do as I bid, Merry, or I promise I will go right back to Broadoaks, swear it was all a hum, a lie, so that you could get your own way, and leave you to face him and his friends.'

She gasped at his perfidy. 'You wouldn't.'

'Would you care to test that assumption?'

She stared at the granite line of his jaw and into the dark of his eyes. No laughter. No yielding. They'd won the day with regard to the house because of him, because Broadoaks wouldn't risk the enmity of one of the most powerful landowners in England. One word and Tonbridge would ruin it all. It was blackmail.

She would not be blackmailed.

Caro had been right to caution her about involving him in her problems. And now there was no going back without losing all the ground she'd gained on Caro's behalf. She gritted her teeth. There were other ways to show him he wasn't going to push her around. She awarded him a tight smile. 'As you wish.'

'Good.' Charlie jumped down. 'Turn them around,' he called out to the ostler. 'I won't be more than a minute or two.'

Merry watched him disappear inside the inn in a swirl of black coat. A three-storey building built in Tudor times, the inn looked tired, its roofs sagging and covered in moss. The curricle lurched as the man manoeuvred the horses in the tight space.

A hollow feeling filled her chest. Hurt because he assumed the worst.

Drat him. Why would she, a Draycott, wish to marry him, just because he was heir to a dukedom? He was judging her by his own standards.

A pang of realisation turned her stomach over. Naturally it would make him look bad if the betrothal became public. If she cried off, people would wonder why a low-class woman hadn't found him worthy. Was that why he'd been so angry? Or was it because people would believe he had actually asked for her hand?

Her. Common as muck, Merry Draycott.

The latter. Definitely the latter. The emptiness seemed to grow.

The carriage ceased moving and Merry watched the door through which he had entered. Would he find out who had damaged her carriage? Lord, she hoped so, then he would go and leave her in peace. She winced. The locals were unlikely to tell tales to a stranger. Perhaps Prentice would have been a better choice for this task. She'd speak to him the moment he arrived tomorrow with his report on the mill.

He couldn't have done anything with Mr Broadoaks, though. Clearly only a duke or his blasted heir could persuade the wily old mill owner to go against the indomitable Maria Broadoaks.

Minutes had passed. Where was he?

She hated waiting. Hated not knowing what was going on. She grabbed the side of the carriage and jumped down. 'Back in a moment,' she said to the ostler.

The courtyard needed a good sweep. If it was her yard, she'd see it done, too. She glared at the ostler, who appeared not to notice, and picked her way around the dung. The door opened before she could put her hand on the latch.

A frowning Charlie took in her presence. 'I told you to wait in the carriage.'

'You've been gone half an hour.'

He grabbed her elbow. 'That's because it takes time to get questions answered.'

She didn't like the grim note in his voice. 'What did you find out?'

'I'll tell you once we are on the road, as I promised.'

She glared at him.

'Someone ought to have taken a birch twig to you as a child,' he muttered.

Her lip curled. 'What makes you think they didn't?'

His eyes widened. 'Damn it, Merry.'

Now what did that mean?

Back in the curricle and heading back for Draycott House, Charlie couldn't stop wondering who could possibly have beaten Merry. While she was utterly infuriating, and had put him in an impossible position with regard to her family, he really couldn't bear the thought.

'Well?' she said.

The anger simmering beneath the surface of his skin would have to wait. The current problem required all his attention. He formulated what he had learned into some sort of order.

'Don't sweeten the medicine,' she said.

He huffed out a breath. 'The landlord said someone got the men stirred up the night of the fire. A small group of them in the corner were muttering about jobs being lost. Men who haven't worked for a very long time. They blame it on the changes in the mills, the new machines. One moment it was the usual complaints and the next a mob ready for mischief.'

'Did he recognise the ringleader?'

'He said not.'

'Did you believe him?'

Charlie made a wry face. 'I offered him a pony to tell me who led the charge.'

She gasped. 'Twenty-five pounds is a great deal of money,' she said, then she shook her head. 'But Yorkshiremen have their pride.

And very stiff necks. I will ask Mr Prentice to talk to him when he comes in the morning.'

Damn. Couldn't she give him any credit? 'He won't get any more information than I did. The man swore he didn't know and looked me straight in the eye. I believed him.'

She pressed her lips together as if to stop herself from saying more. He didn't like that. He preferred her open and honest.

His stomach fell away. He couldn't seem to reconcile the woman he thought she was with the person who had emerged in that meeting. She hadn't been the slightest bit open and honest with him. She'd hidden her noble connections, when most people would have trotted them out to impress. How could he not suspect her motives? And of all people, her uncle had to be Chepstow. The duke's friend. And the father of Charlie's intended betrothed. What a mess.

'I don't think there is any more to be done,' she said. 'Mr Broadoaks will see there is no more trouble and you can be on your way to Durn in the morning.'

'Eager to be rid of me.'

'As eager as you are to be gone.'

He damned well ought to be eager. 'There is the little problem of our publically announced engagement.'

Her mouth fell open. She snapped it shut. 'We agreed. You will cry off as soon as we sorted this out.'

'And what will your relatives have to say about that?'

'They have nothing to say. I am not answerable to them.'

But he was answerable to his father. And he'd gambled Robert's future on a roll in the hay—something Robert would no doubt find humorous and ironic, if he were here to enjoy the joke. It wasn't the slightest bit funny. 'If your family learn of this we will be in the soup.' Especially since he'd proposed to the wrong cousin.

'I can stand the heat.'

Damn her, now she made him sound like a coward. He cursed under his breath. 'I wish you'd told me you were related to an earl. I was blind-sided by Broadoaks back there. And we still don't know who is responsible for the attacks on your person. Until we do, our betrothal must stand.' And the longer it stood, the harder it would be to keep it a secret. As she must have known.

She flashed him a glance of dislike. 'The mill owners have agreed to support the house so there is no reason to continue the pretence. No reason for you to stay.'

He could think of another reason. Not that it was very noble minded. He widened his legs, touching her thighs with his, a simple shift of position that could be interpreted as innocent. 'Perhaps I can convince you otherwise later this evening?'

A low blow. But anger still rode him hard.

She edged away from him, but the narrowness of the seat kept her pinned against his side. 'You, sir, are a blackguard and a scoundrel.'

'So it seems.' They passed beneath the old medieval gate and beyond the cobbled streets of the town. It was colder out here on the moors, the wind fresher. It would have been kinder to bring the closed carriage. And more fun.

The thought of being closed up in such a confined space made his blood run cold. He reached down and pulled the blanket up over her shoulders. 'Warm enough?'

'Perfectly,' she said through gritted teeth. 'Thank you.'

Perhaps it was as well she disliked him. It would make it easier to resist her temptation, make it easier to depart once he discovered who had sawed through that axle. What if the bastard tried again? A woman alone, unprotected, would not stand a chance.

She ought to be married.

His gut twisted at the thought of Merry in another man's arms, even though it was quite clear he was not her first encounter. Why did he give a damn about this aggravating, infuriating woman?

Was it her apparent honesty that had somehow pierced a hole in his wrought armour and continued to do so, even knowing the open gaze hid a devious streak? Or was it her odd blend of strength and vulnerability, which caught him in strangely soft places inside that others had never touched?

'I'm not leaving until I find out who tried to kill you and bring them to justice and that is final.'

A gasp made him smile.

He looked down into her outraged expression, took in the parted lips, and the urge to protect her rose up stronger than ever.

The woman only had to look at him with those bright sapphire eyes and smile, and his blood ran hot. One thing was clear. He needed to get her out of his blood. And soon. He should have accepted her offer and made her his mistress. Used her desire to impose his will. His body tightened. It wasn't too late.

'The more our engagement becomes common knowledge, the more of an idiot you will look when it is called off,' she said with the attitude of a magician who had conjured a rabbit from a hat.

Quick-witted Merry, fighting a rearguard action. She brought her guns to bear without hesitation. 'I will stand the reckoning,' he said.

Father wouldn't like it, of course, but well…too bad. The heir to a dukedom would never be cast off the way Robert had. Not for the triviality of breaking off an engagement to a nobody. People might assume that the duke's pockets were to let for a while, given Merry's fortune, or assume he couldn't hold his nose and bring the marriage off, which would be all about vilifying Merry, but since she didn't move in London circles, either way the damage would be minimal.

'I don't need your help,' she said.

'I'm staying.'

'Not at my house.'

He laughed at the snap in her voice. 'Are you saying you will throw me out in the snow? Now that doesn't sound like true Yorkshire hospitality.'

'Impossible,' she muttered. She hunched beneath the blanket, glowering at the road, clearly brooding on her next line of attack.

A crack sounded off to the right. A shot.

Instinctively Charlie ducked, flicked his whip and set the horses into a gallop.

Merry grabbed his arm. 'What are you doing?'

'Damn it,' he yelled. 'Let go.' It was already hard enough to manage the careening team.

He risked a glance over his shoulder. Some boulders. Scrubby bush and a flock of sheep streaming across the meadow towards the road in fear.

'What is happening?' Merry yelled, looking around her.

'Someone fired at us.' He steadied his horses and they shot over the brow of the hill out of the shooter's line of fire.

He'd recogised the sound. A Baker rifle. Deadly from a distance in the right hands.

Off to his right, the fleeing sheep veered, climbing on each other's backs in their panic. They'd seen something. Charlie pulled the pistol from under the seat. He scanned the roadside. A man rose to his feet on the other side of the wall.

Charlie fired. A wild shot.

The blackguard staggered, then adjusted his aim.

'Get down,' Charlie shouted, shoving her head down into his lap.

Another crack. A stinging pain in his right arm. Right where her head had been a moment before. He flinched. The offside horse stumbled. He regained control, let the team have their heads and prayed whoever had fired hadn't yet reloaded.

The horses galloped at breakneck speed. With no hope of halting them until they exhausted themselves, all he could do was try to keep them straight on the road. Fear-induced foam flew from their mouths. They ran blindly while Merry clutched the side of the carriage, white-lipped and wide-eyed.

His head floated above his shoulders, while the world moved by at a snail's pace. Loss of blood.

* * *

Feeling stunned, Merry looked back over her shoulder. 'I can't see anyone.'

'Good,' he said grimly. 'Hang on, the gates are up ahead.'

Somehow he made the turn into the drive. The winded horses slowed. The carriage ceased to sway.

'I don't think they followed us,' she said.

'Let us hope not,' Charlie said between gritted teeth. He looked terribly pale. He drew the carriage up outside the front door. 'Get inside as quickly as you can.'

Merry saw the blood on his hand. 'You are hurt.'

'Do as I say and get down.' He stumbled out of his seat while she scrambled down on her side.

Jed appeared as Merry climbed down.

Leaning against the side of the carriage, clutching his arm, Charlie called out to the coachman. 'Get the horses inside the stables and bar the door, then bring everyone into the house.'

Startled, Jed nodded. He led the horses away at a run.

'Good man that,' Charlie said. He leaned on her and she helped him up the steps.

Gribble swung the door wide. 'Lock the door behind us,' Charlie ordered. The butler slammed it shut and shot the bolt.

Relieved to be inside, Merry collapsed against the banister.

Caro ran out of the drawing room. 'Merry, what is the matter?'

Merry took a deep breath and gathered her scattered wits. 'We were attacked on the road. We need bandages and basilica powder. His lordship has been shot.'

Caro paled.

Gribble frowned. 'What we need is the constable.'

'Not tonight,' Charlie said. 'No one is going outside the gates before daylight.' Charlie looked at Merry. 'And even then it isn't safe. Who *are* these men?'

'I wish I knew.'

'Luddites?' Caro hazarded.

'Criminals, that's what they are,' Gribble muttered, hurrying off.

Merry turned to Charlie. 'Let me see your wound.'

'It's nothing,' Charlie muttered. 'Give me a brandy and I'll be as right as a trivet in a moment or two.'

She ushered him into the drawing room. He didn't look anywhere near as right as a trivet. Caro rushed to the console and poured a brandy.

He swallowed the glassful in one gulp.

'Let's get you out of that coat,' Merry said.

'Don't fuss. Brian will take care of it.'

Typical male. She hadn't lived with an irascible old gentleman without learning a thing or two. One was to act rather than argue. She attacked the buttons on his greatcoat. First, she pulled it down the uninjured arm. The other side posed more of a problem. It was damp and sticky. 'You've lost a lot of blood.'

'It's a scratch,' he said. 'I've had worse falling off a horse.'

His lips were blue, his face pale.

'Caro, lend me a hand,' Merry said. 'Pull on the cuff while I ease it over the wound.'

Thin-lipped, Caro did as requested. She grabbed the heavy greatcoat as it slipped to the floor and flung it over the chair.

'Now this one,' Merry said, undoing the buttons on his morning coat. She gazed at the sleeve. 'I think it is ruined.'

'I have more,' he said. The coat was so blasted tight she had to pull it over his elbow. His face turned to stone. A hiss of pain escaped his lips.

Her stomach rolled sickeningly as she parted the bloody tear in his shirt. The wound oozed blood.

Caro's face blanched.

'I can't see for all the blood,' Merry said. 'Caro, please request hot water from the kitchen.'

Looking grateful, Caro hurried off.

Merry backed Charlie towards the sofa. 'Sit down.'

He fought her off. 'We don't have time for this. We need weapons. I need to set your men to watch at the windows, front and back.'

She couldn't draw a breath, her chest felt so tight, her stomach roiling at the thought of those men storming her house. 'You think they would dare?'

'I don't know. I am not prepared to take the risk.'

The thought froze her blood. 'Perhaps they want money.'

Charlie stared at her, his eyes dark, his mouth flat and the creases either side deep with pain and with worry. 'Merry, who stands to benefit from your death?'

The breath left her body in a rush. She sank on to the sofa beside him. 'W-what?'

He took her hand in his good one. 'I know this isn't something you want to think about, but we don't have a choice. If you die, who benefits? Do you have a will?'

Her stomach clenched. She shook her head. 'It isn't possible. The townspeople have to be behind this.'

His eyes narrowed, as his grip tightened. 'Tell me, Merry. I need to know.'

'I changed my will in favour of Caro,' she whispered.

'When? What do you know about her?'

'She changed the will the day before the attack on the house in Skepton.' Caro's voice, as cold as ice, came from the doorway. In her hands she had rolls of bandages and a bottle of powders. Her face was as white as the bandages.

She strode into the room followed by Gribble carrying a bowl of hot water. 'Put it there,' she said to the butler.

Gribble deposited his burden and left.

Merry's heart ached at the sight of her friend's distress. 'Caro, I know this is nothing to do with you,' she said softly.

Caro's face was blank, shuttered. 'I will leave tomorrow.'

Charlie narrowed his eyes. 'How convenient.'

Merry glowered at him. 'Be quiet. This is none of your business.'

His dark brows drew together. 'I think it is, fiancée of mine.'

'That is all a hum and you know it.' She picked up one of the bandages, dipped the end in the water and began to clean the nasty gash on his arm. Her hands shook. Not at the sight of blood, but at her fear for Caro. She'd seen how desperate Caro was when they met. For her to go back to that because of his wild accusations would be too much. Kind-hearted Caro wouldn't hurt a fly. She raised her gaze to Caro's tight face. 'Don't worry. I won't let anyone poison me against you. And we are not going to let these people, whoever they are, drive you away. I won't allow it.'

Tears filled Caro's eyes. She blinked them away. 'Your trust means everything,' she said in a low voice. 'I swear, I am not behind these attempts on your life.'

Merry made a 'so-there' face at Charlie. 'I believe you.'

He grimaced.

She stared down at the open wound on his upper arm with a frown. 'You need to see Dr Jessup in Skepton.'

'We are not going back to Skepton,' Charlie said, as she sprinkled the powders over the oozing gash. 'If we are going anywhere, we are going to Durn.'

Merry felt her jaw drop. 'Durn?' Her hand hung suspended over his arm, the powder leaking down in a little pile. 'Oops.' She righted the bottle.

'Yes, Durn. You will be safe there.' He gave Caro a hard look. Clearly, he wasn't convinced of her innocence, no matter what Merry thought. 'I have men there. And guns. From there all the power of the duke can be brought to bear on these blackguards.'

She began winding the bandage around his wonderfully muscular arm. Please God it didn't turn gangrenous. She pushed the horrid thought aside. 'I've never run from anything or anyone in my life.' Not since she'd run from school, humiliated and mortified. 'You need a doctor.'

'There is a doctor in the village on the Durn estate,' he said with the triumph of a man laying an ace and winning the trick.

'He's right, dear,' Caro said, placing her finger on the knot, so Merry could tie it off nice and tight. 'You will be safer there. His lordship can find out who is behind this. You should go.'

'And leave you here? What if they come back tonight? How will you defend yourself? And Thomas?'

Caro's expression turned fearful. 'If it is you they are after, then we will just let them search the house and then they will leave,' she said with a touch of bravado.

It might work. Merry looked at Charlie, whose pallor seemed worse. He must have lost a lot more blood than she'd realised. He gazed at Caro, then let go a breath. 'They would question you. If you refused them the information, they might hurt you or the child.'

Merry leaped to her feet. 'Then I'm not leaving.' She glared at Charlie. 'That is final.'

'Very well,' he said, the corner of his mouth kicking up in a smile. 'We'll all go.'

'Caro's ladies, too?' She couldn't help sounding suspicious.

He chuckled wryly. 'Oh, yes. Everyone. Even the servants if you want. But we have to go soon, before these fellows regroup. We have a couple of hours at most. I hurt one of them, but not enough to stop them.'

'You mean leave tonight?'

He nodded.

'How? We can't all fit in the carriage.'

'If I might make a suggestion,' Caro said, 'the ladies and I could travel in the carriage. You and his lordship could take his curricle. We can leave by the back gate. Gribble and Cook can ride on the roof with Jed. Brian can ride in the tiger's seat on his lordship's vehicle. I think Jed has a shotgun for hunting rabbits.'

Merry frowned. Caro seemed very knowledgeable about methods of escape.

'It would be nice if he had more than one,' Charlie said. His voice sounded less strong than it had moments ago.

'All right,' Merry said. 'Durn it is.' A surge of anger rose in her chest. 'But when I find out who is chasing me out of my home...'

Charlie put up a hand, looking just a little green. 'Merry, do you think you can bring that bowl closer?' he leaned forwards, his head between his knees.

She gazed down at him. Oh, no, he was going to... She shoved the bowl between his feet.

Chapter Twelve

It hadn't taken them long to pack and pile Caro, Beth and poor little Tommy inside the carriage. Jane had disappeared. They'd looked all through the house, until Beth finally volunteered she'd gone for a walk earlier in the afternoon and hadn't returned.

They didn't have time to search for her and Caro had no qualms that the woman could look out for herself.

Not all the servants had wanted to come with them. Cook and Gribble preferred to guard the house with an old blunderbuss they'd found in the stables. The stable boy and the other young footman had run home across the fields with some extra coin to make sure of their welcome. They'd promised to come back the next day and check on the house.

There was no more they could do.

Merry looked back, but could see nothing of Jed and the town carriage. Night had fallen and they'd decided against lighting the carriage lamps.

She had insisted on driving and had been surprised when Charlie hadn't argued. He must feel worse than he openly admitted. The vehicle was beautifully sprung and light bodied; the horses, tired from their earlier race, were docile. Ahead, the rear gate looked extremely narrow.

'I'll get down and walk them through,' she said, slowing the team.

'You'll be fine,' Charlie said. 'Aim for the gap and envisage yourself on the other side.'

His trust in her was quite remarkable. He'd never seen her drive until now.

She took a deep breath, steadied the offside horse, who tended to break step, and shot out into the lane. She made the turn easily. Beside her Charlie relaxed against the seat back. 'Couldn't have done it better myself.'

Brian, riding on the step behind her seat, gave an audible sigh. 'Right gradely, miss.'

She grinned. 'Praise indeed.'

She and Charlie laughed.

'Spring 'em,' he said.

She flicked her whip and the team broke into a nice steady canter. The carriage rocked a little, but held the road beautifully. 'This is as fast as we dare go,' she said, 'or Jed won't keep up.'

Five hours later Merry's fingers were stiff from holding the reins, her feet were numb, the horses were blown. At her side, Charlie looked white around the mouth and he kept shivering. Every time they went over a bump Merry winced, feeling for his pain. A snow squall, one of several they'd encountered, swept in and obliterated the road. Would they never make it to Durn?

'Just around the next bend, you will see the gates,' Charlie said.

'Thank heavens.'

'You did well.'

'It doesn't seem as if we were followed, though it is hard to see. I wonder if they will guess where we went?'

He straightened in the seat. 'Let them.'

'How is your arm?'

'Fine.'

Which probably meant it was hurting like hell.

'There, Miss Draycott,' Brian said from beneath his muffler.

A gatehouse hunched beside imposing wrought-iron gates bearing the ducal coat of arms. Merry pulled the horses up in front of the gates and Brian jumped down to rouse the gatekeeper. An elderly man in homespun hurried out before Brian reached the door.

He rushed to open the gate and stood back as Merry eased the curricle through.

The gatekeeper touched his forehead. 'Welcome, my lord.'

'Wait,' Charlie said to Merry. He leaned over the side of the carriage. 'Good to see you again, Ritson. There is a carriage following—let it through, then lock and bar the gates. No one else is to enter without my permission.'

'I'll see to it, my lord.'

Merry whipped up the tired horses and gamely they managed a trot. The drive was lined with ancient chestnut trees. Bare and limned with snow they looked giant soldiers ready to fight off any intruders. Then the house filled her vision. An enormous castle, all Gothic towers and crenulations. And very gloomy.

'Oh, my word.'

Charlie chuckled softly. 'I know. Dreadful.'

He climbed down from his seat the moment the carriage halted and came around to help her down, while Brian ran to the bridles.

Merry had never felt so stiff or so cold in her life. Her knees creaked when she climbed down.

'Welcome to Durn,' Charlie said wryly.

Light streamed down the steps as the front door swung open. A stiff-looking butler stood framed in the opening, the glow of warm candles behind him. Footmen ran down the steps, taking the horses in hand, pulling down their meagre luggage. Merry stared up at the ducal emblem over the door. Her heart sank.

It was too grand. Too imposing. Coming here was a mistake.

A moment later they were joined by Caro and Beth holding Thomas in her arms. 'Poor little lad,' she said. 'He's fair exhausted.'

Merry knew exactly how he felt.

'Come on,' Charlie said. 'Let's find a warm fire.' He gestured for them to enter.

Behind them, Beth was silent. No doubt equally overwhelmed.

The butler greeted them with a bow. His eyes widened as he took in their party. He recollected himself quickly. 'Welcome home, my lord. We have been expecting you.'

'Days ago, I know, Logan,' Charlie said, striding into the hall. 'I got caught in a snowstorm in Skepton.'

Merry followed him, looking around at medieval armour and weapons, and the banners hanging from enormous ceiling beams. Intimidating.

'What a beautiful home you have,' she said, brightly.

She undid the buttons of her greatcoat, stripped off her gloves and handed them to the waiting footman, as did Charlie and Caro, who then took the sleeping Thomas from Beth.

A footman tried to help Beth with her coat. ''Ere, that's mine, lad. You get your own coat if you needs one.'

'It's all right, Beth, he will hang it up for you and bring it next time you go out,' Caro said.

Beth gave the elderly footman the evil eye. 'Don't lose it.'

The footman whisked the outer raiment away.

'There is a fire in the blue drawing room, my lord,' the butler said. 'And in the library. When would you like dinner?'

'Is there a nursery?' Caro asked. 'Or a schoolroom? I think it would be better if Thomas and I were housed there. Supper on a tray would be all we need.' She gave Charlie a pointed stare.

'Yes, of course,' Charlie said. 'Logan, please make the arrangements.'

Logan snapped his fingers. A footman materialised from the

shadows beneath the stairs. 'Escort the ladies up to the schoolroom.'
He looked at Beth. 'The maids' quarters are in the other wing.'

'She is the child's nurse,' Caro said swiftly. 'She'll remain with
me.' Merry had never heard Caro sound so imperious. It clearly
worked because Logan bowed acquiescence and the little party
followed the footman up the stairs.

Obviously grappling with curiosity, Logan waited for Charlie's
instructions with an expression of polite enquiry.

Charlie drew the butler a little aside and lowered his voice. 'I
have given instructions at the gate that no one is to gain entry to
the grounds without my express permission. Please pass the word
to the other gatekeepers. Have a boy stationed at each entry to warn
me of any arrivals and have the gatekeepers arm themselves with
a shotgun and a pistol.'

Logan's eyes sharpened. 'Are we expecting trouble, my lord?'

Charlie shook his head. 'Expecting, no. But I would like us to be
prepared.' He exuded a quiet confidence. The aura of a man used
to commanding and having his orders followed without question.
The heir to a dukedom.

The duke would be as horrified as the butler looked, if he learned
his son had brought his mistress and her entourage into his home. A
cold chill settled on Merry's heart. It was good of Charlie to want
to help, but he hadn't thought through the implications.

'That is all, Logan,' Charlie said.

'His lordship needs a doctor,' Merry said quickly. 'He was injured
on the road. Please send for one right away. He is to be admitted at
once. In the meantime, my lord, you need to get out of your clothes
and into a warm bed.'

At Logan's wide-eyed look at his master, she flushed. What must
he think of her taking control in such a fashion? Charlie, on the
other hand, blast him, was looking rather smug.

Logan visibly gathered himself. 'I'll send Andrew up to you, my
lord.'

Charlie's smile broadened, becoming wolfish, and Merry wanted to hit him.

'No need,' he said airily.

Merry held her breath wondering what he would say next. 'Brian, one of Miss Draycott's men, has been serving as my valet these past few days. Have him come up to my chamber.'

Logan's moment of utter stillness gave his disapproval away. 'Yes, my lord.' He stood there irresolute.

'Get on with it, man,' Charlie growled. 'Miss Draycott, your arm if you please.'

Logan hurried off, but Merry could imagine what he was thinking.

Charlie had certainly made it clear that he had been staying with her the past few nights, and by implication that she was his mistress. Revenge for her keeping her noble relatives a secret? Merry shot Charlie a glare as they headed up the stairs, but held her words behind her teeth. There were servants standing at every door and in every hallway. What she had to say required privacy.

At the top of the stairs, a footman opened a chamber door as they left the main landing. Not a chamber, Merry realised, but a gallery running along a windowed wall with a suite of rooms on the other side. Medieval style.

'This place must be very old.'

'Fooled you, did it?' Charlie said, striding past a room with a chair on a dais, a sitting room and a small room with a truckle bed. Finally he stopped at a room with a gold-canopied monstrosity of a bed set on an elevated platform at one end and an enormous carved-stone fireplace at the other.

'My grandfather had it built to replace the ruins that once stood here. Completely outmoded now, of course. And just as draughty as the real thing.'

Only someone of enormous wealth could construct such a folly. 'What is along there?' She pointed to the end of the gallery.

'A water closet. The only modern thing in the place. Hot-and-cold running water. I had it put in last year.' He glanced up. 'Beyond it is your room, I hope you find it to your liking.'

She swung around. The devilish look was back in his eyes. Along with a challenge.

Now was not the time for an argument, not with him looking so pale and cold. Their conversation would wait until after the doctor's visit.

He eased one shoulder out of his coat with a wince. She inspected his arm. The bandage showed no evidence of further bleeding, but he was clearly in pain. 'Sit down. Can I get you anything?'

He shivered. 'A brandy, if you please. I find I am quite chilled.' He pointed to a console of inlayed ivory and teak against the wall beneath a tapestry of a boar hunt. It held a variety of decanters and wines.

'Sit by the hearth.' She poured him a glass of brandy, ministering to him when she should be ripping him to shreds for his outrageous words in front of the butler. She handed him the glass.

He tossed off the liquid and a shudder ran through his large frame. She shook her head. 'I think perhaps we should not have risked such a journey with you in this condition.'

'We didn't have a choice.'

'I cannot stay here. I have a business to run.'

He grabbed her hand and held her fast. 'You are not going anywhere, do you hear me? Not until we find out who those men are and why they are trying to kill you.'

She stiffened. 'I still think it is all a mistake. Besides, you have no right to tell me what to do.'

He laughed, a rather chilling sound to Merry's ears, since she could not break free of his hold. 'Oh, but I do. I'm your betrothed, remember? We announced it this morning.'

The bitterness in his voice stung. 'You didn't make it sound as if we were betrothed down below.'

His gaze darkened. 'Nor did you.'

She pulled at her hand and finally tore free. She stepped back.

She did not understand this moodiness. He'd been trying to control her since the day they met, but until now the hand had been light on the reins. It seemed he'd changed to a curbing bit.

'Let us be quite clear. I let you convince me to come here after those men attacked us, but the more I think about it the more sure I am that Broadoaks, or whoever started this, had no time to call off his dogs. That they acted before new orders reached them. By now, everything will have returned to normal. Tomorrow we will return to Draycott House.'

His mouth flattened. 'Is that so?'

'Yes.'

A cough sounded in the gallery just beyond the chamber. 'Who is it?' Charlie snarled.

'Brian, my lord.'

'Good. You are just in time.'

Brian stepped into the room, his face rather stiff. He must have overheard some of their conversation. Merry felt more heat in her face. Drat the man.

'I'm to help you undress, my lord.'

'Yes, you are. But first ring the bell by the fireplace.'

Brian did as instructed, then proceeded to help Charlie out of his waistcoat and cravat.

'I will find my own room now,' Merry said, starting for the gallery.

'You will wait for Logan,' Charlie said. 'He will direct you.'

Imperious beast. If he wasn't so ill, hadn't been wounded helping her, she would have continued on her way. Instead, she went to the window and pulled back the heavy curtains. There was nothing to see. Her ears filled with the sounds of Brian helping Charlie with his clothes, her mind filled with visions of his wonderful body. Her heart picked up speed, her breathing became a little too rapid, her skin too warm. Dash it all, despite his autocratic commands, she felt the need for his strong arms around her. Wanted his body bringing her pleasure, which in turn would silence the fears in her mind.

She ought to be ashamed, knowing she was about to bring shame to the Draycott name again. Grandfather had trusted her with his mill and his fortune, and here she was again proving she was nothing but a weak female as Uncle Chepstow had charged when he learned the terms of her inheritance.

A rather harried Logan strode down the corridor. 'You rang, my lord?'

Charlie sat in a huge armchair beside the fire; his cheeks were flushed, his glittering eyes fixed on her. Dear Lord, he was in the grip of a fever. No wonder he was acting so strangely. Where on earth was the doctor?

He fixed his dark gaze on Merry. 'Logan, I gave an instruction earlier that no one was to enter the grounds without permission?'

'Yes, my lord.'

'No one is to leave, either. Do you understand?'

'Yes, my lord.' Logan's voice held no expression. 'I will bring the doctor up the moment he arrives, my lord.'

'Good. Please show Miss Draycott to her room. Go with him, Merry. You will see that to enter or leave your room, you, or anyone else, must pass by here.' He shot her a dark look. 'We will dine together as soon as the doctor leaves. We have not finished our discussion.' His dark gaze turned to Logan.

Impassivity masked the butler's expression. 'This way, Miss Draycott.'

'Brian will fetch you once the doctor has been.' Charlie's voice followed her down the corridor.

They passed a door. The only one in the suite. The water closet, no doubt. The one new-fangled invention Grandfather had refused to entertain in Draycott House.

The next chamber was a bedroom decorated in the French style. The fire was already lit, along with the candles. Yet no one had passed by Charlie's room. She frowned. 'You surely weren't expecting us?'

Logan glanced back along the corridor and stepped deeper into the room. 'This suite of rooms is made ready when his lordship is expected.' He frowned. 'He has on occasion been accompanied by a…a lady, but not for a long time. Still, we must be prepared.'

'I see.' She wished she hadn't said anything. The thought of being one of many didn't sit well in her stomach. 'Thank you.'

'I'll send one of the maids to attend you, since you only brought a nurse for the child. She'll bring up your valise.'

Merry nodded. 'Where is Mrs Falkner?'

'In another wing. You will have to ask one of the footmen to guide you if you want to see her. Will that be all?'

'Yes, thank you.'

He bowed and left, not back the way he had come, but in the opposite direction. She rushed to see where he went, but the corridor was empty. Charlie was wrong. There wasn't only one way into this suite of rooms. Somewhere a servants' staircase lurked. A secret way in and out.

How could he not know? Because men like him didn't notice servants. They were like furniture, only there to serve him. How they arrived and left was a question that likely never entered his head.

Chapter Thirteen

Charlie suffered the doctor to put his arm in a sling, then he sank into an armchair beside the fire.

'You are lucky, young man,' Dr Wells proclaimed, packing up his instruments. 'The wound is shallow. You should feel as fine as fivepence tomorrow, but to be sure I wish you would allow me bleed you. For sleep, you would be better off with laudanum.'

'Is your patient not co-operating, Doctor?'

Merry's voice. It gave his flagging spirits a lift. He turned his head to watch her glide in. She'd changed from the practical gown in which she'd travelled into something of vivid pink, very low at the neck. Her breasts looked delicious.

He frowned. She was up to something. Damnation, he should not have been so hard on her in front of Logan, wouldn't have been if she didn't fight him every step of the way.

'Is your patient permitted wine, Doctor?' she asked.

'He must suit himself,' the doctor grumbled, buckling his bag. 'He has no interest in my advice, but please do not feed him red meat.'

Charlie leaned back against the cushions, watched her cross the room to the console. She moved with purpose, her curvaceous body supple yet elegant. He also felt wearier than he wanted to admit. A glass of wine would set him up better than all the doctor's potions and pills. 'I will take a glass of wine, Miss Draycott.'

Merry turned and glared at him.

The doctor's heavy white brows drew together. 'Wine might help you sleep, or it might make the fever worse.' He bowed. 'Good day to you, my lord.' He turned to Merry. 'Whoever saw to his wound in the first place did a fine job.'

She smiled. 'Thank you. I will pass on your praise.'

The doctor bowed. 'Send for me if you feel worse.'

'Thank you. Show the doctor out, Brian,' Charlie said. 'Order dinner to be brought up. I am sure Miss Draycott is in need of sustenance.'

Brian ushered the doctor out.

The servants would never dare gossip and not one word would pass Dr Wells's lips about Merry's presence in the house. The duke paid him a handsome sum to serve the Mountfords on their rare visits to Yorkshire.

But Merry didn't know that. She would no doubt be very angry with him for speaking her name. She deserved it after keeping her ancestry a secret. He was looking forward to sparring with her about her intended departure, too.

Despite her wilfulness, and the awkward situation she'd forced on him, she would remain here as long as he chose. As long as there was any chance she was in danger.

Damn, he wished he didn't feel quite so hot, or so bloody weak. And with his arm in a sling, he felt at a distinct disadvantage. If she decided to leave, he wasn't sure he had the strength to stop her.

Merry handed him his glass.

He raised it in toast. 'To the beautiful woman in my bedroom. I had far rather she was in my bed.'

An unwilling smile curved her lips. She shook her head. 'You are incorrigible.'

He sipped at the wine. 'I meant what I said, Merry. You are

not to leave Durn until we find out just who is behind these attacks.'

She shrugged. 'Why did you not allow the doctor to bleed you?'

A sudden change of subject, even for her. His hackles rose, but he let it pass. For now. 'The wound is fine, thanks to you. I have already lost enough blood for one day.'

'Then you should take the laudanum, it will help you sleep.'

The drug left him open to the dreams. He knew from experience. He stifled a shudder. 'I prefer to keep my wits about me.' He narrowed his eyes. 'Did you think to sneak off in the night?'

A scoffing sound came from her throat. 'Another night without sleep? I can't see Caro agreeing to any such thing.'

All the same, she looked a little disconcerted. She'd given it serious thought, he realised. 'No one will be allowed in or out of Durn tonight.'

She rose and went to the hearth, sipping her wine as she stared down into the flames. Plotting more ways to flout his authority.

'It will be interesting to learn if anyone did try to gain entrance at Draycott House,' she mused.

'Yes, it will.'

'How long do you think we should wait before deciding it is safe for us to return home?'

A fair question. 'I don't know. I will have some investigations undertaken first.'

'And in the meantime, I am here in exactly what guise—your mistress or your betrothed?'

Ah, now they had reached the crux of what bothered her. 'What about both?' he said with a grin.

She swung around, a gleam of anger in her eyes. He liked the way her passions rose so quickly to the surface. All of them.

His body hardened. 'Come here.'

In a few quick strides she crossed the room to his side, remaining just out of reach.

'Closer,' he ordered, the urge to bedevil her strong.

She eyed the distance between them without moving.

'I don't bite.'

'I do,' she muttered. The sensual tension between them flared. Never far below the surface, it rose to the temperature of a blast furnace.

He laughed. 'Oh, Merry, don't tempt me.'

'Once your servants realise the sort of woman Beth is, don't be surprised if they hand in their notice.'

'Is that why you had them serving as chambermaids?'

'Partly. Jane made it worse, though, by trying to lure the house-keeper's husband into her bed.'

The one who had disappeared. 'Do you think her departure is suspect?'

Merry shrugged. 'Not really. She's never really taken to the idea of reform.'

'Nevertheless, a possibility.' He'd set his steward to making en-quiries first thing in the morning.

A polite cough heralded the entry of the dinner tray wielded by two footmen in livery. A third pulled out a table from the wall, opened out an extra leaf and placed a chair on each side. In mo-ments, a sumptuous dinner for two was laid out and the men had departed.

He could see Merry was impressed by the widening of her eyes. She thought her grandfather a powerful man, but when it came to a duke, the power was awesome.

He pushed to his feet. 'Shall we?'

She let go a sigh of defeat. 'I could eat a horse.'

Glad to see her practical side win out, he gave her a smile of approval. Female dramatics were such a bore.

'Would you like me to pour you more red wine?' She nodded at his arm in its sling.

'That is kind of you.'

'Sit yourself down, then.' She took their glasses to the console.

Awkwardly, he pulled out her chair and then seated himself on the opposite side of the table. He glanced over when she seemed to take a long time. 'Is there something wrong?'

'I—the stopper is a little tight. There, I have it now.' She turned with a glass in each hand and a smile on her face. A rather strained smile, he thought. Weariness, perhaps.

'Here you are.' She set the glass down beside his plate and settled herself in her chair. She lifted her glass. 'Thank you for your generous welcome and your timely rescue.'

Thank God she'd decided to accept his hospitality instead of fighting him. 'To the loveliest woman of my acquaintance,' he said, raising his glass.

'Very gallant.' She sipped her wine. 'Let us see what culinary delights they have brought us.'

She lifted the cover. A fricasseed breast of chicken, covered in mushroom sauce, filled the room with a delicious aroma.

Charlie took a deep swallow of his wine and set his glass down. He was hungrier than he'd thought. He lifted the cover from his plate and let her help him to some buttered parsnips.

Merry tucked into her food. 'Delicious.'

Charlie tasted from his own plate. The meat was so tender he had no trouble cutting it with his fork. 'You are right. It is excellent, even if there is no red meat.'

'You have a talented chef to prepare this at a moment's notice.'

'Poor fellow, he nearly goes mad stuck here all the time with no one to cook for, except for our annual visit.'

'Why does he stay?'

'Because the duke makes it worth his while.'

'Brass greases the wheels,' she said. She picked up her glass. 'Here's to lots of brass.'

He grinned. 'I love your bluntness, Merry. I really do.' He picked up his glass and tossed back the remainder.

He leaned back to watch her eat, his appetite having already been assuaged. His appetite for food, that was. He also wanted her in his bed.

The question was, having let his fury have free rein, would she now turn him down? Sometimes she made him so angry he spoke and acted without thought. Rashly. A battle it seemed he fought and lost over and over.

He watched her devour her food, her white teeth biting into a morsel of chicken, her throat moving when she swallowed. The red wine staining her lips.

She tilted her head to look at him.

His eyelids drooped. He blinked and forced them open.

'You look sleepy,' she said.

Hell, he didn't feel tired, he felt as if his head was stuffed with wool. A thought pierced the fog slowly building in his mind, a not unfamiliar sensation. He turned his head to look at the wine decanter...and the bottle of laudanum left beside it by the doctor.

'Damn it, Merry,' he said, his tongue thick, 'what did you do?'

'I gave you your medicine,' she said, her voice sounding distant and foggy. Then she was beside him, looming over him, helping him to his feet. 'Time you retired, my lord.'

He staggered to his feet. 'You idiot. You don't know what you've done.'

She put an arm around his waist and helped him to the bed. 'Doctor's orders,' she said. 'That's all.'

He measured his length on the bed. Fought to keep his eyes open, not to descend into the dark wavering at the edge of his vision. He felt the covers slide over his body. He grabbed for her wrist, caught it and held it fast. 'Two things, Merry.'

Her eyes looked huge. She nodded.

'Promise you won't leave in the middle of the night.'

She tugged uselessly at her hand. He gripped it tighter and saw a grimace of pain. She nodded, her lips thin. Angry again. He wanted to laugh.

'I'll take the nod as a yes,' he whispered. 'And hold you to it. Second, light all the bloody candles.'

He couldn't hold on to her any longer. The darkness was winning. His hand went lax. Even as he fell into unwelcome sleep, he heard her move away from the bed.

Blast. He'd trusted her again and once more she'd tricked him.

'Thirsty.'

The voice from the bed sounded hoarse and dry. Merry rose, her back twingeing with the ache of unaccustomed discomfort. A carriage ride and now hours in a chair. She poured a glass of water and went to the bed.

'I can't breathe.' He panted for air and threw the covers back. 'God, it's dark.'

She tried to hold the glass to his lips, but he turned his head away. 'My name is Major Robert Mountford.'

'Charlie,' she said, a trickle of fear running through her stomach.

'Hide. I'll cover us.' He grunted, his head rolling. 'Dear God, the stink.'

His free arm flailed, then he lay still.

A dream. It had to be a dream. Should she ring the bell for help? Try to wake him up? Perhaps the fever was worse. She put a palm to his forehead.

Hot, but not dreadfully so.

He flinched away. 'Lay still. Got to keep still. Will? Talk to me.' He sounded panicked.

'I'm here,' she said.

He quieted. He must have fallen back to sleep.

He stiffened. 'I hear them. They're coming. Why do they come?' He stopped breathing. Terrified, she grasped his arm to feel for a pulse. His limb felt as stiff as a board.

'No. No. Oh God, Will. I'm sorry.'

'Charlie,' she whispered. 'What is the matter?'

'They've gone.' He let go a long breath. 'Will, are you still there?'

'Yes,' she whispered, not sure if it was the right thing to say or not.

'Thrice cursed rain. It has to get light soon. If only I could see.' His chuckle was a horrible gasping sound. 'Can't move. My chest hurts. I'm cold.' He shivered. 'So damnably dark… They are out there. Hear them?'

She couldn't stand it any longer. She shook him hard. 'Charlie, wake up. It is me, Merry.'

'My name is Major Robert Deveril Mountford.'

'Your name is Charles. You are at Durn Castle in Yorkshire.'

His eyes snapped open. He sat bolt upright and put his hand around her throat. 'I will not let you finish me off.'

'Charlie,' she gasped through a throat being squeezed.

His eyes focused.

He let her go and stared at her. He looked around, then back at her face. 'Merry?'

'Yes,' she said, rubbing at her neck.

He glanced around; he was shivering and pale. He clenched his jaw, visibly pulling himself together. 'Did I hurt you?'

'No. I startled you awake. I think you thought I was attacking you.'

He inhaled a deep shuddering breath. 'I remember,' he said. His dark eyes held accusation. 'Laudanum brings bad dreams.'

'I'm sorry. I didn't know.'

He inhaled a deep breath and looked around. 'You couldn't know. Thank you for lighting the candles.'

She nodded. 'What happened to you?'

He stiffened. 'I don't know what you mean?'

'Whatever you were seeing in your sleep has to be real.'

He looked at her for a long moment, then he smiled. 'I thought you'd be on your way back to Draycott House.' He held out his hand and she took it. He tugged her until she fell across the bed.

'Your arm,' she exclaimed. 'Be careful.'

He tipped her chin and briefly brushed her lips with his mouth. 'I know what will make me feel a whole lot better.'

She stared up at him and saw desire in his eyes, but his face was still pale and drawn.

'Not before your arm is healed,' she said.

'But you will stay until then?'

'Yes, I will stay until then.'

He closed his eyes. 'Lie down next to me, Merry, and I am sure I will sleep just fine. I won't be worrying about where you are.'

She settled beside him and he immediately relaxed. Did he think she believed she was the cause of his dream? He probably didn't realise what he had said. Why had he called himself Robert? And what had he feared in the dark?

Blast him, he'd put paid to her questions by falling asleep. She peered into his face. Still flushed, but peaceful. Having given her word, she was trapped. And heaven's above, she was dreadfully tired.

The moment he knew she was sleeping, Charlie slipped out of bed. What the hell had he said? Damned laudanum. They'd given it to him in the army hospital. When he woke all he could remember was the terrible feeling of suffocation, a kind of heart-pounding panic with the stink of human filth and blood fouling his nostrils.

He slipped off the sling, poured water from the ewer into the bowl and washed his hands and face, inhaling the clean scent of soap. His breathing steadied, his head cleared.

Interfering bloody woman. He should have guessed she'd take it upon herself to follow the doctor's orders. He should think himself lucky she hadn't tried to bleed him, too.

Moving quietly, he left the chamber and wandered past her room. He lifted the tapestry and tried the door. Locked.

Logan never let the family down, no matter how much he disapproved.

Beyond the window, the sky showed no sign of dawn, but he'd sleep no more tonight. He went back to his room and settled into the armchair. In the bed, her head pillowed on her hand, her breathing deep and even, Merry looked young and vulnerable. The urge to kiss her awake almost brought him to his feet. He wanted to taste her lips, feel life against his body and lose the presence of death. Lose the horror of his dark dreams within her arms. It wasn't possible, because they weren't dreams—they were memories.

He forced himself to remain where he was. It wouldn't be fair to wake her after such a gruelling day. Only a man lacking control would let such base urges get the better of him. Watching her was all the pleasure he needed tonight.

Would asking her to be his mistress really be the answer to bringing her to heel? Or was reason driven by lust? Whatever it was, he had to find a way to ensure her safety. Tomorrow. He'd deal with it tomorrow.

And with her lovely form tempting him, morning could not come soon enough.

Charlie tossed his reins to the waiting groom in the stable courtyard and strode for the house. His breath hung before his face in a cloud. His cheeks tingled. A ride in the fresh air, despite grey skies, had cleared his head.

The fever of last night had passed. He'd even managed to sleep in the chair until daylight awoke him and he'd carried Merry back to her bed. She'd felt good in his arms. Right. The compulsion to keep her safe as rampant as his desire, which was why he'd gone out riding. To rid himself of lust.

With the light of day, some semblance of rational thought had resurfaced; given his purpose for coming to Yorkshire, the attraction he felt for Merry must be excised.

While it would be impossible to woo Lady Allison with Merry under his roof, the less cause for gossip, the better. If one word of this reached his father, Robert would never be allowed home.

His brother's last piece of advice about having fun was the stupidest thing he'd ever said, because when Charlie had fun everything went to hell.

The sooner he found out who Merry's attackers were, the sooner he could send her home. He entered the house through the side door. The footman stood to attention.

'Miss Draycott up, yet?'

'In the breakfast room, my lord.'

The thought of Merry eating brought a smile to his lips. He strode along the corridor and met Logan coming the other way.

'My lord?' Logan said, holding out a note. 'A letter arrived from the duke, marked urgent.'

Damn. He might have known he couldn't be away for more than a few days before his father would start checking up on him. No matter how hard he worked or what he did, Father no longer trusted him.

He broke the seal.

His heart sunk as he read the cryptic message in his father's scrawl. *Robert is in London. Return by Saturday.*

'Bad news, my lord?'

'I'm not sure.' He couldn't prevent a grin of relief that Robert was found, even as he realised what the request meant. The duke would expect Charlie to make good on his promise right away.

And the urgent nature of the message meant Robert must be in trouble. Again.

Damn it all. Why now? Right at this moment, after all his months of searching?

Hades, Saturday was three days' hence. He'd have to leave right away. What the hell would he do about Merry in the meantime?

There really was only one choice. And she wasn't going to like it. He opened the breakfast-room door.

A frown creased Merry's brow when she looked up and saw him. 'Thomas is ill,' she said. 'Caro thinks it might be scarlet fever.' Her voice hitched on the last words.

'Send for Dr Wells.'

'Do you mind? I will pay his bills, of course, but I could not bear for anything to happen to the child.'

Charlie went to the sideboard and filled his plate with eggs and ham and a thick slice of bacon. 'I, too, have news.'

He sat down. Merry eyed his plate askance and returned to spreading marmalade on her single piece of toast.

He frowned. 'You should eat more than that.'

She gave him a wan smile. 'I'm too worried about Thomas.'

'The boy will be fine,' Charlie said. 'I am sure it is no more than a touch of ague after the long journey. Children come down with them all the time.' He hesitated. 'It would, however, be best if you didn't take him on another journey while he is unwell.'

'Do you think so?' She clung to his words as if they were a life line.

This might work in his favour. 'Positive, he said. 'It happened with my younger brothers and sisters all the time.'

Her tension eased and he felt unaccountably glad he had set her mind at rest.

'What is your news?' she asked.

He glanced down at the letter beside his plate. 'Urgent family business. I am needed in Town.'

'Oh.'

He saw the idea in her head the moment the expression crossed her face. She'd decided to leave.

'You cannot go back to Draycott House.' He spoke more sternly than he intended and she bridled.

'Damn it, Merry, all I am thinking about is your safety, but this urgent business calls me away. You will stay until I return.'

'Will I? Sir, you go too far. I choose where and when I go.'

He wanted to hit something. He kept the frustration out of his face, curled his lip a little. 'Think of the child.'

Her shoulders slumped. He held back a triumphant smile.

She stared at her toast and then glanced up at him. 'How long will you be gone?'

'Six days at the most.'

She stared at him. 'You will scarcely have time to get there and back.'

'My business will not take long. My curricle is built for racing and there are fresh horses in the stable. I've done it in less.'

'Not in the middle of winter.'

'All right, give me two weeks.'

She rose and went to look out of the window. 'Two weeks is a long time to be away from Draycott's. No one knows where I am, except Gribble, and we swore him to silence.'

'Write to your manager.'

'What am I supposed to do here for two weeks? I hate being idle.'

'Ride. Read. Help Mrs Falkner with Thomas. Continue teaching your young…er…lady to read. There are all kinds of things to be done, but promise me one thing?'

She swung around, a refusal on her lips and in her flashing eyes.

He grinned. 'Promise me you won't play billiards until I return.'

Shaking her head, she laughed. A smile stayed on her lovely mouth as she gazed at him. 'My mill needs me.'

If only he could make her want to stay. Perhaps there was one thing that would keep her here. The only kind of promise he could make.

He got to his feet, came to stand next to her. Her perfume rose around him. He dropped a kiss on the place where her pale shoulder met the elegant column of her neck. He put his hands on her waist, lowered his voice. 'I want you here when I get back.'

Desire darkened the clear blue of her eyes to misty dusk. Her eyes closed for a moment, her long black lashes hiding her thoughts.

Deliberately cutting him off. She took a shaky breath. 'Don't do this.'

He tipped her chin, searching her beautiful face for some sign she would yield. And deep in her gaze he saw secrets. Painful secrets. He didn't have time to find out what they were and reach London in time. But he needed her to stay.

'Merry, I beg you, please do not venture off the property while I am away. Before I leave I will speak to my steward. He will undertake some investigations on your behalf. We will find out what is going on when I get back. I promise.' He put every ounce of persuasion he had in his voice.

It wasn't enough. He could see it in her stiff shoulders and her restless hands.

'It is so very awkward for me to remain here under your roof in your absence. No matter how powerful your father, you will not stop the gossip.'

Was this the true reason behind her reluctance? 'I thought you cared naught for gossip.'

She stepped away and waved an airy hand. 'I don't care for myself,' she said. ''Tis your reputation, my lord.'

He looked at her grimly. 'No one will censure me. You are grasping at straws.'

She flushed.

Charlie pulled her close and smiled down into her face, willing her to listen, to hear him. 'Wait for me.' He kissed her lips, then took her mouth and kissed her hard.

The kiss deepened to something far more sensual, an erotic tangling of tongues and breath, the feel of her soft curves against him, her encouraging moans. A kind of desperation overtook him, the need to keep her safe, to know she would be here waiting when he returned.

He pressed one thigh between her legs and heard her intake of breath, a hiss of pleasure that heightened his arousal. He pressed her back against the wall, cradling her face in his hand, pressing against her, until she cried out with longing.

He wanted her in the most primal way. To possess her, to bend her to his will. Roughly he lifted her skirts, slid his hand up the satiny flesh of her inner thigh and found the warmth and dampness of her centre. Lust. She wanted him as much as he desired her.

He stroked her soft feminine flesh, felt her tremble and pant, her desire flaming instantly to his touch.

She arched her neck, her head falling back. He kissed the hollow of her throat, licking and nipping his way to the rise of her breast. He cupped her buttocks, lifting her, pressing her against his erection. He growled low in his throat at the torment.

Her eyes flew open. 'Charlie, your wound.'

'My shoulder is not what aches.'

'What if someone comes in?'

'I'll murder them.'

Her laugh was low and husky. It thrummed a response low in his belly.

He lifted her, supporting her back against the wall, one hand beneath her luscious bottom. She brought her legs around his hips, clinging tight to his shoulder, nuzzling and licking at his ear, nipping the lobe until he thought he might lose his mind.

Fingers tearing at the buttons, he unfastened his falls and guided his shaft into her heated depths.

With a sigh she sank down on to him.

Hot and tight, she enveloped his engorged flesh. He drove into her, hard, again and again, hearing her muffled cries of pleasure against his neck, her fingers digging into his shoulders as he pounded her against the wall.

She was his woman. She might deny it, and resist his will, flaunt her independence, but in this he was her master.

Her fingers ran through his hair, tugging with painful intensity. She flattened her palms against his jaw, lifting his face, and she took his mouth, delving her tongue, tasting him, as if she, too, wanted to stake a claim. Slowly she withdrew her tongue, and when he followed her retreat, probing the hot sweet depths of her mouth, she sucked.

The sensation drove him to the brink. He would not go over without her.

Desperate, he sought her centre with his hand, teased her with his thumb, felt her shiver and tremble and he drove home one last time.

Not her master. She was his equal. The climax rode him hard and as she fell apart, against everything he wanted, he jerked from her body and finished within the tails of his shirt.

Shuddering and gasping, they leaned against the wall, forehead to forehead, her legs lax around his waist. 'You will wait for me,' he ground out.

She nodded.

Slowly, he lowered her to the ground.

She leaned back against the wall, her eyes closed, her lovely mouth rosy from kisses, her delicate cheeks reddened by his stubble.

'Oh, my,' she said. 'I'm going to miss these encounters of ours.' She laughed. But there was heartache in the sound. It touched a soft place in his chest, a tender place that had no place in his life.

'Only two weeks,' he whispered and pressed a kiss to her chin.

He fastened his falls and led her to the nearest chair, pulling her down to sit on his lap. She snuggled down to rest her head on his shoulder. They sat quietly, their breathing slowing, the heat of bliss gradually fading.

'Now give me your promise in words,' he said. 'Two weeks is all I ask.' He kissed her temple.

Eyes smoky, the lids half-lowered, she smiled. 'I will be here when you return.'

He trusted her to keep her word. 'I will return sooner if I can.' Slowly, he lifted her to her feet and rose beside her. He kissed her deeply, savoured her soft pliant body against his. He broke the kiss and left the room, before he lost the strength to leave her at all.

* * *

The journey to London had been hell. Merry had been right about travelling at this time of year and Charlie had pushed the horses far too hard, changing them at every posting house and travelling without stopping. He'd made it as far as Hampstead, then one of his hacks threw a shoe and left him walking two miles to the nearest tavern.

But he'd done the journey in two days. Only to arrive at Mountford House and be met with the news that the family was at church… for his brother's wedding. Not only was Robert found, but he was getting married. Today.

He still hadn't absorbed the news.

He scrubbed at a chin covered in two days' growth of beard. His Grace would not be pleased to see his heir looking so disreputable, but what couldn't be cured, must be endured.

The hackney carriage drew up a short distance from St George's, Hanover Square.

'Can't get no closer than this, gov,' the hackney driver called out. 'Some nob getting married. I hear he's caught himself an heiress.'

Charlie's heart sank. If Robert was getting leg-shackled for money, things must be desperate indeed. He leaped from the hackney and tossed the man his fare. 'I'll walk the rest of the way.'

An odd feeling emptied his chest as he strode through the throng of people on the footpath. Robert home and getting married after years of no word—how could that be?

If Charlie had stood up against his father, Robert would never be in this fix. Perhaps he could stop it.

He broke into a run past the carriages lined up and well-dressed folk mingling with London's riff-raff, all hoping for a glimpse of the couple.

Charlie pushed through them and received some dirty looks. He paused at the bottom of the church steps as the bells began pealing. A joyful sound. He was too late.

The doors swung open. The people around him pressed forwards. A man and his bride walked out into the chilly London air.

Robert. He looked well, if a little weathered. Indeed, he looked as dark as a gypsy, as if he'd spent a great deal of the past three years out of doors.

Charlie had feared seeing his brother starving and gaunt. Instead he looked…happy, even overjoyed, as he gazed into the eyes of the bride at his side.

Standing on the bottom step, Charlie drank his brother's happiness in with a sense of utter relief. The tiny fragile-looking thing beside his tall athletic brother had stars in her eyes and a big smile on her pixie face, while his brother looked positively besotted. Nothing like the jaded rake he'd been the last time Charlie saw him.

The last time they'd met, Charlie had let his brother down. He'd supported Father against his twin, when they'd always stood shoulder to shoulder. At the time he'd thought he was doing the right thing for his brother. Robert's shock, his sense of betrayal, had shown in his eyes. That look had haunted Charlie all these long years.

Perhaps Robert still held a grudge. Perhaps he wouldn't care to see him at all. It would explain the lack of any word. He drew back, unsure.

As if sensing Charlie's presence, Robert's gaze searched the crowd. The moment their eyes met he grinned and waved.

The welcome in his smile swelled Charlie's heart to breaking. He tore up the steps and dragged his brother into an embrace.

The next few moments were chaos. Father taking him to task for being late. His mother hushing Father. An incomprehensible conversation about Zeus with the bride and not a moment for questions.

Somehow, Robert had found the path to happiness. He could see it in his brother's face, but when Charlie tried to seek answers, his brother had sloughed him off.

Apparently a ship to Italy awaited the bride and groom.

Stunned, Charlie stood with his mother, father and siblings and waved as the happy couple departed.

When the carriage disappeared around the corner, the governess gathered her charges and walked them to one of the several waiting carriages.

Father and Mother remained, receiving the well wishes of members of the *ton* who had crowded into the church. Charlie ranged alongside them, shaking hands and muttering appropriate words of thanks.

Finally it was over. Father frowned. 'Glad to see one of my sons still knows what is owing to the Mountford name,' he muttered.

The heavy weight of responsibility strangely missing these past few days descended squarely on Charlie's shoulders. The burden felt heavier than ever before.

'Stantford,' Mother said in warning accents, 'she is a lovely young woman. They will do very nicely together.'

'Who is she?' Charlie asked in awe of any woman who could capture his younger brother's wandering eye and make him look so bloody happy.

'Abernathy's by-blow,' Father said gloomily.

'Oh, really, Alfred,' Mother huffed. 'You promised you would say nothing more. She is Endersley's legitimate daughter. Lord Wynchwood's niece. And an accomplished artist.'

Father snorted.

Charlie wanted to laugh. Of course Robert wouldn't marry a suitable gel. He'd marry where he pleased. And be happy. 'Good for him,' he said, smiling at his mother.

He hadn't seen her looking this happy since Robert had disappeared. The worry had gone from her eyes. She was even standing up to Father.

'How is Lady Allison?' Father asked.

His heart grew cold.

As he'd promised, Father had taken Robert back into the family. Now he wanted his pound of flesh. A trickle of envy ran like acid in

Charlie's veins. No choice for him. No odd little artist or outspoken industrialist's daughter. He had a position to uphold. He'd accepted it on his return from the war, embraced it as a way to make amends. After all, he had no right to expect happiness when he'd destroyed so many good lives. If doing his duty gave him pain, so much the better. It was well deserved. But now, right at this moment, the yoke of responsibility irked.

'I did not yet see Lady Allison,' he replied. 'I barely reached Durn when you called me home.'

Father frowned. 'Unlike you to delay.'

Charlie clenched his jaw, holding in the unreasoning surge of anger. 'You are right, Father. That is why I am returning right away.'

'In the morning?' Mother said.

Charlie glanced at his father's deeply lined face, at the weariness in his eyes and the fear his eldest son would fail. 'No, Mother. Today. Now.' He took her hand and kissed it. 'I'm sorry to rush off, but duty calls.'

She shook her head. 'Life is more than duty, Charles.'

Not for him. He'd seen the results of straying from responsibility when he joined the army against his father's wishes. He gave her a reassuring smile. 'I'll return to town as soon as I can.'

Her eyes misted. 'You brother looked so very happy.'

He had. And Charlie had to be happy he'd been able to heal the breach between his father and his brother, even if neither of them seemed to give a damn one way or the other. Charlie could take comfort in seeing his mother's smile. 'Yes. He did. I'm glad I got back in time.'

Mother's eyes misted. 'I want that for all my children.'

There was happiness, or at least satisfaction, in doing one's duty. There had to be.

His father gave an impatient sigh. 'Tonbridge,' he said, with brows drawn low. 'I'm looking forward to seeing you standing in this church very soon. Hopefully, at least one of my sons knows what is due to the name of Mountford.'

He forced a smile. 'I know where my duty lies, Your Grace.'

'Next time dress in appropriate attire.'

Charlie inclined his head. 'My apologies, Your Grace. It was either change or see Robert and his new wife.'

'Hmmph,' Father said.

'Really, Alfred,' Mother said.

Charlie bowed to his parents, the weight on his shoulders more unbearable than it had ever been, and left for Durn.

Chapter Fourteen

Charlie handed his hat to his butler and shrugged out of his coat. If anything, Logan looked more prune-faced than usual. 'Miss Draycott about, Logan?'

The butler's thin lips pursed. 'In the long gallery, my lord. With that other female and the child. If I may say, my lord, this is not what I expected when I joined the household of one of the first families in England.'

'You may not say,' Charlie said, putting all the chill of a displeased cavalry officer in his voice.

Logan shrivelled a bit, but the resentment in his eyes showed he wasn't completely cowed. Damn it, what were Merry and her ladies up to that they had upset Durn's staff? What was it about the woman that continued to turn all about her upside down?

He took the stairs to the first floor two at a time and made his way through the maze of corridors to the back of the house. The long gallery displayed the pride of generations of Mountfords. Portraits, royal warrants, the odd suit of armour.

As he drew closer squeals of delight echoed along the hallway. The high-pitched voice of a child and women's laughter.

What was she up to?

The cheerful sound brought an unwilling smile to his lips. He approached the wide corridor running the length of the back of the house on silent feet, determined to catch her and her accomplices in the act.

Remaining in the shadows, he glanced along the gallery. Light from the bank of windows flooded the Gothic-style room, which was lined with heavy oak panels and covered in portraits and coats of arms. He'd never before seen all the shutters flung back to let in the daylight, not even the muted daylight of a grey winter afternoon. Bad for the artwork.

Two suits of armour had been moved from their corners to stand at the midway point of the room; a length of line attached one neck to the other. But that wasn't what had his gaze wide-eyed. It was Merry, her skirts looped under a ribbon at her waist, so she showed an extraordinary amount of ankle, calf and knee, with a battledore in her hand, diving for a shuttlecock bashed with great vigour by Beth.

Somehow she managed to hit it back. Beth collapsed laughing as the feathery object fell on the floor at her feet.

'Ten times,' cried little Thomas on the sidelines. 'Now it is my turn.'

Good Lord, he'd forgotten all about those old racquets. He and Robert used to play outside in the summer. Using the long gallery on a winter's day would never have been approved.

This would be how it would be with Merry. Fun. Surprising. Spur of the moment. When she wasn't working, of course. She seemed to have achieved a balance in her life. Duty and pleasure.

Why did he find it so difficult?

Her face was flushed and alive with joy as she tossed her hair back and handed over her bat to the small boy. She looked more beautiful than he remembered.

Frowning, he sauntered towards the players.

Beth shot to her feet with a scared look. Merry turned and her expression of dismay made him cringe inside. With fumbling fingers she untied the ribbon at her waist and, disappointingly, her skirts fell to the floor with much brushing and tweaking from their owner.

'Lord Tonbridge,' she said, sounding breathless. 'We didn't expect you back so soon.'

'Clearly.' He raised a brow and glanced at the wooden-and-vellum bat in Tommy's hand.

'Oh, er…I hope you don't mind,' she said. 'Tommy was restless. Caro has come down with the ague, but he is so much better.' She pointed at the battledore. 'I found these in the schoolroom. I made the shuttlecocks from corks and pens from the library.'

No wonder they flew so badly. Beth and Tommy were looking at him as if he was an ogre. He couldn't hold his serious face any longer.

He chuckled, then he laughed out loud. 'If you could have seen yourself just now. I thought you were going to break your neck trying for that shot.'

Merry grinned back. 'I used to be champion at this game as a girl, I'll have you know.'

'I bet you were.'

He ran a finger along the string. 'Interesting innovation.'

She chuckled. 'Tommy kept running into us. We put that there to keep him back at bit.'

'Does the shuttlecock have to go over it or under it?' he asked.

'It doesn't matter,' the boy said. 'Just so long as you stay on your side.'

'Can I have a turn?' Charlie asked.

'Of course,' Merry said.

'You can have my turn,' Beth said, bobbing an awkward curtsy. 'I really ought to see how Mrs Falkner does.' She handed her battledore to Charlie and scurried away.

Tommy pouted. 'He's too big.'

'All right,' Charlie said. 'You play with Miss Draycott, and I will keep count.' He lowered himself to the floor and rested his back against a priceless tapestry. 'Off you go.' He gave Merry a saucy look. 'Feel free to adopt your new style of clothing, Miss Draycott, if it makes it easier to play.'

'Rogue,' she said.

Sadly, she didn't. But from this angle Charlie had plenty of glimpses of her shapely ankle to keep him happy, as well as the view of her lovely bosom bouncing beneath her gown. Her ready smiles and laughter were even better.

It was like watching poetry. It brought back the flashes of happiness he'd had before Waterloo. He sat on the floor and smiled until his cheeks ached.

He counted out each hit and was delighted to see how carefully Merry knocked the flighted shuttlecock back to Tommy so he could hit it. The boy was wild in his returns, but Merry was agile and light on her feet.

Finally, after twelve hits back and forth, Tommy let the bird drop to the floor.

'Oh, well done, sir,' Merry cried. 'That is the longest number of hits we've had all afternoon.'

The little boy instantly cheered. He grinned.

Merry dabbed at her face with her handkerchief. 'My word, I am hot. I think we will call it a day.'

'What?' Charlie said, leaping to his feet. 'Just because it is my turn? You fear I will best you.'

Tommy giggled at his expression of outrage.

Merry laughed. 'You take unfair advantage, sir. I have been playing for almost an hour.'

'And I have been driving neck or nothing for several.'

She made a mock curtsy of defeat. 'Count for us, will you, Tommy?'

The boy took up Charlie's position on the floor.

Charlie released the string around the neck of one of the suits of armour. 'If I remember correctly, there is a lot of dashing about in this game. I don't want to knock these fellows over. Logan will have my hide.'

Merry covered her mouth with her hand. Her eyes twinkled above her fingers. 'I'm sorry. I should not have moved them.'

'He's cross with us,' Tommy said.

'He's always cross with me, too,' Charlie replied. 'I shall pay it no mind. Please serve, Miss Draycott.'

He loved the way her cheeks flushed red, and the frown on her brow above her sparkling blue eyes as she determinedly returned each of his shots. She was good at this game, as she was good at so many things, and she kept trying to catch him off guard, sending her shots in unexpected directions. It wasn't so much about how high the count went, but about who would miss the first shot.

Tommy's voice rose in pitch as they exceeded twelve and headed for twenty.

But Merry was tiring, he could see her energy flag and he was about to miss her next shot out of sheer kindness, if he could do it without making it obvious, when she tripped on the carpet.

She went flying at the suit of armour in front of the fireplace.

He dove to catch her, somehow managing to pull her clear of the hearth and land beneath her. A very sharp elbow jabbed him in the ribs as he hit the floor. Winded, he lay gasping beneath her. Laughing so hard, he couldn't stop.

'It's not funny, ye great lummox,' Merry said. 'You made me miss my shot.'

Tommy dashed over, his face terrified.

'I made you miss it?' Charlie said. 'I thought you had abandoned the game in favour of a waltz with Lord Stanley there.' He tickled her beneath the ribs.

'Oh, stop.' She dissolved into helpless giggles and Tommy joined the heap on the carpet, his little fingers more like claws as he tried to tickle them both.

Charlie gathered them up, one under each arm and staggered to his feet. 'That's it, you two. You are going in the duck pond for insulting the heir.' He whirled them around, aware of a twinge in his arm, but not giving a damn for the sheer joy of the moment.

Merry, the little wretch, blew in his ear, bringing him up short.

'Enough,' she commanded. 'Enough, both of you. Put me down,

my lord. It is time I retired from the lists to change my gown and tidy myself.'

Charlie grinned down into her face. The pull of desire left him hard and wanting. Not at all suitable in front of a child. He put them both down.

'Run along and see your mama,' Merry said. She smiled at Charlie and there was tenderness in her gaze. 'Thank you for playing with him. He lacks for male company.'

She looked lovely. Beautiful. All flushed and happy. And beyond his reach.

He bowed. 'Thank you for the game. When you have freshened up, I would like to talk to you, if I may.'

Her face sobered. 'Did your steward find out any information? I have tried to speak to him once or twice, but he has been too busy to see me.'

'I called in on him on the way home. He found no news of the men who shot at us. Nor anything about Mrs Falkner before she arrived at the inn where you met.'

She gasped. 'I did not ask you to poke around in Caro's life.'

'She is hiding something, Merry. Who is she?'

'My true friend. And that is all you need to know.'

Until someone proved her wrong. Frustrated, but admiring of her loyalty, he bit down on the words. 'Very well. But we do need to plan our next course of action.'

'I'll change and join you in the drawing room in half an hour.'

Heavy hearted from what he knew he had to say, he watched her walk away and pulled himself back to business. He also needed to freshen up after his journey, but he'd use one of the guest rooms. Their affair had to end and he'd decided he would hire someone to guard her at Draycott House while they continued searching for the attackers.

He didn't have an alternative. Her staying at Durn made it impossible for him to follow through on his promise to Father. Her

Purtefoy connection added yet another dimension to the complications. Agreeing to her plan had been a mistake of epic proportions, for them both.

Merry started down the stairs for her meeting with Charlie. She was still smiling after their game. She'd never seen him so unreservedly happy. But the joy had faded as swiftly as daylight left the evening sky. Something was troubling him.

'Psst,' a voice said, bringing her head around to the source of the noise. Beth.

She retraced her steps to where Beth hovered in the doorway to the other wing.

'Did you need me?' Merry asked.

Beth glanced at a stolid footman. 'I wants to speak to you in private. I was going to do it afore, but his lordship came along.'

Her heart gave an uncomfortable thump. 'Is Mrs Falkner worse?'

'No, miss.' She winced and again glanced at the footman who was looking down his nose.

Merry gave him a haughty glare. 'Would you mind stepping further down the hallway? Out of earshot.' She spoke with calm authority. The man's ears reddened and he strode away, all offended dignity.

'What is it, Beth?'

'I made friends with one of the kitchenmaids.' She grinned. 'Never know when an extra bit of food might come in handy. She snuck out to see her man last night. This mornin' she said there's a woman staying at the inn asking about visitors here at Durn.'

'What sort of woman?'

'I thinks it's Jane. I was wondering if she wants to come back, like. Changed her mind and followed us here. She weren't very keen on t'house when we was there, but mayhap she's thought better on't.'

'How did she know to look for us here?'

'We all saw how it was between you and his lordship. April and May, she said. Seemed a bit put out by it. But she must 'ave guessed he'd bring you here.'

Hardly April and May, but the attraction must have been more obvious than Merry thought. She frowned. How could a woman like Jane afford a room at the inn? Unless she'd returned to her old work. One of Caro's rules had been no more male customers.

Beth was watching her eagerly. 'Shall you tell them to let her in?'

'I can't override his lordship's orders,' Merry said, suddenly glad for Charlie's autocratic edict. Every instinct told her not to trust Jane, but Caro had always accused her of prejudice and Merry, unable to deny it was something about Jane's hardness that troubled her, had pushed the feelings aside. 'But I will see what can be done when I talk to his lordship in a few minutes. I will let you know what he says.'

Beth shifted her feet. 'You won't tell him about the maid?'

Heaven help her. 'No, Beth. I won't give your friend away.'

Beth bobbed a curtsy and ran back down the hallway. Merry continued down the stairs.

Charlie was waiting for her in the drawing room. Oddly, Logan followed her in, though she had not heard him behind her. He'd been following her around quite a bit. Her and Beth. Making sure they didn't run off with any valuables, no doubt.

Charlie glared at him. 'What is it, Logan?'

'My lord, I'm sorry, but a party of visitors have been admitted through the front gate. The lad ran all the way here to let us know, but they are not far behind.'

Charlie's face darkened to thunderous. 'I instructed no one was to be admitted.'

Merry froze. 'I had better return to my room.' She hurried out into the hallway and headed for the stairs. Charlie followed her out. 'Logan, hold them off until Miss Draycott is upstairs.'

Before Logan could move, the door swung open.

'Honor Draycott,' a shocked voice said. 'Is that really you?'

Merry swung around and stared at the fair-haired young man and fashionably attired lady in the opening.

The Purtefoy siblings. Digby and Allison: blond, blue-eyed, beautiful and aristocratic. They looked horrified.

They stepped into the entrance hall.

'Tonbridge,' Digby said, removing his hat. 'I knew it was you who passed us in the village. The stupid fool at the gate tried to tell us you were absent.'

'My lord,' Allison said, stepping into the vestibule and making an elegant curtsy. 'And my cousin. How delightfully unexpected.' Her smile was sweet. Her eyes glittered like glass. Lady Allison was furious.

Merry couldn't move. She couldn't speak. Her throat simply didn't have enough moisture to utter a word. She looked helplessly at Charlie, who seemed equally shocked.

She swallowed hard. 'Good morning, Digby. Allison.'

Allison raised a brow. 'I hardly know what to say. Although, perhaps we shouldn't be surprised, should we, Digby? We do sometimes hear of your exploits.'

Merry felt herself flush at the poison-laced words. She drew herself up to her full height. 'You should not believe all you hear.'

'I should hope not,' Allison said, batting her eyelashes at Charlie. Her heart-shaped face looked particularly pretty beneath the brim of a green velvet bonnet with its dashing ostrich feather dyed to match.

'When we saw your curricle haring through the village, Tonbridge, we came to make sure you hadn't forgotten our invitation,' Digby said. He glanced at Merry and winced. 'If you are free, that is?'

In other words, Merry wasn't invited. Good thing, too. There was no way she would ever enter her cousins' house. Not for a thousand pounds, or if she was starving in the street.

A faint look of embarrassment crossed Charlie's face and then his jaw hardened as if he'd come to an unpleasant decision. He faced his visitors and squared his shoulders.

'We weren't expecting callers this morning,' he said, rather pointedly, Merry thought with a flash of glee. 'However, since you are here, and are now practically family, you might as well be the first to hear the news.' He gestured to Merry, calling her back to his side. 'Miss Draycott has done me the great honour of accepting my offer of marriage.'

Allison gasped. Digby's jaw dropped.

As did Merry's. Her heart stumbled strangely. Her head felt oddly light. Trembles shook every bone in her body, fear and hope mingling. Hesitantly she walked back down the stairs to stand beside him. He pulled her close and gave her hand a squeeze. His smile, when he looked at her, didn't reflect in his eyes.

A blade twisted in her chest. He was keeping to his side of their bargain. Nothing more. And she should be grateful, not feeling hurt.

Lord Digby recovered first. 'Congratulations, old man. Father will be pleased. Finally, he'll be able to boast a duke in the family.'

A flush appeared on Allison's cheeks. Of course. She'd hoped to be the one to catch the ducal heir. That was why they'd hurried over here at the news of Charlie's arrival.

Merry found herself smiling. 'By gum, Purtefoys is going up in t'world.'

Allison narrowed her gaze on the hand tucked beneath Charlie's arm. No ring. Not that there need be one, but it was unusual for a family like the Mountfords not to provide the heir's future bride with a promise ring. 'A sudden decision, I assume,' she said with a sneer.

Charlie must also have seen her gaze, because he covered Merry's hand with his. 'I am the luckiest man alive.'

'When is the wedding?' Digby asked, still having trouble controlling his jaw.

'We haven't yet set a date,' Merry said, before Charlie made up another monumental lie that would have to be explained away.

'The sooner the better,' he said, giving her a wolfish grin that made her heart lurch and her insides clench. So inappropriate.

More heat scalded her face. She tried to tug her hand free, but found it held fast.

Allison's head tilted to one side. 'Did you two lovebirds travel here alone?' A wealth of suspicion tainted the sugary-sweet voice.

'Certainly not,' Charlie said. He seemed to have recovered his wits very nicely and Merry was quite happy to have him respond to her cousin's barbed words. 'Miss Draycott is accompanied by her companion, Mrs Falkner.'

'Perhaps we should introduce ourselves to the lady,' Lady Allison said with a sweet smile that dripped acid. 'Invite her to our party. You will both come, won't you? It will be a wonderful way to celebrate your approaching nuptials, which seem to have been a well-kept secret until now.'

They were done for. Allison knew they weren't betrothed. The Purtefoys, with their close connections to the duke, would have been the first to know.

Before she could refuse the invitation, Charlie smiled. 'It isn't public knowledge, I'm afraid. We haven't yet spoken to His Grace.'

The look of triumph on Allison's face was a sight to behold. 'Oh, I see.' She surreptitiously nudged Digby in the ribs. 'We really ought to make the acquaintance of your companion before we go.'

'Mrs Falkner is indisposed at the moment,' Merry said. 'The doctor fears scarlet fever.'

Charlie made a sound like choking, then coughed.

'Scarlet fever?' Allison's voice rose. 'Why did you not say so at once? It is very dangerous. Why, my aunt died of it in less than three days.' Allison's pretty face changed to sly. 'How very inconvenient of your chaperon to be ill right at this moment.'

The aunt she spoke of so cavalierly was Merry's mother. Merry wanted to bash her over the head with her green parasol.

The last time she'd done so, she'd been expelled from school. Although it was not the reason given. The hours spent with Jeremy in the garden shed had provided the excuse they needed to make her *persona non grata*, courtesy of Allison. The girl had a knack of making herself look like a saint.

'We do not yet know for sure,' Merry said.

Charlie had a strange look in his eye. 'Perhaps you would like to join us for tea,' he said. 'If Mrs Falkner has a debilitating condition, I am certain we will not be going out in company.'

Digby looked as if he might agree, but Allison grabbed his arm. 'No, no. We wouldn't dream of putting you out with illness in the house. Good day to you both.'

She turned and trotted down the steps. Her brother had little option but to follow. At the bottom, they climbed quickly aboard their brougham.

Like a long-married couple, Charlie and Merry stood on the front steps watching them depart. It seemed odd. And somehow right. And completely impossible.

'It seems we stirred the mud at the bottom of the pond,' Merry said, half-laughing.

The grim expression on Charlie's face said he couldn't agree more, but not in a good way.

She let him escort her to the drawing room without saying a word. What was he fretting about? The betrothal could be dealt with right away. The sooner they ended this terrible farce, the better. Dash it. If Caro hadn't fallen ill, they would have been on their way before the Purtefoys arrived on the doorstep.

She sank on to the sofa and looked up at his distant expression, his tight shoulders. He looked as if he carried the weight of the world. 'How did your family business fare?' she asked in what she hoped were calm accents.

A faint bitter smile curved his lips. 'Everything was fine.'

A lie.

'Right now we have a more pressing problem,' he said.

Their betrothal no doubt. Merry Draycott solved her own problems. 'Simple. One of us will cry off, now, today, and I will return home. It would have been better if you had said nothing at all about our supposed engagement to the Purtefoys just now, but the damage can be soon undone.'

He looked taken aback. 'What other explanation could I have given for your presence in my house?'

'Do you think they didn't draw their own conclusions? And besides, our agreement was for Broadoaks. For the mill owners in Skepton. People who don't move in your circles. Now the news will be all over London. You will be a laughing stock.'

He frowned. 'I hardly think so.' He sat down beside her and took her hand in his. He gazed into her eyes with a smile she could only describe as puzzled. 'The thing is, Merry, I find myself unwilling to let you go without assuring myself of your safety.'

A bubble of something light and warm filled her chest. She felt as if she might float away. And beneath it was an odd sort of longing. The bond between them seemed stronger than ever, despite his absence. No doubt about it, she'd missed him dreadfully.

He dipped his head for a kiss. She fought the insidious longing in her body. Fought the desire to melt into him, to surrender to the drug of his kiss. Fought the lonely ache in her heart. Her hand pressed against his chest to push him away; instead, it crept up around his neck and she kissed him back with the passion he aroused.

Long moments passed. His tongue swept her mouth. Her body pressed close to his hard length, loving the strength and the power against her soft pliant curves.

He broke the kiss and held her by the shoulders. His smile was just a little smug.

All she could think of was getting him in her bed.

'Why on earth did they have to show up right at this moment?' He rubbed his chin. 'It would serve them right for barging in if we did get married.'

What would it be like to be married to a man like Charlie?

The heir to a dukedom. A man who moved in the first circles of society—the kind of society that looked on the Merry Draycotts of the world with scorn.

The thought chilled her to the bone.

He wasn't serious, though. He couldn't be. He was just angry at her cousins' intrusion. She struck at his shoulder with her fist. 'You gormless lump. I can't marry you.'

'There you go, hiding again.'

She pushed him away. 'You have no idea what you are talking about.' One thing she knew for certain: for him, marrying her would be a disaster.

Rueful regret filled his eyes. 'I certainly can't force you if you don't want it.'

Not want it? How could she explain what she didn't want were all the trappings that went with the dukedom. Just the thought of it made her shudder. 'All I want is to go home.'

He pressed his lips together and drew away. 'As you have said before. I wrote to a friend of mine. A soldier stationed at York. I asked him to recommend a couple of good men no longer employed by the military who will guard you until we get to the bottom of these attacks.'

She shook her head. 'I don't want to be surrounded by guards. People will think I'm afraid.'

'You should be afraid.' He held up a hand. 'Don't argue. Wait until we see who he suggests. It will make it easier for me, Merry, if you go along with me in this.'

This is what it would be like if she married him. He would control her life. But it was because he cared. She let go a breath. What harm would it do, to put up with a couple of retired soldiers underfoot for a while? They probably needed employment. At the moment, her desire to have speech with Jane was a more pressing issue, because Charlie's hints that he thought Caro responsible for the attacks still worried her.

If Charlie discovered Caro was to blame, she feared for her friend's life. Charlie would have no problem having her incarcerated, whereas Merry would prefer to give her friend enough money to send her away.

Not that she believed Caro was guilty of such a betrayal. She didn't. She just had to know for sure. If Caro was involved, then Jane must be, too, and Merry needed to talk to her—before Charlie found her himself.

She let her shoulders sag in defeat. 'Very well. I will leave my decision until we have your friend's reply. In the meantime, I would like to go to the village.'

He frowned.

'Caro is ill. The doctor suggested willow-bark tea, but there is none to be had here at Durn.'

'I'll send one of the footmen.'

The blasted man had an answer for everything. She shuffled her feet. 'She also has need of other things. Female things. She brought very little with her, we left in such a rush, and Beth tells me she is too proud to ask. I would like to make her a gift.'

He started to look uncomfortable. 'Give the footman a list.'

She gave a disappointed shrug. 'I can, I suppose. It would not be the same, though. Such intimate apparel needs a woman's touch. I hoped you would come with me. I should not have troubled you with such a trivial request, you must be tired after your journey.' She rose to leave.

'Merry, no,' he said, stopping her mid-stride. 'I'm sorry for being such a dreadful host. I will be happy to drive you to the village.'

Now she felt terrible. But the die was cast. 'Thank you.'

In a few swift strides, he drew close and captured her face in his hands. He gazed down into her eyes with a frown, as if seeking assurance. Then he kissed her gently, briefly, on the lips. 'I was rough on you earlier.'

'I was a shrew.'

They laughed at the same moment. He stroked her cheek. 'May I make it up to you properly later?' he whispered, his dark gaze hot. Again he brushed her lips with his mouth.

She felt worse than ever. Heartsick at playing off such wiles, when he was being so sweet, and the thought of one last night in his arms made her weak. 'I shall look forward to it.'

He gave her a swift kiss. 'Enough of this or we will not be going anywhere.'

'Shall I ask Logan to have the carriage brought around?'

'Please. Ask for the closed carriage. For safety.'

She hurried away before guilt made her admit her request was all a plot.

The carriage ride passed delightfully, despite the sinking feeling Merry had every time Charlie smiled at her with approval. Twice she almost owned up but then bit her tongue. Fortunately, their swift arrival at Durn village, a collection of stone houses with slate roofs, occurred before she plucked up the courage.

The village boasted an inn, a mill, an apothecary and a haber-dasher's, which also served as the post office. Numerous cottages wound along a fast-running beck, with the grand Norman church set at one end. They started at the haberdasher's. While Charlie enquired after the mail, Merry picked up an assortment of items. Handkerchiefs, a nightdress of serviceable cotton, stays, a matronly cap of the sort Caro favoured, some stockings. Soon her arms were full. Pretending to browse, she made her way to the back of the shop where an open door led to a storeroom.

'What are you doing?'

She spun around at the sound of his voice. 'Looking for buttons.'

Charlie raised an eyebrow at her collection of items. 'Mrs Falkner needs all of those?'

Merry couldn't help her blush. Lying to him felt horrid. 'She does,' she said firmly. She carried them to the clerk at the front of the shop and dropped the pile on the counter. She picked up the nightgown. 'It is very plain.'

'Ah...' the clerk nodded. 'Most ladies makes their own.' He

pointed to the bolts of cloth behind him. 'I have some nice white linen.'

'How much is the nightdress?'

'One and six.'

'Daylight robbery,' she exclaimed. 'I'm no bairn wet behind the ears, you know.'

He grimaced. 'All reet. A shilling.'

'Give him what he asks,' Charlie said, clearly embarrassed by her haggling.

She frowned. ''Tis my brass,' she said. 'And I'll not be gilding his lily.'

The clerk muttered something under his breath.

Charlie winced.

Merry turned to face him. 'Why don't you wait outside in the carriage? It will probably be quicker.'

Brow furrowed, he looked doubtful, though she had the feeling he was dying to leave her to her negotiations. 'Better yet, why don't you see if the apothecary has the willow-bark tea?'

His expression cleared. 'Good idea.'

No doubt he had a vision of her trying to bargain with the apothecary, too.

He strode from the shop.

Merry picked up the stays. 'I'd like to try these on. Do you have a private room?'

'In t'back.'

'I won't be a moment. If his lordship comes back, tell him I'll be quick.'

The storeroom had a screen secluding one corner from view. It also had a door into the laneway, which traversed past the Red Lion. If she hurried, she could be back before Charlie noticed her absence. Perfect.

She picked up her skirts and ran along the rutted alley and, breathing hard, entered through the side door.

'I'm looking for a Miss Jane Harper,' she said to the lad

sweeping the parlour floor. 'She is expecting me.' She tossed him a sixpence.

'First room at the top of the stairs,' the boy said, pocketing the coin and returning to his sweeping.

Beth was right. Jane had followed them. Hoping there was an innocent explanation, she ran up the stairs. Pressing down on the latch, she pushed the door open into a private parlour with Jane sitting at a table in front of the window beside a swarthy young man with close-cropped hair and a brutish face.

A premonition all was not well made her heart race. 'Jane Harper, what are you doing here?'

The man rose to his feet, a nasty look on his face. 'Now here's a surprise.'

Merry narrowed her eyes on the woman. 'I heard you were here and wondered if you wanted to return with us, but now I see you have other friends.'

A rather unpleasant smile split Jane's narrow face. 'Nice of you to call, Miss Draycott.' She gestured to the man. 'Why don't we make our guest comfortable?'

He pulled out a chair.

'No, thank you, his lordship is waiting for me.'

The man lowered his beetling brow and pulled a pistol. 'Sit.'

'All right,' Merry said, sitting down opposite Jane. She eyed the woman warily. 'Are you working alone, or is someone paying you to cause me harm?'

'I'm saying nothing,' Jane said, her lips tight.

Merry's heart sank. 'Then tell me if Mrs Falkner is involved?'

Jane's eyes widened a fraction. Surprise? Because Merry had guessed wrong or because she'd guessed right? 'Tell me. I'll pay you well and tell no one how I found out.'

'There isn't enough money in the world to pay me off.'

How odd? 'It is not the marquis, is it?'

Jane openly laughed. 'Guess all you want, missy.'

Chapter Fifteen

The trip to the apothecary should not have taken Charlie more than five minutes. Unfortunately, Mr Quire, the owner, had served the needs of the Mountford family for years. Charlie could not escape without a full accounting of the health of his family and a discussion of his brother's wedding, which had appeared in *The Times*.

Twenty minutes passed before he returned to the carriage outside the haberdasher's. He glanced inside his coach.

'Not back yet, my lord,' the footman said.

'Blast women and shopping,' he muttered.

'Yes, my lord.'

She was probably still bargaining. His mother had always complained about the haberdasher's exorbitant prices, but she had always paid him without comment. He should have done the same and dragged Merry out. He squared his shoulders and entered the shop. The pile of goods lay where Merry had dropped them. The clerk was busy tidying a tray full of brightly coloured ribbons.

'Where is the lady?' Charlie asked.

The clerk gave him a disgruntled glance. 'Trying something on in t'back room.'

Charlie heaved a sigh. He leaned one hip against the counter and folded his arms across his chest. Minutes passed. The clerk went around to the other side of the counter. 'Do she want these or not?' he asked.

Oh Lord, if she was going to start haggling when she came back, they were going to be here all day. He'd decided he'd rather spend the afternoon in bed, with her, because they had very little time left.

'Tot up the bill, package them and I'll pay while I am waiting.'

The man's eyes gleamed. Clearly, he was going to pay far more than any of this stuff was worth. The man was a Captain Sharp. He would speak to Father about not renewing his lease the next time it came up.

The clerk parcelled up the goods and handed Charlie the bill. He forked over the dibs.

Still no sign of Merry. 'What was she trying on?'

The man coughed. 'Stays.'

Why on earth…? 'Where did you say she was?'

The man pointed to the door leading to the rear of the building. As Charlie made his way back there a band around his chest tightened. He had no doubt what he'd find when he entered the back room full of boxes.

'Merry?'

No answer. Of course there was no answer. The little minx. She'd given him the slip. Reckless. The woman had no care for life and limb. But where the hell had she gone? He dashed through the back door and looked up and down the lane. Nothing suggested where she could have got to. The only other building of any size nearby was the inn.

The inn had horses for hire. Could she really be that desperate to leave? It made no sense.

'Hey,' the clerk called. 'What about your parcel?'

'Have it put in the carriage,' Charlie said. Anger balling in his chest, he strode down the lane and into the inn.

A lad stood at the bar tossing a coin in the air.

'Did you see a young lady come in here in the last few minutes?'

The boy's grubby face took on a crafty expression. 'Wot if I did?'

'Sixpence if you tell me where she went.'

'It's my lucky day,' the lad said. 'First door at the top of the stairs.'

Not renting a horse then. Charlie dropped the promised coin in his hand. 'If she's not there, I'll want it back.'

'She ain't come down yet.'

What game was she playing? Who was she meeting? The hairs on the back of his neck rose. A warning. Not to be ignored.

Cautiously, he climbed the stairs. The door stood ajar a fraction. He pulled the pistol from his pocket and pushed it open.

The first face to meet his gaze was Merry's. She was seated at the table facing the door. Pleasure did not describe her expression when she saw him.

The other woman grinned. Jane. The missing lightskirt. 'What in hell's name is going on, Miss Draycott?' He stepped into the room.

Merry's gaze darted off to the right. She had an odd look on her face as if she was trying to tell him something.

The door swung closed.

He whipped his head around. Too late. The cold metal of a pistol muzzle pressed against his neck. 'One move and you're a dead man,' a coarse voice said.

'It seems we have a stand off,' Charlie said, keeping his pistol levelled on Jane.

'Nah,' another voice said. 'See, if you don't put down your pop, I shoots Miss Draycott here.' A second man, a lanky pockmarked fellow, stepped into his line of vision from the other room, a bedchamber, with his weapon directed at Merry.

With a curse, Charlie lowered his gun. He'd walked into an

ambush like some Hyde Park soldier fresh on campaign. 'What is it you want? Money?'

The first man snatched the weapon from his hand.

'They are nothing but cowards,' Merry said, her voice full of scorn. 'They won't even admit who they are working for.'

'Whoever it is, I'll offer you double to let us go,' Charlie said swiftly.

The second man laughed. 'You ain't getting off so light.'

Charlie glanced at Jane with a frown. 'Are they holding you hostage, too? Is that why you disappeared?'

Jane rose. 'Certainly not.' Her voice was cold enough to freeze a pond in mid-summer. 'These men work for me.' Her voice no longer had a nasal whine and her clothes were better quality than those she had worn at Merry's. She looked more like a housekeeper than a maid. Or a prostitute.

'What do you want?' Charlie asked.

She smiled. 'I have everything I want.'

None of this made any sense. 'And that is?'

'The end of Merry Draycott.'

Blunt and to the point. Merry's face paled and Charlie's fists bunched in futile rage. He should have brought reinforcements. He'd been so annoyed with Merry for giving him the slip, he'd not stopped to think it through. *Too bloody hot-headed.* His colonel's voice rang in his ears. It chilled his blood. He could not let the past tie him in knots.

'Don't you know who I am?' he said. 'Do you know what will happen to you, if you harm me or my betrothed?'

Jane laughed. 'Your whore, you mean.'

Merry flushed red.

'I'll have none of your lip,' Charlie said, clenching and unclenching his fists, watching for some sign of weakness, some lack of attention on the part of the men.

'Don't worry about your skin, my lord. We've no axe to grind with you. We just need you not to interfere for a day or so. Tie them up.'

Poor Merry. Her lower lip trembled, showing her fear. He gave her an encouraging smile, though what the hell he had to be encouraging about he didn't know.

The two men pushed them to the floor roughly and bound them hand and foot. The ropes were tight about his ankles and his arms. Merry winced as the other man pulled at her restraints.

'Be careful,' Charlie growled. He wanted to tear the man apart for that wince. 'My men will come looking for me,' he warned. 'My coachman is standing out in the street. He will wonder what has happened to us.'

Jane looked thoughtful. 'He's right.' She pointed to one of the men. 'Go give the coachman a message from his lordship, here. Tell him they've decided to spend the afternoon at the inn and he's to come back for them after dinner.' She fumbled in Charlie's coat and pulled forth his purse. She fished around and found a half-crown. 'Give him this. Tell him mum's the word. He'll know. The servants all know what the two of them are like.'

Merry gasped.

'Servants talk, Miss Draycott.' Jane curled her lip. 'They say what they think when they know you're not listening. They know his lordship's had you in his bed and they won't be a bit surprised to hear he stopped off to dance a blanket hornpipe after an absence. You always were a slut.'

'You are a nasty piece of work, Jane Harper,' Merry said.

'Blindfold and gag them,' Jane said. 'Take them down through the cellar until tonight. Just make sure no one sees you. Be careful with the girl—he wants her in one piece until he deals with her himself.'

Charlie's blood ran cold. 'If you value your life, you won't do this.'

Jane grinned.

The man closest uncocked the pistol in his hand and raised it by the barrel.

Merry's eyes widened. 'No!'

The sharp blow to Charlie's head sparked stars behind his eyes. Darkness descended.

Merry screamed. One of the men heaved Charlie up on his shoulder with a grunt. 'Bloody heavy, he is,' he said, looking at Jane.

She waved him away. 'Get on.'

The other man approached Merry. 'You don't have to knock me out,' she said.

He looked at Jane.

'We don't want her hurt,' she said. 'A blindfold and a gag will do, if she doesn't struggle. Then cover her with a sheet.' The blindfold came first, followed by a rough cloth shoved in her mouth.

The man hoisted her over his shoulder like a sack of coal. His shoulder ground into her stomach, making it hard to breathe. She held still.

The journey to the cellar being carried like a bag of washing was something of a nightmare. When Merry was carried outside, she began to worry. They weren't out there long. The smell led her to think they had entered a barn. After another set of stairs, they seemed to turn in circles and the direction became muddy in her mind.

She was dumped on a cold damp floor. Her ribs felt bruised from the rough handling, but at least she could catch her breath. She inhaled the stink of stale beer, mould and rodents. They must be underground. She shivered.

The men walked away, leaving them alone in this horrid place. But why? What had she done?

Jane had let slip the word 'he', so she hadn't acted alone. Did it mean Caro was not involved? Lord, what did it matter? The situation was hopeless, whoever it was. One thing she was sure of. Charlie was not part of the plot.

And the man who was involved was coming tonight. One of the mill owners? Grandfather's friend? One of her employees? Bile rose in her throat. The gag tightened. She swallowed hard. A hollowness filled her chest. Stupid tears burned the backs of her eyes.

Dash it, she would not cry. Despair would not help them escape and she feared if she was here when the *he* arrived, things would go very badly indeed.

She couldn't see a thing through her blindfold, and her hands were going numb, but she could hear Charlie's breathing. A harsh rough sound through his nose. At least they hadn't killed him when they hit him.

She lay still in the dark, listening. He was panting as if he'd run a mile and making the same kind of noises she'd heard him make in his nightmare. Sounds of terror.

Was he conscious?

She wriggled backwards, towards the sound. 'Charlie,' she mumbled. It sounded more like 'Uhhhn uhhhn', but his breathing slowed as if he was listening.

He groaned when her legs touched him and flinched away. She tried again, slowly running her bound feet up and down some part of his body. His legs, she thought.

He inhaled a deep noisy breath and shifted closer. Something touched her arm. He was trembling. Shaking as if he had the ague.

'Mmmmm?' she mumbled.

His breathing picked up speed again like a startled horse. The sound of panic.

How could he be so afraid? What did he know? Her heart raced. Her breathing shortened.

No. There was nothing to be afraid of. Not yet anyway. No sense in getting into a lather until they knew what they were dealing with, as Grandfather used to say. 'Stop it,' she snarled, furious he couldn't understand the stupid sounds coming from her throat.

He stopped breathing.

Damn. What was the matter with him? Was he afraid of the dark? Was that why he left the candles burning all night? A grown man fearful of his dreams? Dreams like the one he'd had the other night?

When she used to be afraid at night after her parents died, Grandfather used to sing her to sleep. It took her mind off all she'd lost. It had always felt comforting.

She started humming an old lullaby.

He drew closer, touching her down her length. She felt him relax. She hummed 'Lavender's Blue', then 'Sweet Lass of Richmond Hill'. He joined in, his deep hum echoing off the walls. They sounded more like a church choir than a couple of terrified prisoners.

After a while her dry throat gave out. 'Sorry,' she said. He rubbed his forehead against her shoulder blades in acceptance. He wasn't shaking any more and his breathing had slowed.

They lay still, bodies touching, for a long time.

Then he moved, pressing his knees into the small of her back.

'Uhhn?' she said.

'Uh,' he said. It sounded like a command.

How was she supposed to know what he wanted?

He pushed her leg with the toe of his boot.

'Uh?' she asked.

He pushed her again. Harder. Why was he kicking her? He had boots on. The same boots he'd worn when he cut her traces and when they were attacked. The boots where he hid a knife.

'Ooooh,' she said.

He made a sound like a chuckle followed by 'ugh ugh'. That had to be *good girl*. Had to be.

She wriggled until her bound hands found the tops of his boots. He pushed one at her, so she concentrated on it. Found the hilt of the knife with her fingertips. After much grunting and muffled cursing she managed to pull it clear.

'Now what?'

He seemed to understand because she felt him move away, then he was hard up against her again, his fingers feeling her sleeve. Back to back. Oh God, he was going to try to cut the ropes against the blade. His fingers passed over her hand and she felt the blade shift.

'Careful.' Oh, this stupid noise coming out of her mouth was so annoying.

'O I,' he said.

Hold still.

'Mmmm,' she agreed.

She gripped the hilt hard in her palms and prayed she wouldn't drop it. The pressure of him sawing back and forth made it so difficult to hold the knife. She hoped he was cutting hemp and not flesh. She swallowed at the stomach-wrenching thought.

After what seemed like an age, the pressure stopped. He scuffled around beside her.

He stilled.

Footsteps. They were too late. Someone was coming. She heard him move again. His breathing becoming rapid. Oh, no, don't say he was going to start panicking again.

'Mmmm,' she said.

'Mmmm, mmmm,' he murmured softly. He didn't sound upset. Then what was he doing?

Light pierced the blindfold. She turned her head in its direction.

'Dear God,' a well-educated voice said in horrified tones. 'Do you know who you've got there?'

Merry strained to hear something familiar in the voice, but the echoing chamber distorted it. Oh, well, she would see who it was soon enough, when they set her free. And then he'd get a piece of her mind and some besides.

'Naught we could do, your lordship.' Jane. 'They came looking for me. They know who we are.'

A lord? What lord?

Some whispered mutters. Merry held her breath, waiting for Charlie's signal.

'That's no good,' Jane said, sounding furious. 'He's seen us. You have to do away with them. Today. Now.'

'You people are idiots. Kill Tonbridge and the world will be looking for you. Let them go as soon as I am clear,' the new man said in a harsh whisper. 'I'll deal with her later.'

Merry shivered. If only she could recognise his voice, but the echoes and the whispering made it impossible. He had recogised Charlie at a glance, though.

The muttered voices drew further away. Footsteps drowning out their words. They were leaving.

And Charlie, beside her, was moving. He took hold of her wrist and began sawing at the ropes.

No, someone was coming back. A light hurried step. Had Jane returned to set them free?

'Mmmm,' Merry said. Charlie must have heard, too, because he stopped cutting at her ropes.

Liquid splashing on the floor. The smell of brandy hit the back of her throat.

'Mmmmm,' she said.

He kicked her foot. She lay still.

'Bloody coward,' Jane said. 'He'd see us all hang. But not me. 'Tis bad enough she caused the death of my brother.' The voice receded. Then the sound of a striking flint, followed by a woof of rushing air. And heat.

'Hey,' Merry yelled through her gag.

'That'll teach you,' Jane yelled and then she was gone, running after the others.

And Charlie's hands were on her ropes, cutting frantically, then pulling at her blindfold.

Merry blinked at the dazzle of flames. Jane had set a fire. It licked up the side of a barrel. They were surrounded by barrels on racks. The flames ran like rivers along the liquid Jane had poured. Fumes filled Merry's head and made her feel dizzy.

'Come on,' Charlie said, working on the ropes at her feet. 'We have to get out of here.' He freed his own ankles and pulled her up.

Pain. Hands, feet, legs—all prickled with the rush of blood. She rubbed at her wrists.

Charlie grabbed her hand and they headed for the doorway. Flames curled up around the doorposts.

They broke into a run.

With a crack and a rumble, the rack nearest the door collapsed. Barrels rolled off it to the floor. One, maybe more than one, split open. Flames roared up to the ceiling.

Heat. Merry put her arm up, to protect her face. 'We are trapped.' There was no way out.

'This way,' Charlie shouted.

He ran to the racks on the other side of the cellar. He put his shoulder to it.

She ran to help. 'What are you doing?' She pushed at the wooden structure and felt it move.

'I think there's another way out,' he said, heaving with a grin that looked demonic in the blaze of flames. With the place lit up like Guy Fawkes's night, he looked positively happy. She wanted to strangle him.

'Come on, Merry, together. Heave.'

She pushed with all her might. It shifted a little. She was sure it moved. The flames were spreading to their side of the cellar.

'Again,' he panted.

She put her shoulder beside his and grasped the wood frame.

'Heave,' he said.

The rack rolled, picked up speed, slid away from the wall.

A gaping black hole. A tunnel. A draught of sweet fresh air fanned the flames behind them. Shadows danced on the wooden ceiling.

'Come on. Before those explode.' Charlie grabbed her hand.

Explode made her legs work really well.

They ran for their lives, only stopping to catch their breath when they could no longer feel the heat of the fire, or hear its horrid roar.

She put her hands on her knees and bent over, gasping for air. 'She meant to burn us alive.' The horror of it made her want to throw up.

Charlie put an arm around her shoulders. 'It's all right. You are safe. I remembered this when we were singing; my brain started working instead of panicking. Robert and I found a smuggler's tunnel in the riverbank years ago. It led to a barn. This barn.'

'Thank God you remembered.'

Her mind froze, refusing to think about what would have happened if he had not.

He took her hand. 'The tunnel comes out below the mill. Smugglers row the contraband upstream and bring it this way to the inn. If you don't mind, I'd rather like to get out of here.'

Merry glanced back down the tunnel at the distant glow of flames. 'The innkeeper is going to be very upset about losing his wares.'

'If I find out he is part of this, he'll lose more than contraband brandy. And if he isn't, Father will be furious. He's one of his best customers.'

Merry giggled. Then started to laugh. She couldn't stop. It just sounded so ridiculously funny.

Still laughing, she let Charlie drag her along by one hand, using the other to guide himself along the wall. Walking this time, thank goodness. If she tried to run, she'd fall down.

The exit appeared as a small circle of grey and grew swiftly. A few moments later they were standing in snow in the gathering dusk. Never had Merry been so happy to see snow. Luckily the tunnel did not end in the river, but in the bank a few feet above water level.

She heaved a sigh of relief as they climbed up beside the mill.

'Nothing,' he said, striking his fist in his hand. 'All that for nothing.' There were soot streaks on his face. His face was grim, his eyes dark. 'No Jane and now this other man. This lord.'

She winced. 'I suppose you didn't recognise his voice.'

Thin-lipped, he shook his head. 'No. We go back to Durn.'

'Shouldn't we find the constable? Tell him what happened? Start a hue and cry for Jane?'

'You forget the man who set all this in train.'

'We don't know who he is. Catch Jane and we can catch him, too.'

'In the meantime, he is still at large and you are in danger. You heard him. He planned to deal with you some other way, and when Jane learns you did not die in the fire, she will come after you again. I can't take that risk.'

Across the field, a pillar of smoke was beginning to rise. 'Everyone will be too busy with the fire to look for our criminals for a while,' he said. 'And I will not be sure you are safe until we are inside Durn's walls.'

'But—'

'I mean it, Merry. I'll put you over my shoulder and carry you all the way home if you won't come willingly.'

Exhausted, she let him lead her along.

'Bully,' she muttered, but never in her life had she felt so protected as she was leaning on Charlie's steady arm.

They met the carriage returning for them just beyond the mill. To his coachman's obvious shock, Charlie refused to help the people trying to put out the fire and insisted on speeding back to Durn. His servants would think him heartless. Hopefully, he would be able to set their minds at rest at a later date. Given the amount of brandy burning there was no saving the barn, but no lives would be lost, since he and Merry had got out.

He'd almost got them both killed by charging after Merry. Always impetuous. His commanding officer had said so and his father had said so. It seemed he had learned nothing by his experience in the army.

The thought of Merry burning in the fire sent cold chills down his spine every time his mind wandered back to the scene in the bowels of the earth. Hell could not have looked worse.

The carriage halted outside the front door of Durn.

Charlie looked at the glower on his coachman's face. 'Take some men, return to the village and see if you can help,' he said. 'But say nothing about picking up Miss Draycott and me on the road, if you please. Also remind those at the gate of my orders. No one other than members of the household are to be admitted tonight without my express permission.'

The man gave him a look that said he thought Charlie touched in the head, tugged his forelock and set his team in motion.

Charlie guided Merry up the steps. She'd sat with her eyes tight shut all the way home. He'd been glad of her silence. There had been too much going on in his head for sensible conversation.

Logan opened the door. For once his expression showed shock. 'Has there been an accident?'

'Oh, no,' Merry said, before Charlie could speak. 'It was all quite deliberate. If you'll excuse me, I would like to see Mrs Falkner.'

'Perhaps you will scare her, appearing covered in soot.'

Merry narrowed her eyes. 'Perhaps she will be shocked if I appear at all.'

She headed for the stairs.

Charlie caught her halfway up the staircase. 'All this time you have defended her. What makes you suspect her now?'

She looked on the edge of breaking. Tears stood in her blue eyes. The tears of betrayal, and fear and pain. He wanted to hold her close and comfort her. When he tried to put his arms around her, she pushed him away.

'She brought Jane into my home. She insisted she stay when I said I didn't like her. And she is so damned secretive. She is the person who will benefit by my death.' Her voice broke. She covered her face with her hand. 'I can't really believe it but I just don't know any more.'

So this was why she'd been so quiet in the carriage, brooding about her friend. Damn it, he should have asked her what was wrong. She'd been so brave up to now, so courageous—he couldn't bear to see her so utterly lost.

'If you confront her and she denies it, how will you know if she is telling you the truth?'

She swallowed, blinking back the moisture before it spilled. He wanted to hold her close but feared too much sympathy and her spirit would break entirely. 'Would it help you to know I am starting to doubt her involvement?'

'You are?'

'I believe our man in the cellar is behind it all. And Jane was acting out of revenge. You heard her speak of her brother.' He frowned. 'Have there been any accidents at your mill? Lives lost?'

She gazed up at him. 'None. I swear it. Grandfather ran the safest mill in Yorkshire and I have kept to that standard. There have been a few accidents, but nothing fatal. And all victims well compensated, I swear.'

'And I believe you.' He kissed the tip of her nose. 'You are covered in soot and dirt. You are cold, you are tired and these things are playing on your mind. Questioning Mrs Falkner can wait.'

'It can't. I have to hear it from her lips. Will you come with me?'

He sighed. He'd learned that if Merry Draycott made a decision, he might as well go along with it, because she was stubborn and determined and rarely took no for an answer. 'If that is your wish.' They walked up the stairs together. 'First, though, we wash and change. Quite honestly I can't stand the smell. I don't think I'll ever be able to drink brandy again.'

She managed a small chuckle.

* * *

When Beth met them at the door to the nursery, Merry was feeling a little less shaken.

'How is Mrs Falkner?' Merry asked. All her old fears about fevers and sickness that she'd had since her parents' deaths pressed down on her. She pushed them away. She needed to look into Caro's eyes when she asked her questions.

'Better, miss. Sitting up, giving orders.' Beth grinned.

With Charlie behind her, Merry crept into the dimly lit room. The flush of fever lay on Caro's cheeks and her eyes were unnaturally bright.

'What are you doing here?' she croaked.

'Nice welcome,' Merry said, surging forwards, forcing the dry panic in her throat down with a quick swallow. 'How are you?'

'Better.' Caro smiled. 'Poor Tommy has been worried, but Beth has been a wonderful nurse.' She glanced at the girl with a fond smile. Beth bobbed and left. 'I will be up and about in a day or so.'

'Thank goodness.'

'You look pale,' Caro said. 'You should not be here. We do not want you taking ill, too.' She gestured to Charlie, who had remained in the doorway.

'We need to talk to you. Whoever attacked us at Draycott House has followed us here to Durn,' Merry said.

Caro's blue eyes widened; she paled beneath her flush. 'What happened? Are you hurt?'

Merry took her hand, felt the dampness and the heat. 'I am fine, Caro. But I must ask you some questions, if you would agree?'

A shuttered expression passed over Caro's face. It always did whenever anyone questioned her. Merry clenched her hands, trying to believe her friend had nothing to do with what was happening.

'We wanted to ask you about Jane, Mrs Falkner.' Charlie's deep voice was gentle. 'How did she come to be in your company?'

Caro swallowed.

'Would you like water?' Merry asked.

Caro nodded and sipped from the glass Merry held to her lips.

She pulled her shawl tighter around her shoulders. 'She arrived at the house in Skepton two days before the fire. She said she had heard it was a refuge and begged admittance.'

'You had never met her before?' Charlie pressed, stepping closer to the bed.

Merry watched Caro's face, looking for anything—guilt, fear.

Caro looked Merry straight in the eyes. 'Never. Nor had the other girls.' She pressed the back of her hand to her forehead. 'Are you saying Jane has something to do with this? Wretched woman. I wish I had never set eyes on her.'

'We were captured by Jane and some men, one of whom spoke like a gentleman,' Merry said.

Caro gasped and looked horrified. 'Captured? What do you mean captured?'

A wave of relief washed over Merry. She knew people. She'd studied them. Caro was genuinely shocked and concerned. Merry turned her gaze to Charlie. His expression was unreadable, his eyes shadowed.

Caro stared at him. 'You think I—?' Her voice broke. Her eyes swam with tears. 'I had something to do with this?'

Merry picked up the water, but Caro waved it away. She struggled upright in the bed. 'If you believe such a thing, I must leave.'

'I don't believe it,' Merry said, feeling her own throat become thick and damp. She sniffed. 'Not for a minute.' Well, it was only a small white lie. She gazed up at Charlie. 'And nor does his lordship.'

'Not any longer,' he said abruptly, as if he'd finally made up his mind. 'I keep thinking I had heard the man's voice before, though. Did you recognise him at all, Merry?'

Merry thought back to the dank cellar, to the few words she'd heard, before the conversation became muffled.

She shrugged. 'He sounded like a toff. And he knew you right away.'

Caro frowned at Charlie. 'A friend of yours?' She tilted her head. 'An odd coincidence. Was it also merely chance you found her on the road, my lord?'

Charlie's lip curled. 'Nice try, Mrs Falkner.'

'Stop it, both of you,' Merry said. She stared at the counterpane, a gorgeously embroidered work of art. She ran her fingers over the threads, tracing the outline of entwined roses. 'We know Jane is involved. If we find her, we will find our answer.'

'I don't agree,' Charlie said. 'I think it is the man we need to find. He was clearly in charge.'

'But Jane will surely lead us to him. Or her accomplices will. They would probably betray their mother for a guinea or two. I know their type.'

'I don't doubt you are right on that score,' Charlie said. He looked down at Caro. 'I am sorry if I was overly harsh, Mrs Falkner. My concern is for Merry.'

Caro looked at him for a moment. One of her all-too-rare sweet smiles curved her lips. 'Mine too, your lordship. I apologise for voicing my suspicions also.'

He grinned at her. 'We will leave you to rest. Come, Merry, you are exhausted. We will decide our next step in the morning.'

There he went, ordering her about again. But it had been a gruelling day and her head felt filled with thick wool; she could do nothing more than take his arm.

Aware of Merry sleeping in her chamber upstairs, Charlie paced his study. He would not go to her. She needed her rest.

God, she'd seen him naked, his very soul exposed, and she'd been wonderful. Calm, courageous and kind. Unbelievably, the sound of her voice in that cellar had held his dark visions at bay.

He'd found a light in the darkness and now duty required he let her go.

Earlier today he'd proposed they marry, out of a sense of frustration, but then when he thought she might say yes he'd felt an unexpected flood of joy. Until she turned him down.

Why shouldn't he be happy? Like Robert. Nothing Father could do would harm Robert any more. He had married an heiress.

What harm would it do if he also married where he willed? Where he—God was he even thinking this?—where he…loved.

Was love this strange restlessness inside him, this need to meld with Merry, to be as one? Or was this just him again trying to escape? Had he lost any sense of himself, who he was, what he owed his position, his father, the men who had died because of him? Had sleepless nights and guilt finally taken their toll?

It seemed more than likely, given that men in his position did not marry for love. They married for political reasons. For reasons of power and increased status. To acquire a suitable hostess. And to beget heirs.

They married women like Allison Purtefoy because the arbiters of his world said women like Merry weren't good enough.

They were wrong. So bloody wrong.

Merry was worth twice most of the females of his acquaintance and three times the vapid Lady Allison. He pressed his fingers to his aching temples in an attempt to ease the residual headache from the blow to his skull.

Only Merry had no interest in marrying him. She'd made that perfectly clear.

He rubbed at the pain in his chest.

She was right not to want him. He was little more than a shell since Waterloo, going through the motions, clinging to his duty to stop himself from tipping into darkness.

Which meant he had no right to hold Merry to their promised betrothal. The only thing he could do for her was rid her of whoever was trying to harm her. He'd at least have the satisfaction of knowing she was safe.

Damn it. All that torture in that bloody black cellar and he'd walked away with nothing. He put his glass down on the table.

The man who had come to their prison beneath the barn had spoken with power and authority. He was a far more dangerous opponent than Jane Harper. Merry was right, though, the woman was the key. And he needed to find her quickly.

He rang the bell.

While he waited for Logan, he went to the pigeonholes at one end of his bookshelf and pulled out a map. He spread it flat on his desk. He stared at the map of the moors and villages around Durn. 'Where are you hiding, Jane Harper?' he muttered.

'My lord?' The butler looked as if he'd dressed hurriedly.

'I'm sorry to disturb your rest,' Charlie said. 'I have need of men tonight. Grooms, footmen, anyone you think useful in a brawl.'

Horror filled the butler's eyes, though he clearly tried not to look as if he thought his master had run mad. 'Yes, my lord.'

'Have them meet me in the gunroom in half an hour.'

'Right away, my lord.'

Poor Logan, he might never be the same again.

He stared at the map. He'd start at the inn. There might be tracks in the snow. If he found nothing there, he would visit every farmhouse and hovel within ten miles. There was nowhere she could hide.

At the inn, the smell of smoke hung in the cold night air, oppressive and choking. While his men waited outside, Charlie spoke to a very disgruntled landlord. Not only had he lost his stores, his guest had disappeared, leaving behind her belongings and her unpaid shot. 'You have no idea where she went?'

The man glowered from beneath his nightcap. 'She ain't been seen since yesterday afternoon. Her and the bully boys she had with her ran off and left me trying to save my barn. Not a hair of 'em have I seen. They must have done it. I'm ruined.'

Charlie felt a twinge of guilt. He'd have to do something to help the fellow. But not now. 'I will inspect her chamber, if you please.'

'Help yourself, my lord. An' if you finds her, you leave her to me.'

'The magistrate will deal with her.' Charlie ran up the stairs to the room from which he'd been so rudely carted that afternoon. The smell of smoke seemed worse up here than it had below.

He rifled through her meagre belongings. Her valise contained a few clothes and some old yellowed letters tied in a ribbon. Love letters? It seemed odd that she'd left without such personal items. Very odd.

He lifted the mattress. Nothing. The pillows. He opened the drawer of a small roll-top desk. Among her handkerchiefs, he found a note in a bold hand. Dated two days ago, it set up a meeting at an abandoned cottage a short distance outside of the village. No signature.

The mystery man? Perhaps he'd find the pair of them at this cottage? He stuffed the correspondence in his pocket in case it gave some clues as to where she might have gone if the cottage proved a dead end and headed down to his men.

The ride took mere minutes. The cottage was dark and silent. He huffed out a breath, the fog of cold drifting away on a breeze. 'I'll take a look,' he said to the head groom, Fred, who had leaped at the idea of a nightly adventure. 'If anything happens, ride for the magistrate.' He dismounted.

The man drew a pistol from the holster in his saddle and climbed down. 'I'll come with you.'

Charlie tried the door. It swung open. Sprawled on the floor in a patch of moonlight from the window, a bullet hole in the middle of her forehead, lay Jane Harper. The stink of death hit him in the face. A too-familiar odour. His gut churned. Images rushed into his mind. Darkness edged his vision. He fought down the panic. 'Hold the torch higher,' he growled at the man at his back.

'Dear God,' his groom said, looking over his shoulder. 'What sort of fiend would dispose of a woman in cold blood that way?'

It had been a long time since Charlie had seen a dead body, but he had no trouble recognising its lack of life. Bile rose in his throat. He swallowed. 'Someone who feared discovery. Someone she trusted.'

He was no closer to discovering who that someone was than he had been yesterday. In fact, now Jane was dead, perhaps further away.

After a cursory glance around the cottage, he and Fred returned to the waiting men.

'Fetch the constable and the magistrate,' he said to Fred. 'Take a couple of men with you. I'll search around here to see if we can find anything to tell us who might have done this.'

Fred grabbed his horse, picked two of the four men they'd brought and set off for the village.

'You two can help me search for tracks,' Charlie said to the others. 'You in that direction, you over there. I'll take the centre. If you see anything, call out and lift your torch high so we can find you.'

The men nodded their understanding and fanned out.

Charlie swung his torch in an arc around him after each step. He'd gone about five yards when one of the other men sang out, 'Found something.'

Charlie retraced his own footprints back to the cottage, then followed the footprints of the man signalling. The other man followed suit.

'What have you got?' Charlie asked. The man, another groom, pointed. 'Someone tied a horse here earlier this evening.'

Hoof-flattened snow and a pile of dung. Whoever had tied his horse here had not stayed long. The man pointed to boot prints leading away from the horse. 'He must have circled around and taken her by surprise.' The boot prints could have been anyone's. The horse was large. That was all Charlie could tell.

'Damn it,' he said. 'Not a thing to say who the murderer might be.' And Charlie would have to explain to the magistrate exactly why he was prowling around in the middle of the night and had just happened on the grisly scene.

He also had to decide what to tell Merry.

It was ten in the morning when he handed a distinctly disgruntled Logan his greatcoat. 'Miss Draycott is in the breakfast room,' the butler said with a slight curl to his lip.

Charlie ignored the butler's tantrum. He'd get over it. 'Wondering where I am, no doubt.'

Logan bowed. 'I wouldn't know, my lord.'

He was starving. He flung open the door and caught Merry tucking into ham and eggs.

The smile on her lips drove all thought from his mind. He wanted to hold her close, kiss her lovely lips, nuzzle against the column of her throat.

'You were up early?' she said.

He picked up a plate and helped himself to some ham and a couple of coddled eggs. He sat down beside her. 'I couldn't sleep.'

A soft smile curved her lips. Sympathy. No doubt she thought him in need of comfort. A weak puling creature. A chilling thought. 'I had to find Jane.'

She frowned. 'Are you saying—'

'I went looking for her.'

'Alone? Are you mad? Why didn't you wake me?'

'Not alone. I took some of my men. We found her.'

'You did?' Her voice rose in excitement. 'What did she say?'

'She's dead.'

The pallor in her face grew worse. 'No,' she whispered. 'You can't—'

'Blast it, Merry. What do you think I am? I didn't kill her. She was dead when we found her.' He spoke more harshly than he intended.

'I…I'm sorry.' She bit her lip. 'So we have no way of knowing who employed her?'

'None at all. The men with her have disappeared. Likely left the county if they've any sense.' He pulled the letters from his pocket. 'We found these at the inn. Letters from a brother, forced to leave England from the sound of it, and instructions for a meeting, presumably from our mysterious man. But no clue as to his identity. I went back to her room at the inn to make sure.'

She picked up one of the letters. 'It seems rude to pry, but perhaps there is some clue as to her identity. Perhaps a family who should be informed.' She winced.

'There is an address in Cumberland.'

Merry's hand stilled. 'Cumberland?'

He nodded.

'It can't be.' Her hand shook as she unfolded the letter.

'What can't be?'

She scanned the note, stopping when her gaze reached the signature. She picked up the next one and the next and with each reading her face held more and more pain.

She let the last one fall to the table. Charlie covered her limp hand with his. It felt cold. Freezing. He picked it up and held it within his palms. 'What is it, Merry? Do you know something of this woman?'

She turned her gaze to meet his and he had never seen her look so devastated, not even the first time she'd realised someone wanted her death.

'She was Jeremy's sister.'

'Jeremy?' A cold fist clenched in his chest.

'A gardener's boy from school.' Her voice choked with tears.

'Merry.' He put an arm around her shoulders, but she shrugged him off. Rose to her feet and strode to the window.

He wanted to go to her. He wanted to hold her close, but something held him back, as if a shadow stood between them. The shadow of this man Jeremy.

He hadn't read the letters, just the address. He'd been focused on the note from the man to whom Jane had reported.

'I never meant him any harm,' she whispered to the glass.

'What are you talking about?'

She turned and gestured to the letters. 'We were close. At school. There was a scandal.'

Charlie winced, his imagination running riot and a sudden surge of anger making him hot. Jealousy. How could he be jealous of something that happened so long ago?

'It seems Grandfather had him shipped off to the West Indies.' She covered her mouth with her palm, her eyes wide and moist. She blinked a couple of times and, removing her hand, took a shaky breath.

'He hated it, according to those letters, but he repeats over and over to Jane not to hold a grudge against the Draycotts. He meant me. Jane must have railed about me in her replies.'

She wrapped her arms around her waist. 'The last one is started by him and finished in another hand. He died from a fever. By the date, he can have been no more than twenty.' She lifted her sorrowful face, her eyes focused in the past. 'So far from his home and his family,' she whispered. 'No wonder Jane wanted me dead.' She bowed her head and covered her face with her hands. 'I didn't know.' Her muffled voice was full of tears. 'Grandfather never told me. I kept wondering why Jeremy never wrote to me. I even wrote to the school once asking for news. They never answered.'

He felt sick, not for himself, but for her, for the sorrow he saw on her face. Was this why she'd never married? She'd been waiting for this man to return? 'You loved him.' The thought was a blow to his kidneys.

She uncovered her face and there were tears on her cheeks. He'd never seen her cry. 'Passionately.' She choked down a sob. 'As young people do. I wondered over and over why he never tried to contact me. And now there is nothing I can do.'

Her shoulders sagged. She stared at the letters as if seeing the boy she'd loved.

Charlie strode to her side and put his arm around her shoulders. He inhaled the lavender fragrance in her hair and ignored the anger at her grandfather for keeping her in the dark and Jane for wanting revenge. 'We can find out who killed his sister. Who used her against you. We can do that much.'

She leaned into him, and he held her gently against his chest, lightly in case she would break. Slowly the tension eased from her body. Her warmth felt good in his arms. He wanted to keep her there forever.

She raised her face. 'Thank you.'

He bent to kiss her lips. Something wrenched in his chest. Loss. But you couldn't lose what you never had. 'Come sit down. You look exhausted. Worn to the bone.'

She managed a shaky laugh. 'Thank you for the compliment.'

'Eee, lass,' he said softly. 'Would you have me lie to your face?'

Her eyes shone with tears, but her smile was sweet. 'No. That I would not.'

'Come then, drink some tea. We will find this man, I promise.'

Logan entered with a silver tray.

Charlie frowned at him.

'I'm sorry to disturb you, my lord, but a reply by return is requested.'

Charlie took the note. 'From Purtefoy,' he said glancing at Merry.

Her mouth tightened.

He broke the seal. 'He's apologising for his sister's lack of courtesy and requesting that the family be permitted to show their pleasure at our betrothal at the ball. He begs our attendance.'

'Really? When they know my chaperon is laid low? It will be yet another opportunity to prove my lack of breeding.'

'Show them they are wrong.'

'By playing off our sham on members of society? We must not continue this pretence.'

His gut rolled. Unfortunately, she made perfect sense, but... He glanced down at the note. 'Everyone in the county will be present.'

'Precisely.'

'Including perhaps the blackguard from the cellar.'

Her eyes widened. 'Of course. Why didn't I think of it?'

'I might recognise his voice.'

'All right, we will go.'

The sudden about-face made the hairs on his nape tickle. 'I can manage alone.'

'What, and speak to every male guest? Also you might need my confirmation, once you think you have found him.'

There was excitement behind her reasoned words. He raised a brow. 'He...he may try again. Give himself away,' Merry continued.

'Are you suggesting I use you as bait?' His back stiffened. Outrage. He would never knowingly endanger a woman. He'd led enough people to their deaths. 'Certainly not. The man is dangerous.'

'And he will continue to be dangerous until he is caught. This time, we will be the hunters.'

A cold chill ran across his shoulders. 'As well as the hunted. No, Merry. I will not allow it.'

She rose to her feet and he followed suit. 'What can he do in a ballroom full of people? As long as we stay together, a loving couple besotted with each other, nothing can happen.'

'I will not put your life in danger again.'

'Then I will go alone.'

'You forget, your chaperon is indisposed.'

A gleam of triumph lit her eyes. 'I do not need a chaperon to visit family.'

He tipped her chin and gazed down into her defiant eyes. 'Miss

Draycott, you truly are the most infuriating female it has ever been my misfortune to meet.'

'Because you know I am right.'

'I really think it is better if I go alone,' he said into her hair, knowing full well her answer.

'I'm going with you.'

'Then we must take great care. I'll send a note to my soldier friend.'

'And I will enlist Caro's help with my gown. I think it a little *risqué*.'

'Never.'

She grinned, but there was a touch of sadness in her eyes. 'Still, I would not wish to disgrace you.' She got up and strode to the door. She turned back. 'For what time are we invited?'

'Eight of the clock. It will take at least an hour to get there.'

She nodded. 'I will be ready.'

So would he. Forewarned was forearmed in more ways than one.

As the carriage drove up the drive to the Chepstow country seat, Caro's admonition rang in Merry's ears. *Trust no one.* She trusted Charlie. With her life. She leaned against his broad shoulder in the dark of the carriage and he pulled her comfortably close. Her heart, that stupid organ, squeezed painfully. Because this was a bit like Cinderella's ball, but this time there would be no happy ending. No prince on her doorstep. He would go back to his life and she to hers.

It was the only possible outcome. Neither would be happy in the other's world.

The carriage halted and a footman opened the door. Once again snow threatened. She could smell it in the air. Any sensible Yorkshire person would remain home on a night like tonight. It seemed being sensible was incompatible with being a member of the nobility. They only cared about entertainment. She pulled her fur-lined cloak around her, stepped out of the carriage and looked up at the sprawling red-brick Tudor mansion.

'Looks like quite a party,' Charlie said, taking her arm. Every window blazed into the night and carriages lined the driveway.

'It does.'

An elderly butler opened the door and took their outer raiment.

'Welcome.' In the entrance hall, all black-and-white tile and medieval beams, Digby looked very much the viscount. He smiled in lordly greeting. 'Merry, you look lovely. Good to see you, Tonbridge.'

The bonhomie felt forced, but at least the man was making an effort. Her cousin Allison likely would turn up her nose.

'Through there to the ballroom,' Digby said. 'You'll find Allison in there somewhere. You've never been here before, have you, cousin?'

Merry shook her head. 'No, indeed. Are your mother and father here?'

'No, Father stayed in town for the holidays and Mother is visiting relatives.'

'While the cat's away, mmm?' Charlie said cheerfully, peering into a ballroom filled to capacity with every conceivable member of Yorkshire aristocracy. Feathers bobbed, diamonds winked and perfume thickened the air.

Her cousin laughed. A little too heartily, Merry thought. 'No, no. We always host a ball at this time every year.'

'And Merry was never invited?' Charlie's tone sounded just a little dangerous.

'Glad not to be,' Merry said quickly. 'All these nobs. I've nowt to say.'

Digby winced. Charlie touched her ankle with his toe. A be-good admonition. She remembered her promise not to put him to shame with a flicker of resentment, but she didn't really blame him for wanting her to behave like a lady, not when she was supposed to be his betrothed.

'Shall I take you around?' Digby said. 'Introduce you?'

'I pretty well know everyone,' Charlie said. 'Don't worry about us. We will be fine.'

'All right. It will soon be time to start the dancing, and I still have guests to greet.' He hurried off.

Charlie placed her hand on his arm and walked over to the nearest group. 'Lord Tonbridge,' a pretty blonde lady in a gown of pink crepe, hemmed with enormous twining roses, cried. 'I heard you might attend.'

'Allow me to introduce my fiancée, Miss Merry Draycott,' he said, pulling her forwards. 'Merry, this is Lady Argyle.'

Merry curtsied.

Lady Argyle ran her gaze from Merry's head to her heels and, seeming to approve, introduced her to the rest of the party. It seemed that Tonbridge gave her an entry where none would have been possible before.

Wouldn't they be surprised when they learned the engagement was off? Perhaps even insulted. Her heart sank a little.

Soon they were moving from one group to another, Merry being introduced and conversations rippling around them. She did not feel quite as out of place as she expected. Many of these people were pleasant, and were anxious to talk about the manufacture of cloth. Many of them depended on it for their livelihoods. While she and Charlie conversed, she strained her ears to hear that one voice.

When the dancing began, not only did they have to listen to male voices through the general chatter, they now had to contend with the music. Not once did she hear a man she recogised as being the one in the cellar; judging from Charlie's air of frustration, nor had he.

'Perhaps he wasn't invited,' she murmured as they strolled around the dance floor, looking for people they'd not yet spoken with.

His lips thinned. 'Perhaps he disguised his voice.'

'Then him taking the bait might be our best chance after all.'

He didn't look any happier.

The orchestra announced a waltz. 'Dance with me,' Charlie said.

'How do you know I can dance?' she said, smiling up at him.

His eyes crinkled at the corners and gleamed wickedly. 'A man canny enough to send you to the most exclusive girls' academy in England is hardly likely to neglect the rest of your education.'

'Touché.'

He swept her into his arms and they circled the floor in fine style. He was the best dancer she'd ever encountered, including her teacher.

'I see you had lessons too,' she said.

'Required curriculum for ducal heirs.'

'And also for rakes.'

'Who are you calling a rake?'

She smiled. He looked charmingly boyish. You would never know he was trying to catch a murderer.

Beneath the air of sophistication, beneath his cool reserve, resided a man with a very good heart. If only she had been of his world, things might have been different, but she wasn't. The ache in her chest for what could not be made no sense, so she smiled as he whirled her around.

She relaxed in his arms, living the dream of being his fiancée for one more night.

And when he smiled down at her, the gold burst around his pupils as bright as a guinea, she could almost believe it would last forever.

But it didn't.

The orchestra played the final notes and, looking down into her face, Charlie slowly released her. Was it regret she saw in his gaze, sorrow in the slight tightening around his lips, or was it all wishful thinking?

She gave him a bright smile. 'That was grand.'

He smiled. 'Thank you. You dance like an angel.'

'More like a baby elephant.' They laughed and linked arms.

Many eyes followed their progress off the floor. Men and women. Wondering eyes.

Did one pair belong to the man in the cellar? Would he strike? The joyful mood from their dance dissipated as if a cold wind had blown through the room.

Charlie guided Merry to the refreshment table.

'Mountford,' a male voice said behind them. 'I got your letter.'

Charlie swung around. The man before him held out his hand.

'Blade,' Charlie said. 'I'm Tonbridge, remember?'

'Sorry, I forgot.' Blade grinned beneath his magnificent brown moustache.

'Merry, this is Captain Bladen Read. Read, this is my fiancée, Miss Draycott.'

'Delighted to meet you.' The captain bowed.

'So, Blade, how are you finding Yorkshire?'

He grimaced. 'Cold on more than one front. Several of us from the York camp are here tonight. Out of uniform. The army is not popular at the moment.' He spoke carefully, like a man well on the way to half-seas over and his twinkling hazel eyes looked a little bleary.

Everyone dealt with the aftermath of Waterloo in their own way. Charlie could only wish brandy worked for him.

Blade turned his charming smile on Merry. '*The* Miss Draycott?'

Merry's eyes widened. 'I don't know of any others.'

'Don't tease her.' Charlie knew Blade of old. The man was an incorrigible flirt. And a confirmed bachelor.

Digby sauntered up. 'May I have this waltz, coz? Show family solidarity and all that?'

Merry glanced at Charlie. He nodded. A private word with Blade was just what he needed.

They watched Merry dance with her cousin. 'She's a lovely woman,' Blade said. 'An heiress and not a wart or bristle on her chin. Can't think why she's not been snapped up before.'

Charlie's nape hair rose. 'Well she's snapped up now.'

'No need to poker up, old fellow. I'm not in the market for a bride. Although with a fortune like hers, I'd be tempted. Not that you are in need of money,' he added swiftly at Charlie's glare and rigid shoulders. 'She's a very attractive woman in her own right.'

They moved a little apart from the dance floor, seeking a quieter place for conversation.

Charlie flexed his fingers. 'How have you been?'

'Well enough. Regiment's gone downhill. We lost too many of the good ones.'

Cold steel twisted in Charlie's gut. He glanced down at his friend's left hand.

Blade grinned when he saw the direction of Charlie's gaze. He raised his arm and the sleeve fell back, revealing a wickedly sharp hook. 'Makes a great weapon. And holds the reins just fine.'

The recollection of Blade's screams when the women took his finger sent a shudder of revulsion across Charlie's shoulders. He hoped Blade didn't see it. But of course he did, because his grin widened. 'I was one of the lucky ones. If you hadn't stabbed that old crone, who knows what she would have cut off next?'

'If I hadn't led that bloody charge, you wouldn't have ended up off your horse.'

'It was glorious, though, wasn't it?'

Glorious and foolhardy. Utterly mad. Their commanding officer had been beside himself with anger, when he'd finally found Charlie in hospital.

So many good men lost, because Charlie lost his head.

Bitterness rose in his throat like bile. He swallowed it down. He lived with the guilt as best he could. 'As I wrote, I need your help.'

'Name it.'

'Someone is trying to do my heiress harm.'

Blade's eyes sharpened. 'Gad, an adventure. Who?'

'I don't know. But he may well be here tonight. I might need you to watch my back.'

'Like old times.'

'You will need your wits about you.' He looked pointedly at the glass tucked inside Blade's left elbow.

Blade shrugged and set the glass on the windowsill. 'I'm better than I was.'

'Glad to hear it.' He scanned the dance floor. He couldn't see Merry. She had been there moments ago, waltzing with her cousin in prime style. She'd drawn many envious glances from the other women. But now she was gone.

He cursed under his breath.

'What is it?' Blade asked.

'Where is Merry?'

He frowned. 'I didn't see her leave.'

'Look around, will you? I don't see her damned cousin either.' They circled the ballroom in opposite directions.

Anxiety closed his throat. How the hell could he have let this happen?

'There you are,' Lady Allison said, appearing at his elbow. 'There are young ladies dying to meet you.'

'In a moment,' he said. 'Have you seen Miss Draycott?'

She smiled brightly. 'Ladies' withdrawing room. Digby stepped on her train. She went off to pin her lace.'

He let go a sigh of relief and let Lady Allison introduce him to a group of debutantes—vestal virgins he always called them because he never could remember their names. They all giggled and blushed and peeped sideways over their fans. Unlike Merry, who looked him straight in the eye.

He shot a not-to-worry grin at Blade across the room.

His friend nodded.

Several minutes passed and still Merry didn't return.

Worry returned, more intense than before. 'Excuse me, ladies. I see an old acquaintance.' They chorused their dismay as he strode from the ballroom.

'Ladies' withdrawing room?' he said to the footman at the door.

'Down the hallway to the right.'

Blade caught him up. 'Still no sign of her?'

'Or her cousin. Lady Allison said she'd gone to the withdrawing room.'

'With her cousin?' Blade said, meaningfully.

Charlie stopped. 'They are family.'

'Family members don't always like each other. More betrayal in families than anywhere else.' He sounded bitter.

Charlie's heart stopped. The educated voice in the cellar could easily have belonged to Purtefoy. The undercurrents of dislike had been palpable when he and Allison visited Durn. But what would he gain by her death? Even if the family thought her a dirty dish in their cupboard, it hardly counted. Everyone had one or two of those.

His heart drummed louder. His chest tightened. 'We'll check the withdrawing room first. No sense in yelling "fire" before it happens.'

They sped down the hallway. A woman emerged into the corridor. She smiled at them vaguely.

'Is Miss Draycott in there?' Charlie asked.

The woman looked startled. 'No one is in there.'

Charlie closed his eyes. Damn. His stomach churned. Merry had gone off with her cousin. She could be anywhere. How like Merry not to let him know.

'Where next, old fellow?' Blade said.

Charlie narrowed his eyes. 'Lady Allison.'

They hurtled back to the ballroom, but she also was nowhere to be found.

'If they meant to do Merry harm, where would they take her?' Charlie asked, looking around as if the walls might give him a clue.

'Somewhere away from the guests, where she wouldn't be heard. Lots of people staying tonight, because of the snow.'

'The stables?'

'The attic.'

'Bloody hell.'

Blade grinned. 'I have an idea.'

He went back to the footman at the door and leaned heavily on the wall beside the man. 'Whersh your mashter?'

'I don't know, sir.'

'Got to know. Servants always know. Thing ish, see, I'm a war hero.' He held up his hook. 'Losht this at Waterloo. Want him to help me find it.'

He put an arm around the man's shoulders and leaned hard. He stroked his cheek with the pointed metal. 'Where ish he, old chap? Don't want to damage anything, but I need hish help.'

The man turned bright red. 'He is otherwise engaged, sir.'

'Where?' He placed the hook against the man's throat.

'In the library. But he won't appreciate being disturbed.'

'Too bad.' He clumped the man over the head with the base of the hook hidden beneath his coat sleeve and the man slumped to the ground. Blade showed his teeth. 'Great weapon in a brawl that hook. Give me some help here.' They dragged the unconscious footman along the hallway and pushed him into a niche.

Blade always was a ruffian at heart. 'Did you have to hit him?' Charlie asked.

'You are getting soft, Major. Don't want him raising the alarm, do we?'

Charlie shook his head. 'Right.'

They hurried down the corridor to a set of double doors. Charlie placed his ear against the door and heard voices. He pulled his pistol from his pocket.

Blade grinned and produced his pistol. 'In case of insurrection, don't you know.'

They tried the doors handle very carefully and quietly. Locked.

A scuffling sound could be heard on the other side of the door. Charlie's blood congealed.

'We have to get in there.'

'Take more than a boot to smash that lock,' Blade said. He fired his weapon and they went in through the puff of smoke.

'Good God.' Purtefoy, bending over the fireplace, whirled around to face them. 'Oh, it's you, Tonbridge. And Captain Read.' His gaze shifted from one to the other. He smiled awkwardly. Guilt flashed in his eyes as he sank into the nearest chair. 'Can't a fellow blow a cloud in peace?' He waved the cigar he'd been lighting from the coals in the fire.

'Where is Merry?' Charlie said.

'Cousin Honor, you mean? I left her in the ballroom moaning about her gown.' He shook his head. 'I can imagine why you might fancy a roll in the hay with her, but engaged? You really can't, not unless the Mountford fortunes have plummeted.'

The insult drove a spike of heat to Charlie's brain. Somehow he kept a grip on his temper and prowled closer, his pistol cocked. 'Mountford fortunes are as they ever were, Digby. What have you done with her?'

The other man waved a languid hand. 'She's probably tupping a footman, or one of the stable boys. You do know that's why she was expelled from school.'

Charlie recoiled.

'Didn't you know?' Digby sneered. 'You do now. Everyone else will, too, if you continue with this engagement. You were supposed to be courting my sister.'

'Shut your filthy mouth and tell me where she is.'

'She's nothing but a thorn in my family's side, but as for her whereabouts, you are welcome to search for her.'

The man was just too confident. Charlie's gut dipped. Wherever Merry was, she would not be easily found. In an old house like this there could be any number of secret staircases and priest holes. If she was still alive. His stomach did a sickening roll.

No. He wouldn't believe it. The man hadn't had time. Had he?

He looked around. 'I heard voices. She has to be here.'

'Check behind the curtains, why don't you, or under my chair,' Digby mocked.

Blade was looking distinctly annoyed, his smile all teeth and cold eyes. 'So you don't have a clue where she went, old fellow?'

Digby shook his head. 'As I say, ask the stable boys.'

'I'd sooner have a drink.' The soldier pointed to the decanter at Digby's elbow. 'D'you mind?'

'You've had enough,' Charlie said, wondering what his friend was up to.

'None of your business,' Blade said and closed in on the decanter with a slight stagger that hadn't been there a moment ago.

Charlie tensed.

Blade poured a glass and turned to look at Charlie. 'Looks like you've tangled yourself with an unsavoury young woman, my friend. If you want my advice, you'll forget all about her. Cry off.'

Charlie clenched the grip of the pistol. Digby didn't know just how much danger he was in.

Digby nodded agreement. 'Leave her to us,' he said. 'I'll sort her out. As head of the family, it is my responsibility.'

Blade took a long swallow from his glass and leaned on the high back of Digby's chair. 'Good advice,' he said, patting Digby's shoulder with his hook.

Digby glanced down at the sharpened metal and swallowed. He started to rise. 'Well, if that is all, gentlemen—'

'Not so fast,' Blade said. He patted Digby's cheek. The man paled.

Blade chuckled. 'What are you afraid of, man? This old missing hand of mine?' He ran the tip down Digby's cheek, leaving a red line on the pale flesh. 'It's taken out an eye or two and leaves a nasty scar.' He traced a path from the corner of Digby's mouth to his ear. 'Accidentally, of course.'

Charlie curled his lip. 'And who wouldn't believe two heroes of Waterloo that it wasn't an accident?'

Digby sat still. Utterly frozen, his eyes wide and terrified.

Blade moved the hook to hover over Digby's eye. 'One eye, I think. A drunken stagger, an arm outstretched for balance, drags right across his face. Nothing left to sew together. I've seen it many times.' The words were as chilling as his face.

The coward shuddered. 'No! She's in there.' He pointed at the fireplace. 'A priest hole. Twist the cherub to the right.'

'You bastard,' Charlie said. He tossed his pistol to Blade. 'Keep him covered. He's going to pay for this. And for Jane's murder.' He released the catch and a portion of the wall swung clear of the chimney breast. Gagged and bound, Merry dropped to her knees.

Charlie pulled his knife from his pocket and cut her free.

'Charlie, thank God.' Her face was ashen.

'You have nothing to tie me to any murder,' Digby cried out. 'No evidence at all.'

Charlie picked a dazed-looking Merry up and put her in a chair. He chafed her hands. 'Don't be so sure. The simple fact of your treatment of Miss Draycott is evidence of wrong doing.'

'The bitch brought it on herself. She as good as killed Jane Harper's brother. Then she changed her will in favour of some destitute whore. Our family was supposed to inherit Draycott's. The old man's will left it to us on her death.' His face twisted in disgust. 'Now Father insists I marry the slut.'

'What?' Merry gasped. 'I wouldn't marry you if you locked me in that place for a hundred years.'

Charlie looked at the dark and narrow place beside the hearth and bit back a curse. He wouldn't want to be in there for a hundred seconds.

Digby's lip curled. 'Forget marriage. All I wanted you to do was change your will in my favour.'

'And if she refused?' Charlie asked.

He shrugged, the sneer on his face more pronounced. 'She's a woman. Any judge learning of the reckless way she's behaved, setting up a house for whores, trying to run a business by herself and losing money hand over fist, would put her finances in the charge of her male relatives. To protect her interests. It stands to reason. She'd be thanking me for stopping them from incarcerating her for operating a damned bawdy house.'

'It was not a bawdy house.'

He looked morose. 'Jane would have testified otherwise.'

'You beast!' she yelled.

Sickened by the man's machinations, Charlie put up a hand. 'It looks as if you are the one going to prison. For murder.'

Digby pressed his lips together briefly. His blue eyes flashed. 'Prove it.'

'I don't think I'll have much trouble convincing a jury,' Charlie said. 'A duke's heir trumps an earl's, you'll find.'

Digby paled. 'You are a disgrace to the title. You should be supporting me, not her. I will be a peer. Your equal. Hell, you were going to marry my sister, for God's sake. What an insult, turning up here with that.' His scornful gaze turned on Merry.

She wilted under his gaze.

Charlie clenched his fists. Hitting Digby wouldn't help their case against him.

Blade waggled his pistol. 'I suppose we'll have to see what the magistrate says.'

The viscount pushed to his feet. He pulled a pistol from his pocket and pointed it at Merry.

Charlie's heart lurched. He stepped in front of her. 'You will have to kill me first.'

The man's chin bobbled. 'You self-righteous bloody bastard.'

Charlie glared at him.

Digby's face crumpled. Resignation filled his eyes. 'Allison knew nothing of this.'

His gaze begged for belief. Charlie nodded, his gut rebelling as he saw in those eyes what came next and would do nothing to stop it.

Digby turned the pistol to his temple and fired. He fell to the floor with a hollow thump.

Merry screamed.

'Don't look,' Blade said, kneeling beside the body. 'He's gone.' He picked up the edge of the carpet and tossed it over the fallen man. 'We'll leave him for the magistrate, who luckily is here at the ball.'

'His father wanted him to marry me,' Merry whispered. She gave an odd little laugh and covered her mouth with her hands, her gaze tangling with Charlie's. 'And he killed himself.'

'It's over, Merry. He was mad,' Charlie said.

'As queer as Dick's hatband,' Blade agreed. 'Come on, Miss Draycott. I think you should go home.'

'My house,' Charlie said.

Durn's front door swung open. The stiffness in Merry's shoulders eased. A sigh escaped her lips. She wanted to crawl into bed and stay within the circle of Charlie's arms. Arms that had held her all the way home. Strong protective arms. Only there would she be able to forget the happenings of this night.

She smiled up at him. 'Home at last.'

He smiled. The warm light in his gaze said he would be very happy to have her in his bed one last time.

Logan took her cloak. He gave Charlie a worried look. 'The duke and duchess are waiting for you in the drawing room.'

Charlie stiffened.

The bubble of comfort surrounding Merry burst. She swallowed. 'I will retire.'

'They asked to see you too,' Logan said with a flicker of emotion on his face. Triumph, Merry thought.

'Very well.' Charlie straightened his shoulders, a small movement, but Merry felt his discomfort, his expectation of trouble. He took her arm with a hard set to his jaw and a martial light in his eye.

Cold gripped Merry's stomach. The duke must have heard rumours of the betrothal and come to stop it. It would not take long to set their minds at rest. She stiffened her backbone.

A footman Merry didn't recognise threw open the drawing-room door. Merry stepped inside.

She stopped and stared.

Behind her, Charlie cursed softly.

Caro and Beth were perched on the edge of a sofa, their gazes pleading for rescue.

A tall grey-haired gentleman stood by the hearth, his face lined and grim.

A small but vital lady sat opposite the girls with a cup of tea in her hand. She smiled at Charlie. 'How was the ball?'

'Mother.' He bowed stiffly. Merry's heart twisted at his obvious chagrin. 'Your Grace,' he said to his father with a deeper bow. 'What brings you to Yorkshire? May I introduce my friend Miss Draycott. I see you have already met Mrs Falkner and her child's nurse, Beth.'

The grey eyes of His Grace bored into Merry. His lip curled with distaste. 'I knew your grandfather.'

'Come, child,' Her Grace said. 'Sit down. May I offer you tea?'

Merry would have preferred a hole to open up in the floor. She glanced at Charlie. His face was expressionless, his eyes dark and unfathomable.

She took the chair indicated. 'No tea, thank you.'

Charlie stood, feet apart, his hands clasped at his back. Rigid. Formal. 'As I am sure you know, Miss Draycott has kindly agreed to accept my proposal of marriage.' The harshness in his voice, as if the words had been forced from his throat, caused Merry to cringe inside.

The duke glared at her. She lifted her chin. He turned his cold gaze on his son.

'So, the rumours are true,' the duke said.

'They are not rumours,' Charlie said. 'We were waiting to inform you before making an announcement. You have saved us the trouble of returning to London.'

'Lord Tonbridge,' Merry said, 'I—'

Charlie crossed to her side and picked up her hand. He kissed it, deliberately displaying the ring on her gloved finger, one he'd given her that afternoon. He was making it worse. Why did he not just admit the truth?

'I beg you to excuse me,' Caro said, rising, then making a deep and elegant curtsy. 'My son is alone upstairs. I would prefer to go to him than take tea.'

Her Grace turned her gaze on Beth squirming on the couch. 'I found this young lady in the servants' hall kicking up larks. I understand she is one of your servants, Miss Draycott?'

Caro turned a reproachful gaze on Beth.

'I weren't there for more'n a minute or two,' Beth said. 'I've been locked up in the nursery for days.'

Caro smiled gently. 'You have been a great help. And you deserve a little fun. I beg your pardon, Your Grace. It was quite my fault.'

'Bad influence, she is,' His Grace said. 'Found her sitting in a footman's lap.'

Beth flushed scarlet. 'Sorry, Mrs Falkner.'

'What kind of woman employs—?' His Grace began.

'Father,' Charlie said.

'Please do go to your son, Mrs Falkner,' Her Grace said mildly, but with the authority of a woman who is sure of her place in the world. 'I know what it is to worry about children. I suggest you take your nurse with you.'

Head down, Beth scurried to the door with Caro close behind. Cowards. And Merry didn't blame them one little bit. She felt quite cowardly herself and rose to follow them.

'I wonder if I might have a moment more of your time, Miss Draycott,' the duchess said.

The command hung in the air. No way to refuse, it was uttered too softly. Merry sank back into her chair. She swallowed against the rawness in her throat.

The door closed behind Caro. Lucky Caro.

'Hmmph.' The duke cleared his throat. He looked at Merry, then at his son. 'Why did you bring these females into my house, Tonbridge?'

Charlie stiffened, muscles flickering in his jaw, his hands opening and closing. 'You will not speak in that tone of voice about my fiancée's friends.'

There was something in his eyes. Embarrassment, perhaps? Regret? Whatever it was, it was Merry's fault for letting his chivalry overcome her objections. She didn't belong in his world. She never had. And never would.

The dryness in her throat made it hard to speak. Her voice sounded rusty. 'Your Grace, Lord Tonbridge gave us needed sanctuary. Please be assured we will be leaving first thing in the morning.'

She removed the ring from her finger and placed it on the tea tray. 'I hereby relinquish any claim to your son's hand. We find we do not suit.'

'I'm witness to your statement, miss,' the duke said.

'Oh, my dear,' Her Grace said. She glanced up at Charlie. 'Have you argued?'

He stared at Merry, his face grim. 'No. The engagement stands,' Charlie said.

'What?' His Grace roared, his face flushing with an unhealthy colour of puce.

The room blurred. Charlie's face wavered in and out of focus. She could not quite make out his expression, but she knew what was there. Determination. Perhaps even a desire to protect her feelings. Chivalrous kindness. She could not let him do it. She swallowed the hard lump in her throat. Forced the shake out of her chest with a deep breath.

She rose to her feet and brushed the wrinkles from her skirt. 'Tha's been reet kind, Charlie. Helpin' out with the Purtefoys an' all.' She cast him a saucy smile as she headed for the door. 'If you ever need a favour, or a tumble, Merry Draycott's your lass. But I'll not hand over my brass to any man.'

'Damn it, Merry,' he said.

She turned at the door and swept a magnificent curtsy. 'It was a pleasure to meet you both.' Dignified and straight-backed, she walked out.

The footman quietly closed the door.

Heart in her throat, so large and painful, Merry hesitated, listening, praying everything would be all right between Charlie and his father.

'How dare you bring a common trollop into *my* house?' The duke. It seemed her little act had worked.

'You are wrong about Miss Draycott,' Charles said, his voice low. 'She deserves nothing but respect.'

'What about you, Charles?' The duke's voice, harsh, angry. 'How can I respect a man who forgets his promises so quickly? Did I not keep my part of the bargain? Have I not paid out a fortune to widows and orphans from the last time you ran from your obligations? At your request? Based on your promises to do your duty?'

What on earth could he be talking about?

The footman shook his head, his face disapproving. Merry glared at him.

Charlie cursed. 'This is different.'

'Charles,' his mother said sharply.

'Is it?' his father said, overriding his apology.

'Please, both of you,' Her Grace said. 'Can we not discuss this sensibly?'

'Sensibly?' the duke roared. 'He doesn't understand sensible. Or honour. He destroyed a regiment and with it our good name with his foolhardiness. I'll be damned if I let him destroy anything else with this latest peccadillo.'

Merry covered her mouth with her hand, shock catching her by the throat in a vice. The footman inched closer, his face red beneath his peruke. She held her ground.

'Damn you, Father,' Charles said. 'Miss Draycott is worth a dozen Lady Allison Purtefoys as you will soon discover.'

'Oh, I know you burnt your bridges there, Tonbridge. Ruined my hopes. But I'll not let you marry that woman. I'll cut you off without a penny. You'll get nothing that isn't entailed, d'you hear me? Not a thing.'

Merry whirled away. She'd heard enough to know exactly what she had to do.

Charlie wanted to plant his father a facer. And he might have if the old fellow had not looked as sick as a horse. He crossed the room and glared down at him. 'Do it. Cut me off. See if I give a damn.'

Father glared back. 'You are a Mountford. Act like one.'

'I am also a man.' He looked at his mother. 'There is more to life than duty.'

'What about Robert?' Father said. 'Don't you care about your brother now? Are you so blinded by lust you'd abandon him?'

The realisation hit Charlie like a blow to the solar plexus. 'He doesn't need you or your title or your money. Any more than I do.'

Father's jaw dropped. He narrowed his eyes. 'Don't test me, my boy.'

'I'm no boy, Father, to be bullied by you or anyone else. If you'll forgive me, I have your apologies to make to Miss Draycott.'

'Damnation, Charles. You will not leave this room.'

Oh, but he would. It was time he and Merry sorted out just where they stood.

He walked out of the door and ran up the stairs.

He found Merry in her chamber, folding a gown into her valise. She did not look up.

'What are you doing?'

Merry turned to face him. 'Preparing for our departure.'

He felt something tear in his chest. 'Marry me, Merry.'

Open-mouthed, she stared at him and he swore he saw a yes in her gaze, and yet there was a brittleness about her smile he couldn't quite understand. 'A tempting offer, my lord, but, no, thank you. I am more grateful for your help than I can say, but it is time to return to reality.'

Refused. Again.

Damn it all. 'Why not?'

She looked over at the valise and then back to him. 'I'm not the marrying kind. I have a business to run. I have been away too long.'

Unable to look at the regret in her eyes, Charlie turned away. He crossed to the window and looked out. Ice frosted the panes. Merry wouldn't be speaking of her business if she felt as he did. Perhaps this was his punishment for all those lives lost. He was to be deprived of the one thing he really wanted. No doubt he deserved it. 'I will come with you,' he said. 'See you safe home. Stay a while.'

Try to get her out of his blood. Except he had the feeling it would never happen.

'Running the mill keeps me far too busy for such distractions.'

'Damn it.' He crossed to her, pulled her into his embrace and looked down into her lovely face. 'You know I will miss you.'

She stroked his cheek. 'I'll miss thee, too. But duty is duty. You have yours and I have mine. The reason for our bargain is over. I thank you for standing up for me to your father, but I have cried off and there is no sense in drawing this out.'

Regret shadowed her eyes, as if she was holding something back. Something she didn't want him to know.

Of course. It hit him like a blow between the eyes. She'd seen him cowering in the dark, seen his weakness and wanted no more to do with him. It had to be something, because if Merry wanted to stay with him, nothing would stop her.

'Then there is no more to be said.' His voice was hoarse, his throat tight.

She nodded and raised her brows. 'We do have one last night, before we set our feet back on the path of duty. Should we waste it talking?'

His blood heated. His body hardened. How could she still have this effect after all she had said? He should walk away. At least he'd retain a shard of pride.

She must have seen the thought in his face, because she gave a wry smile. 'Happen you are right. I'll move into Caro's apartments in the other wing.' A small sniff undid him.

Tipped her chin and brushed a tear away with the ball of his thumb. 'Oh, Merry, why are you crying?'

She cupped her hands around his face. 'I need you tonight, Charlie,' she whispered. 'I need you to hold me and make me forget.' Inevitability shone in her eyes. This or nothing.

He looked down at her, and his heart felt full and empty at the same time. He felt as if a step in any direction was the wrong one, but he did know he wanted Merry. And probably always would. He pushed aside thoughts of the empty future, because tonight he would hold her, bring her bliss and pretend she was his. Something in his chest stretched tight like a bowstring. No matter what happened, it would break. 'So be it. We will not waste these last few hours. Instead we will make memories neither of us will forget.'

He let her see the heat of his desire.

Merry tipped her face for his kiss. Her heart ached. The pummelling it had received from her betraying family seemed insignificant to the tearing in two she felt now. He'd stood against his father and defended her honour, but the sacrifice he faced was too great. The scorn in his father's voice, the threat of banishment, were too much for her shoulders to bear. She'd already separated one man from his family—she could not do the same thing to Charlie. She loved him too much.

Love? How had love happened? Wasn't it gratitude? Friendship?

The pain in her chest increased. If she truly loved him, she had to let him go. For his sake.

He plied her lips with his until she opened to admit him. The kiss was delicious, expert, teasing and demanding. She let her senses drift on sensual delight, until they were both breathless.

'Let me help you out of that gown,' he whispered in her ear. Delicious shivers ran down her spine. Sensations she would never feel again. Regret flowed through her veins, an aching sadness. The urge to weep caught at her throat. Burned in her eyes. Pain she must not let him see.

'Tha's a bad lad,' she said with a smile that felt forced. To hide it she turned her back to grant him access to her ties.

He made short work of the hooks and the laces. 'Oh, Merry,' he whispered, 'I am going to miss you.'

She would miss him too.

He slipped the sleeves of the gown down her arms and held it there. 'Now I have you,' he whispered wickedly. 'You cannot get away.'

She chuckled low in her throat.

A shudder of pleasure ripped through her body. Helpless, she waited for the onslaught of his lips.

Slowly, he pulled the pins from her hair. Heavy black tresses fell down around her shoulders. From behind, he cupped her breasts covered by her chemise, rubbing her nipples with his thumbs while he buried his face in her hair, nuzzling until he found her nape. He licked and nibbled at her neck and shoulders until the sensations had her writhing with pleasure.

He breathed a soft laugh against the tender place beneath her ear. 'Patience, my lovely.'

'You will suffer for this,' she gasped as his tongue explored her ear and shivers ran across her spine.

'I'll look forward to it, sweet darling.'

His endearments tugged at her heart. Unbearably sweet as well as sensual. Wanting to see his face, hold him in her arms, Merry twisted around. He'd trapped her arms at her sides within the gown. Left no option, she attacked his mouth with her lips and pressed her body to his hard length.

With a grin, he relaxed his hold, allowing her to ease her arms free. She flung them around his neck and showered his face with kisses as light as butterfly wings.

While she kissed him on his lips and cheeks and jaw and chin, he pushed the dress down over her hips. It slid to the floor. Taking her shoulders in his hands, he pushed her a little away. 'You are beautiful,' he said. 'Do you know what word came to my mind when I saw you out on the moors?'

She shook her head.

'Perfect,' he breathed. He shook his head. 'Nothing else. Simply perfect.'

Thrilled and honoured, she wanted to melt. She forced herself to grin. 'Now you know better.'

He laughed. 'Yes. I do. You are sublime.'

The reverence in his voice smashed through her defences tearing down walls, crumbling armour to dust, yet she could not let him see. She forced a smile and hoped he would not hear how close she was to breaking. 'Thank you,' she murmured. *I love you*, she whispered in her heart.

Brightening her smile, she cocked her head on one side. 'You are behind in the undressing department.' With trembling fingers, nerves and excitement tangling together to render her awkward, she attacked the knot at his throat while he shrugged out of his coats.

The strip of muslin followed them to the floor. Obliging her, he pulled his shirt off over his head. She looked her fill at his chest, so broad and manly, at the scar gleaming silver in the candlelight, and branded it all on her mind and in her soul.

A corner of his mouth lifted. A purely male arrogant smile. It hit her low in her belly and her blood raced through her veins, hot with desire.

It hurt to know she would never see him like this again. She wanted to see all of him.

Her fingers went to his waistband, hesitated. Would he think her too bold. 'May I do the honours?'

'Please.' His voice sounded strained as if he, too, battled with words he could not say.

The buttons came undone with a little tugging. Free of the confines of tight fabric, his shaft rose proudly between them. She took it in her hand, curled her fingers around his width and stroked hard and firm. A hiss of indrawn breath tightened her insides with a steady pulse beat of blood. She slipped her hand beneath the base of him, and rolled his testicles, heavy and hot, in her palm. Exquisite velvety heat. He groaned his pleasure and sent hers rocketing out of control.

She leaned close to his lovely sculpted chest and grazed his nipple with her teeth.

'Careful, sweet,' he said on a sharp exhale of breath. 'You will undo me too quickly.' He picked her up and laid her on the bed, before slipping off his shoes and peeling off his evening breeches and stockings.

Magnificent man lit by candlelight. Sculpted warm skin and muscle. A god of love bearing the scars of a warrior. She would always remember him like this.

His expression softened as he gazed on her. Regret filled his eyes. It echoed in her heart and her soul.

Then he covered her with his body.

Her core ached for his entry, but her mind yearned for more. This would be the last time they would lie together and she longed to bring him more pleasure that he had ever known. A gift he would never forget.

He didn't resist when she pushed at his shoulder. He rolled on his back, the candlelight and the wicked smile curving his lips making him less angel and more devil. She straddled his hips.

He grinned up at her. 'Feel like going for a ride?' He reached down to lift her up.

'Lie still,' she ordered. 'If I am the rider, you must obey my commands.'

His jaw clenched. For a moment she thought he would refuse, but he let his hands fall to his sides. 'Tally ho.'

She dipped her head and kissed his lovely mouth, nibbling his lips, tasting with her tongue the fruit of wine and his own special flavour. When he responded with his own darting taste, she sucked hard, holding him fast, punishing him for his boldness. Immediately he held still, clearly understanding.

Her insides tightened deliciously. This would be a night to remember for them both. She faltered at the thought of never seeing him again. Never knowing his touch again. Or the feel of his mouth on her body. Agony speared between her ribs. She fought a cry of anguish.

Now was not the time for sorrow. There would be years and years to feel sad. Now was the time for taking pleasure and giving pleasure and sharing pleasure.

She broke free of his mouth, pressed her breasts to his hard wall of chest, moving her lips over his cheekbone, his stubble-hazed cheek and jaw, feeling the roughness of beard and the strength of bone beneath. She licked the rise of his Adam's apple and the hollow beneath and inhaled the faint scent of bay and musky sweat.

She learned every dip and contour, every bone and pulse point, where he had hair and where his skin was silken smooth and warm beneath her hand.

She tweaked first one nipple, then the other, feeling his groan of pleasure laced with pain deep in her core.

Reaching down between them, she found his shaft hard and eager. Felt his need to drive home in the tension of muscle and sinew as he drew in a swift gasping breath.

'There is something I have always wanted to try,' she whispered.

He looked down at her, one of those male considering glances that is full of amusement laced with a healthy dose of wariness.

'You'll think me very strange. You might not like it. Perhaps it is better left unasked.'

His expression changed, became more heated. Feral. 'Try me.'

Dare she? She took a breath. 'I've had the dream of a man who obeys my every command.'

His eyelids lowered a fraction and she looked away, suddenly embarrassed, wishing she hadn't spoken.

A warm hand gently drew her face around. 'I'm hard just thinking about it. If it is your wish, it will be my very real pleasure.'

Excitement clogged her throat. 'Put your hands above your head,' she ordered in a husky voice.

She sensed a slight hesitation, but he did as requested.

'Open your legs.'

'Merry—'

'No talking.'

He pressed his lips together and widened his thighs.

A generous relinquishing of control for a man who liked to be in command. The heat of shared passion in his eyes drove her to heights of arousal such as she'd never encountered before. She could scarcely breathe for the thrill of it.

One hand on his shaft, she brought him to her entrance, the other she used to torment his erect nipple. His chest rose and fell on ragged breaths as he fought to hold still beneath her hands. His eyes squeezed shut. His lips drew back in a grimace, revealing white even teeth. She traced the outline of muscle on his chest with the tip of her forefinger. She stroked him against her folds. 'Do you want to be inside me?'

'Yes,' he said, hoarse and low.

'I don't think you are ready.'

He opened his mouth to protest and then must have thought better of it, because he simply gazed at her from eyes hazy with pleasure and sadness.

'Raise your knees.'

He followed her order. Straddling his groin, she rested her back against his thighs. His shaft jutted straight up between them. She circled the tip with her finger. So silky soft. She bent forwards and flicked it with her tongue. He pressed upwards, seeking more prolonged contact.

She straightened and looked down at his face. 'Bad boy,' she said. 'Is that what you are? A wicked boy? You can answer.'

'Yes.' He grinned wickedly. 'I'm evil.'

'I like bad boys.' She leaned forwards and took him in her mouth. She licked and sucked and tormented his shaft until his body shuddered beneath her. He was hanging on by barely a thread and not once had he tried to wrest back control. The man was a god. She would adore him forever.

She released him. 'Please, Charlie, join with me.'

Pride filled his face and he helped her rise up. She guided him to her entrance. Slowly, delicately, she slid down his shaft, a gentle glide when he wanted hard pounding force. Each time his hips shifted, she pulled away. He groaned his frustration, the sound zinging through her blood to heighten her tension.

When finally he was seated deep within her, she held perfectly still, squeezing him with her inner muscles, each new pull a little harder than the one before.

He panted with the effort of remaining immobile beneath her, his shaft twitching and throbbing until she thought she might go mad with the tiny sensations tormenting her insides.

Nothing remained of her mind, every fibre of her being focused on their joining.

In a steady rhythm she began to ride. Lifting and lowering herself with smooth long strokes, leaning back to increase the pressure where it felt unbelievably good, watching the pleasure in his eyes and expression as he submitted to her enjoyment of his body.

He lifted his lashes and gazed into her face with smoky eyes, his lips curved in a sensual smile, and all control left her as she rode him hard and wild, driving to completion. The tightness within stretched to breaking point.

She shattered.

He followed her over the edge with a moan deep in his throat, a sound of joy and despair.

She caught the cry in her mouth and collapsed against his chest as his hips pumped his hot seed into her body.

Shivering and shuddering, they lay together in heat and bliss. The shadow of their parting returned, like a presence in the room. Merry tried to pretend it wasn't there.

Charlie lay beneath her, his gaze following the shadows and patches of light cast by the candles. Never in his life had he felt so drained and replete. Or so alive. His skin prickled with excitement, while his limbs remained languid and heavy beneath her sleeping form. Tonight they'd become one. Losing her was like losing part of himself.

Regret left an empty space beneath his ribs. A hollow in his stomach. This was goodbye. Sorrow filled him. A black emptiness. A knowledge that he would never find another woman like his Merry. Except she wasn't his to have and to hold. She was quicksilver. Beautiful to look at. Impossible to grasp.

But he didn't know why.

She stirred. Her hand tracing circles on his chest. 'What happened at Waterloo?'

The urge to deny tightened his throat. The thought of putting his guilt into words made his spirit shrink. She'd despise him. As she should. Hell, he despised himself for the suffering he'd caused because he'd rebelled against his lot in life. He'd done so much damage.

She more than anyone ought to know.

He drew in a breath. 'Against my father's wishes I joined the cavalry. I commanded a troop of horse at Waterloo. My orders were to take a French cannon. We charged. The French saw what we were about and sent a troop to meet us. We clashed right in front of the cannon's mouths. The French broke really fast. In hindsight, some of us think it was a trap.'

'Who thinks?'

'Read, for one. A good friend. And a good soldier.'

The caresses ceased. 'I didn't think heirs of dukedoms went to war any more. I thought they left it to their younger brothers.'

'I switched places with my twin, Robert. He took my place here. I went to war as him. Looking for excitement.'

'Didn't you get found out?'

A smile pulled at his lips. 'We are like peas in a pod. We changed places so often as lads, it was like second nature. Father always hated it when we were young.'

'What happened next?'

'When the French turned and ran, we followed. Half of my men took the cannon. The rest of us, on my orders, followed the French over the hill straight through a company of their infantry waiting to cut us to pieces. A more experienced officer would never have continued the charge. I led them to their deaths.'

'No wonder you have nightmares.'

'The worst came later.' He swallowed the dryness in his mouth. 'I was cut down by a French officer's sabre. My horse fell on top of me and I lost consciousness. When I came to my senses, I was still beneath my horse, crushed, having difficulty breathing. It was dark and it was raining. All around me men were screaming, begging for water, unless they were dead. The appalling stink, the horror. The fear. It's all there waiting every time I close my eyes. I called out. Read answered from a few feet away. We talked to keep our spirits up. Then the women came. The camp followers.'

'They helped you?'

'Hell, no, Merry. If they find you alive, they kill you for whatever they can find on your body.'

'How could they?'

'Mostly because they are starving. In daylight I don't blame them.

In the dark, they are unholy horrors. Blade and I lay very still, pretending to be dead whenever a party of them came by. Hours passed. Every now and then you'd hear a man cry out and know they'd finished him off. I let them finish off what was left of my men and did nothing to stop it, terrified I was next. I even played dead while one of them dragged me out from under the horse and stole every stitch of my clothes.'

She gasped. 'No wonder you have bad dreams. You could have been murdered.'

He should have been. 'She started hacking at Blade's finger for his ring. He screamed. She lifted her knife to cut his throat.' He shuddered, then chuckled grimly. 'I stabbed her with my knife. I'd been using it to try to keep the rats away. I tied up his hand as best I could, but I was so damned scared they'd hear him and come back and finish us off I stuffed his mouth with a rag to keep him quiet. He almost suffocated.'

'But you saved his life.'

'Hardly. He would not have been there but for me. My men trusted me to see them safe and I led them to their deaths.' Guilt roiled through him, bitter and black, writhing in his gut as the visions filled his mind. An older wiser officer would have seen the danger.

'What happened then?'

He shrugged. 'They found us at first light. Me and Blade and a couple of the others.' Then, only then, in the grey dawn, had he realised the full extent of his mistake. 'Twenty good men died or were badly injured because I didn't follow orders.'

'But you captured the cannon.'

'We captured the cannon, but my commanding officer was furious. Even more so, when he realised I wasn't Robert. He half-expected Father to have him put in the Tower.'

'I think you have to stop blaming yourself. You did your best. War is terrible, but it is over now and because of men like you the world has peace.'

He kissed the top of her head and inhaled the scent of her hair. He felt easier within himself than he had for years. Never had he talked about the horror of that night, the fear, not even with Blade who had been there, and while the guilt would never leave him, some of the darkness in his soul had faded.

Because of Merry. It was as if by listening she had taken some of the worst of it into herself. Relieved him of the worst of the burden.

He rolled on to his side and took her face in his hands. He thought he saw the sheen of tears in her eyes. He kissed her mouth, her cheek, her eyelids and tasted salt. 'Don't leave, Merry.'

Her answering half-laugh, half-regretful sob wrenched at his heart. 'I can't stay. You know I can't.'

He didn't, but the finality in her voice blocked his objections. She didn't want to stay.

For the last time, he enfolded her in his arms.

A fortnight had passed since Merry's departure when Charlie joined his mother for afternoon tea in the drawing room. She always looked lovely, but in the sunlight from the window, and wearing her favourite pale lilac, she positively glowed. Robert's news, no doubt. They'd had a letter from Italy announcing a grandchild in the autumn.

He hoped his decision would not dim her sparkle.

'Did you enjoy your ride, dear?' Mother asked as he sat beside her on the sofa.

'I did.' He stirred the tea. Then put the cup down. There was no sense in procrastinating. 'I went to visit Lady Allison.'

'That was kind of you. I really must call in again myself before we leave for London.'

'You are going soon?'

'In two days' time. Your father is needed in town.' She sighed. 'Politics. How is poor dear Lady Allison?'

Charlie gritted his teeth. Poor dear Lady Allison had been

horrendously unkind to Merry, even if she didn't know of her brother's plans. 'Her brother's death hit the family hard. While she has my sympathy, she knows any chance of a betrothal is out of the question.'

Mother frowned. 'Is this your father's decision?'

'No. It is mine.'

Mother sipped her tea, then, head tilted on one side, looked at him. Her grey eyes twinkled. 'Do you have some other gel in mind?'

He grimaced. 'You know I do. But she won't have me.'

Mother made a scoffing noise. 'What girl wouldn't have you?'

Mother never could see anything wrong with any of her children.

'I'm going to try once more to change her mind.'

She put down her cup and put her hand over his on his thigh. Her hands were small and the skin fragile. She gave his hand a pat. 'Why, Charle? Why this girl?'

It was a question he'd been torturing himself with for days. Why couldn't he just get on and do his duty as he'd promised his father when he came back from Waterloo? It wasn't a matter of honour. She'd refused him twice. The answer had come to him in the middle of the night.

'She makes me laugh. She makes me remember there is more to life than abiding by the rules.' He turned to face his mother full on. 'With her I believe in myself.' He thought about speaking of love, but decided that could only be spoken of in one person's hearing.

'I wish you good fortune, my son.'

For a moment, Charlie stared at her serious face in bemusement. She raised her brows above twinkling eyes. 'I hadn't seen you look happier for years, than I did the night before she left. Until your father got in his high stirrups.'

He took her hand and kissed it. 'Captain Read is travelling to Skepton, I am going with him, then on to Draycott House to seek out Merry.' He let go a sigh. 'I'm sorry if this upsets Father. I just hope he doesn't take his spleen out on Robert as well as me.'

The thought of being cast adrift the way Robert had left a bitter taste in his mouth, but Robert had survived and so would he.

Mother picked up her teacup. It hovered at her lips for a moment, then she looked at him with a frown. 'Your father gets a bee in his bonnet sometimes, you know. Why he thought I would permit him to cut Robert out of the family, I cannot imagine.' She sipped.

'Permit?' Charlie said cautiously.

Mother looked at him with surprise. 'Power has a way of corrupting a man, Charles. Makes him think he can never make a mistake. Don't let it happen to you. Though I doubt a woman as strong as Miss Draycott will allow it.'

'I'm not sure I understand what you mean.'

Mother put down the cup and picked up her embroidery. 'Alfred can pass laws and write bills—' she smiled a small smile '—but our family is my concern.' Mother cut a skein of blue silk with a decided snip. 'You leave your father to me.'

An odd feeling, something like horrified laughter, rose in Charlie's throat. He managed to keep it behind his teeth. When he finally managed to breathe, he was able to ask his question. 'Are you saying you have Father under your thumb?'

'Not when it comes to important matters of State. But here in this family, your father is not the one in charge. Believe me, none of my sons will ever be cast out again. Not if your father plans to live to a peaceful and ripe old age.'

Side by side with the laughter in his chest, hope blossomed that no ill would come to his twin as a result of what he was about to do. Not that he was sure his efforts would be rewarded.

Merry was a conundrum he hadn't yet solved.

Mother set a stitch, peering at it closely, then her grey eyes flashed up to meet his. She touched his hand. 'Be gentle, son. She's been hurt, I think.'

Merry? Strong outspoken Merry? Was that what she hid behind

her blunt exterior? She had a kind heart. And a courageous soul. The thought she might be in pain tied his gut in knots. That he might have added to it...

Mother flapped her embroidery in front of his face. 'Stop blaming yourself and go and make amends, Charles.'

He grinned. His mother might be small, but she was exceedingly formidable and clearly very wise. 'There is one thing I would like to say, Mother, if I may.'

An eyebrow shot up. 'Indeed?'

'Heaven help anyone who crosses you.'

Laughing, Charlie went off to set his affairs in order, because who knew how long it would take Merry to change her mind.

If she would.

He pushed that cold thought aside.

Chapter Sixteen

'Let me show you the refectory,' Caro said, leading the way to the back of the new house Merry had acquired in Skepton. 'The workmen finished yesterday. It is perfect.'

Perfect. The word struck a painful chord. Somehow Merry managed to smile. 'Then lead the way, my dear.'

In the two weeks since she'd returned to Draycott House, Merry's life had settled back into its old rhythm. At least, outwardly the rhythm remained the same. Inside, she felt like a clock with a broken spring, with little rushes of time full of busy work and long empty gaps in which the seconds ticked by like hours.

Even here, visiting Caro's new refuge for needy women, she couldn't feel any excitement. It was as if a piece of her was missing.

Charlie. Each day she scanned *The Times*, looking for word of him, dreading to see the announcement of his forthcoming wedding and steeling herself to read it and smile.

Caro flung open the door to a long room, with a bank of windows down one wall, a polished plank wood floor and furnished with a rectangular table surrounded by chairs. A door led off it to the kitchen. 'We can feed at least six ladies in here,' she said with obvious satisfaction. 'Once they have real work and can afford to rent accommodation, we can take another batch.'

'The workmen did a good job. It looks very welcoming.' Prior to the renovations, there had been three small rooms at the back of the house.

'They will start the dormitory next week.'

'Mummy, Mummy.' Tommy rushed into the room, his face flushed with excitement. 'There's a soldier at the door.' He shot off again. Tommy loved all things military and was no doubt intending to ogle their guest. If he was a guest.

Caro looked at Merry with consternation in her eyes. 'Not more trouble.'

'I haven't heard any grumblings. Mr Broadoaks tackled the other mill owners and their wives. He promised money, too.'

Beth appeared at the door. Her face held suppressed excitement, but no concern. 'Two gentlemen to see you, Miss Draycott.'

'Me?' Merry said. 'Who on earth knows I am here?' Instead of working in her office as usual, she'd used the finished refectory as an excuse to leave her empty house. Not that she was getting much work done even when she was there. Her mind wouldn't focus. It kept wandering off to think about Charlie and the events of the past few weeks.

Beth had a secretive smile on her round face. 'I've put them in the front parlour, miss.'

'Did the gentlemen not give you their cards?' Merry asked. She really didn't want to see anyone. Making small talk took too much energy.

'They did, mum, but I couldn't read them too good.' She sauntered off with a swing of her hips.

Merry glanced at Caro and laughed. Beth's role as housekeeper had it drawbacks, but she was learning.

'We should see who it is, I suppose,' Caro said.

'Yes, we should.' Merry tucked her arm through Caro's and they strolled back to the front of the house.

Merry gestured for Caro to go ahead. It was, after all, her house. Merry had put it in her name.

Caro came to a sudden halt with a gasp of shock. Merry almost bumped into her. She stepped around her friend.

Two gentlemen rose to their feet. Tommy hung on the arm of the chair from which Captain Read had risen, hero worship on his angelic face.

And looking haughty and reserved across the room was... Charlie.

Merry's stomach pitched. Her heart stuttered to a halt, then broke into a gallop. She grabbed the doorpost for support. 'Lord Tonbridge?' Her voice sounded reedy. She swallowed and realised the captain was staring at Caro open-mouthed.

Charlie bowed. 'You remember Captain Read, don't you, Miss Draycott? Mrs Falkner, Captain Read is a friend of mine, here in Skepton looking into rumours of unrest at the mills.'

The captain glanced down at the boy and back at Caro. 'Mrs Falkner?' He looked stunned.

As did Caro, who backed towards the door, her hands fluttering at the ribbons of her cap. 'If you gentlemen will excuse me, I have remembered an urgent appointment. Thomas. Come along.' She made a stiff curtsy and left the captain frowning after her.

Tommy dragged his feet in her wake.

'If you do not mind, Miss Draycott,' the soldier said. 'I would like a word with Mrs Falkner.'

Whatever the captain wanted to say to Caro, the desire for speech was clearly not mutual. Merry put out a staying hand. 'Please, Captain, may I not take the opportunity to express my deep thanks for your help the other evening?'

Reed glanced down at his coat sleeve tucked inside his jacket. His mouth curled in a wry smile. 'I wouldn't have missed it for the world, my dear Miss Draycott. Quite like old times, eh, Tonbridge?'

'Quite,' Charlie said drily.

The captain bowed. 'If you will excuse me.' He marched off.

'Oh, dear,' Merry said. 'I think he knows Caro.'

'I shouldn't be surprised. Blade is a bit of a rake. And the hand doesn't seem to hold him back.'

'Perhaps I should go and make sure she is all right.'

He blocked her from leaving. 'She won't come to any harm. He's an officer and a gentleman.'

'Why are you here?' Merry asked, struggling to ignore her quickened heartbeat. 'Are you visiting in the neighbourhood or passing through on your way to town, perhaps? It is very kind of you to call and see how we do.'

'Merry,' he said sternly, 'I came specifically to see you.'

A lump rose in her throat. She swallowed. 'We have nothing left to discuss.'

He looked down at his hat, turned it in his hands and set it on the table. 'I think we do. Or at least I have things I need to say.'

She really didn't want to do this again. Her heart was aching quite enough at the sight of him without adding further pain. Nothing had changed. He was still heir to a dukedom. She was still common-as-muck Merry Draycott, a mill owner's daughter. She had done the right thing for him. Left him with his own class of people. Why could he not let it lie?

'Please, Charles, can we not do this?' She went to the window and looked out. Dark grey clouds hung over the moors beyond the edge of town. 'My business in Skepton is concluded. I called in on Caro on my way home, but I really must be going. It looks like snow.'

'It doesn't smell like snow,' he said.

She spun around and just caught the flicker of a smile on his lips. Teasing her? The wretch. Didn't he know how painful it was for her to see him again? Probably not. He was likely doing what he considered his duty. A courtesy call.

She managed to draw a shaky breath, something to sustain her next words around the pain. 'If the captain needs information from me, he may call on me at Draycott House.'

'But I may not,' he said, his voice low.

'No. You may not.' It hurt, but still she smiled. 'I am not looking for an affaire at the moment.'

He smiled. 'Are you sure?'

His voice was low and husky. Sensual. His eyes hot. Heat fired beneath her skin, her body tingled where it should be quiet and still. 'Perfectly sure,' she said coolly. She couldn't bear the thought of it, knowing eventually he would leave her.

In three steps he was at her side, his hand holding hers to his lips. His brown eyes regarded her steadily, intently, as if he would look into her soul. 'I miss you, love.'

The words melted her insides. Her arms yearned to hold him. What good would it do? There would be more pain, more longing when he left. Nothing good could come of it, but a few fleeting hours of passion.

Surely he understood. 'We are not children, Lord Tonbridge. We are adults. We know that it is not the end of the world if we are denied the thing we most want at any particular moment. Find somewhere else to cast your eye. Lady Allison, perhaps.' Oh, dash it, that sounded terribly bitter.

The twinkle did not leave his gaze. 'Lady Allison is in mourning.'

Merry recoiled, forced herself to remain calm. 'There are many others, I am sure.'

'Yes,' he agreed, smiling, his face devilish. 'There are.'

'Well, then.' She tried to recover her hand, but he held it fast.

His gaze searched her face. 'Unfortunately, there is only one Merry Draycott.'

Captain Read charged into the room. He winced when speared by Charlie's glare. 'Mrs Falkner has disappeared.'

'And you are telling us this because…?' Charlie said coldly.

'I thought Miss Draycott might know where I should look.'

'If Mrs Falkner does not wish to be found, Captain Read,' Merry said, 'don't you think you should leave her unfound?'

He swallowed and turned red. 'I...I... Yes. I beg your pardon.' He bowed and left.

'Idiot,' Charlie said.

The interruption had allowed Merry a chance to gather her scattered wits. She pulled her hand free, put a few feet between them, where she found air enough to draw breath, and escaped his sensual pull. 'It's reet kindly of you, my lord. Flattering. If you are concerned for my reputation, you needn't be. It is as ever it was.'

'Merry, dearest Merry. It is no good hiding behind that accent. It is music to my ears, love. I have done a great deal of thinking these past two weeks about what is right and what makes sense.'

He'd been thinking? She'd been going round in ever-decreasing circles. 'Nothing between us makes sense.'

'I know I am not happy while we are apart. And I know I was never happier than when we were together.'

A rush of tears filled her eyes. She turned her face away. 'Please, I am begging you, do not ask this of me.'

'What am I asking, Merry? You have to tell me, so I understand.'

'How can you understand? You are the son of a duke.'

'Try me. Give me a chance. Please, Merry.'

Oh, he knew her too well. If he had commanded her, she could have called on anger and resisted, but this gentle question was so much harder to fight.

She took a deep breath, panicked and grabbed the first thought in her mind. 'I won't be the reason for estranging you from your family.'

'Heard that, did you?' he said grimly. 'I should have guessed. This has nothing to do with my father. I am talking about *our* future, *our* happiness. Doing my duty, as Father calls it, won't make up for past mistakes. I know that now. Nothing can. I can only trust I have learned enough to do better in the future. Merry, I want that future to include you. I need you there with me.'

Oh, it wasn't fair, that he should be so wonderful, so sweet, so terribly tempting. She sniffed and he handed her his handkerchief. She dabbed at her eyes. 'But I don't fit in your world.'

'How can you know if you don't try? With me beside you—'

'I did try.' The old hurt rose up like a poisonous mist, clouding her mind with the anger, the hurt. 'At school. When I first arrived, they laughed at my speech. I'd been copying Grandfather, you see. I learned quickly. I said nothing out of turn. I was a model pupil. I even bought things for the other girls. Grandfather sent me whatever I asked for, money, hair ribbons. A puppy.' A hard laugh escaped her at the memory. 'Can you imagine the stir? I was the centre of attention.'

She tugged her hand free and paced to the other side of the room. She forced a smile to her lips and turned to face him. He was watching her gravely, trying to understand. How could he understand? He had never known what it was like to feel rejected, unworthy. 'I loved how they gathered around me.' A hot lump formed in her throat. She breathed around it, her chest rising and falling painfully. The schoolgirl of those long-ago years, curled up in a ball. Curled around the hurt, protected it from view.

'All the while I was trying to fit in, those girls were laughing behind my back.'

'You don't know that for sure.'

'I do know it. Lady Allison kindly told me. Why do you think I sought comfort from Jeremy?'

'No one will laugh at the Marchioness of Tonbridge.'

'You don't understand, Charlie. They expelled me from school because I wasn't the right class of person. Not because of what I did in the potting shed. I wasn't good enough. Nothing has changed.'

He shoved a hand through his hair. He looked tired and frustrated. 'All right, we will live in seclusion. We don't need to mingle with the *ton*. It will be just us. You and I and our children, if we are blessed.'

She grabbed on to his words like a life line. 'You'd hide me away, you mean. You see. You know I'm right. You'd be ashamed of me.'

'You are twisting my words.'

'And what of the children? Will they be laughed at, too, when they go to school?'

'Of course not.'

'You don't know that. You can't know that.'

'I'm sorry you had such a bad time of it. Children are cruel. And, yes, the *beau monde* is rabid about guarding their privileges. Show weakness and they will tear you to pieces. But you aren't weak. And nor will our children be weak.'

'I can't do it.'

His jaw hardened. His eyes grew bleak. His expression turned to granite. 'Merry, these excuses of yours encourage me to think I can find a solution, but if the real truth is you don't want me, then say so. Put me out of my misery.'

She wanted to weep. To see him looking so hurt, so confused, and to let him suffer. She wrung her hands. 'You don't understand.'

Sadly he gazed at her. 'No. I don't. I have tried. But I really do not understand why you would care more about the views of a pack of jackals than about us.'

Layer by layer he peeled away the fabric she'd woven to protect her innermost secrets until she could no long hide the raw and bleeding bitter truth.

'Do you know what I did?'

Silent, watchful, he waited for her to tell him.

'At the end of term, I asked Grandfather not to come to the school to collect me. I told him to meet me around the corner, so no one would see him. I was ashamed of him. The man who gave me everything. I didn't want them to meet him.'

'Oh, Merry, a child's mistake.'

'I was old enough to see the hurt in his face when he realised what I had done. The kindest, most generous man in the world and he knew I was ashamed. And yet I did nothing, said nothing.'

He took a half-step forwards as if to offer comfort. She held up a hand to ward him off.

'I knew it would hurt him. I knew. And still I did it.'

'But he forgave you?'

'We never spoke of it. He was kind and cheerful as always. But he knew what I had done.'

'Then he forgave you. And you must forgive yourself. He would not want you to dwell on such a small thing.'

She curled her lip. 'It sounds simple when you say it, but what about you? You haven't forgiven yourself for what happened at Waterloo and you came home a hero.'

'That is different. Men died because of my stupidity. And to tell you the truth, since we talked, I seem to have come to terms with it.'

'I'm glad.' She was glad. Thrilled that she might have been of help. She smiled brightly. 'At least something good came of our time together.'

'Merry, I love you. I want to marry you. Don't push me away.'

Love? She stared at him open-mouthed. She thought he'd come for honour and duty's sake. Because he'd taken her to his bed. He loved her?

'Oh,' she said. Her legs felt weak. She sank on to the sofa.

'I should have told you before. It took me a while to work it out. It took your leaving for me to understand my own heart.'

'You honour me,' she said.

'But?'

'It can't work.'

He took her hand and kissed her gloved knuckles. 'It can if you want it, too. If you love me.'

Everything she'd ever wanted shone from his eyes. Love. Affection. Honesty. She shook her head.

'Why, Merry. Give me a reason I can understand. Tell me you don't love me in return and I will never bother you again.'

She loved him with all her heart.

The tears, pushing up in hot waves in her throat, spilled over. 'Charlie, what if our children are ashamed of me? I don't want that for them. The shame and later the guilt.'

He put an arm around her shoulders and drew her against his wide chest. 'I won't allow it, love. They will love, honour and respect their courageous, beautiful mother or I will cast them off without a penny.'

A shaky laugh pushed its way through the tears. 'You sound like your father.'

'Don't I just.' He gave her a squeeze. 'It won't happen. If your parents had lived, do you think your mother would have been ashamed of your father?'

'Oh, no. Grandfather said it was love at first sight.'

'And do you think either one of them would have left you to the mercies of callous schoolgirls like Lady Allison? No. Your mother would have given you the tools you needed to deal with their ilk. Instead of that you had to work it out for yourself. Our children will not be ashamed of their mother because not only will they love her, but their father will make sure they respect her. They will know how brilliant you are and how beloved.'

It sounded plausible when he said it with such conviction. 'Your father won't like it.'

'Father will come around.' He shrugged. 'And if he doesn't, then I'll find some gainful employment. After Waterloo, I swore I would follow the rules and never risk harming anyone else. God, I even tried to make my brother fit the same mould. He tried to tell me a life of only duty is no life at all. I wouldn't listen. You taught me to listen, Merry, and gave me joy. Something I thought I didn't deserve. Don't send me back to an empty life. I need you. Together we can face the world. I would be proud to call you my wife.'

Proud? Of her? 'How can you be?'

He kissed the tip of her nose. 'Because you are clever and kind. You stand up for what you believe in no matter what others say. And because I love you.'

'I love you, too.' The words held so close to her heart she hadn't known they were there spilled forth like heady wine. 'I love you, Charlie.'

He let go a sigh of relief. 'Thank you.' He slid off the sofa and on to one knee. He withdrew a ring from his pocket. The one she'd left on the tray at Durn. 'Merry Draycott, will you do me the honour of becoming my wife?' He slipped the ring on her finger.

She stared down at it. Everything clicked into place, her heart, her mind, her soul, joining together with his, like some well-oiled lock. The little schoolgirl who everybody had scorned danced in circles of happiness. What had he said earlier? They would face the future together. With Charlie at her side, no one could cause her hurt. Because no one else counted. Only Charlie.

She lifted her gaze to his eyes, saw the question and the hope and the love. 'Yes,' she said. 'Yes, please.' She flung her arms around his neck.

He found her lips with his and she lost herself in his kiss.

After a while he broke away and tucked her against his chest, his arm around her shoulder. 'Miss Draycott, you certainly know how to lead a man a merry dance.'

'Mmmm,' she said. 'And I am looking forward to many more dances with you.'

He grinned. 'Other things too,' he said. 'After our wedding.'

'About the wedding. Do we have to have a grand affair in London?'

'I want everyone to see you. To know you are the woman I have chosen as my wife. To see my pride and my happiness and gnash their teeth.'

A laugh escaped her. 'Oh, Charlie. You couldn't have said anything better.'

He grinned. 'Let us be off, sweet. We can reach Durn tonight and break the news to my parents before they leave for London.'

She winced.

He rose, pulled her to her feet, and kissed her forehead. 'Courage, love. That is what I admired about you from the first, your courage as well as your beauty.'

She raised a brow. 'You thought I was a lightskirt.'

'Instead you are the light of my life.'

He drew her into his arms and kissed her lips. Happiness was a bright golden thing in her heart. It filled her with warmth. True love didn't care who your parents were, or what had happened before, she realised. True love was a beginning.

'Has he gone?' Caro asked, peeping around the door.

They separated like naughty children.

Caro flushed scarlet. 'Oh, I am sorry. I didn't mean to interrupt.'

Merry held out the hand with the ring. 'You are here just in time to hear my news. I am to be married.'

Caro's eyes widened. 'Really married?'

Charlie grinned. 'Leg shackled. Permanently.'

'Oh, Merry, I am so happy for you.' Caro rushed forwards and hugged her. 'So very happy.' She stepped back and there were tears of joy in her eyes.

'Why did you run from Captain Read?' Merry asked.

Caro paled. 'He is someone I knew a long time ago.'

Merry glanced at Charlie. 'Perhaps I should stay and—'

'No,' Caro said, her voice firm. 'I should not have run. He never did me any harm. It was just the shock of seeing him again.' She smiled. 'I have made a new life for myself and it is past time I stopped hiding.'

Merry sensed an underlying disquiet beneath the calm face. 'If you are sure?'

'Merry,' Charlie said, capturing her hand, his face serious. 'If Mrs Falkner finds herself in any difficulty she must send word to me. I will do all in my power to help her. But now we must speak with my parents.'

'Go,' Caro said, laughing. 'Invite me to your wedding and I promise I will come.'

The fear for her friend lightened. She kissed her cheek.

'Come,' Charlie said, urging her out of the door. 'The sooner we get this over, the sooner we can be wed.'

Wed. Common-as-muck Merry Draycott, wed to the heir to a dukedom. It hardly seemed possible, but when she gazed up into Charlie's face, she knew it had nothing to do with who he was and everything to do with the love shining in his eyes.

She reached up and kissed his cheek. 'No need to fuss, love,' she whispered. 'We have the rest of our lives.'

'We do.' He swept her up in his arms and carried her out of the house. 'And the sooner we get started, the better.'

He'd brought the closed carriage she noticed with a sigh of anticipation and a flood of heat. The ride back to Durn couldn't start soon enough.

She twined her arms around his neck and smiled.

* * * * *